J.
Jade
Slash
Laverna

Jade Slash Laverna

Anne Montagnes

a novel

Anansi

First published in 1995 by
House of Anansi Press Limited
1800 Steeles Avenue West
Concord, Ontario
L4K 2P3
Tel. (416) 445-3333
Fax (416) 445-5967

Canadian Cataloguing in Publication Data

Montagnes, Anne, 1935–
Jade Slash Laverna

ISBN 0-88784-169-4

I. Title.

PS8576.068J3 1995   C813'.54   C95-931163-7
PR9199.3.M65J3 1995

Cover Design: Bill Douglas at The Bang
Computer Graphics: Tannice Goddard

"The Wild West Is Where I Want to Be," page 64, © 1953 Tom Lehrer,
copyright renewed. Used by permission.

Excerpt on page 169 from Death of a Salesman, by Arthur Miller.
Copyright 1949, renewed © 1977 by Arthur Miller. Used by
permission of Viking Penguin, a division of Penguin Books U.S.A., Inc.

Excerpts from Encyclopaedia Brittanica on pages 171–74 reprinted with
permission from Encyclopaedia Brittanica, 14th edition, © Encyclopaedia Brittanica, Inc.

Every reasonable effort has been made to contact the holders of copyright for
materials quoted in this work. The publishers will gladly receive information
that will enable them to rectify any inadvertant errors or omissions in
subsequent editions.

All characters and events in this book are fictitious, and any
resemblance to actual persons, living or dead, or actual events
is purely coincidental.

House of Anansi Press gratefully acknowledges the support
of the Canada Council, the Ontario Ministry of Citizenship,
Culture, and Recreation, Ontario Arts Council, and
Ontario Publishing Centre in the development of
writing and publishing in Canada.

For Al, Donna, Jeanie, Joan and Vivette

One

Kuan Yin Buddhist Temple
Steveston Highway
Richmond, B.C.
Friday, June 28

Sakyamuni! Gleaming gold god, silent, huge up there above your candles in this echoing, busy, red and gold temple. It's me, Polly. Breathless, wet from the dash in from the taxi through the rain, shivering, grungy. Wearing the same clothes I had on yesterday when Zeeb phoned — old olive Marks and Sparks skirt, scuffed beige tie-ups, Hawaiian print shirt. I've taken flight, Prince, run from them all back there in Toronto. I need you, Lord. I've come for sanctuary, help.

Oh, male manifestation, teacher, listen! My beloved Zeeb has had a fight with Leslie. He phoned to say he was going up to the farm. I should phone Uncle Paddy, tell the old man Zeeb is coming.

Can't bear to.

Can't stop shivering.

Can't bear to see what I foresee.

Oh, Lord, what bad karma cursed me with clairvoyance and deprived me of the gift of non-attachment?

There will be violence up there, Sakyamuni. Rape, murder. The girl in the bush. No exit, no answers. They're going to be hurt — Zeeb, Paddy, my dear ones — and I can't help. You can't save people from their destinies. You can't live other people's lives for them.

Yet how I crave their safety. Who will steady my boy now?

Hardly a boy any more. Twenty-six? Twenty-eight? How many years since Sibyl died?

Only you know my heart, Sakyamuni. It's you I keep coming to, to learn how to live, how to bear life, since Sibyl died, my love, my one love. Only you know the pulse of my love. Your words, Sakyamuni, I read and re-read them. I sit in the dark in front of your image, legs twisted under me, numb, staring at a candle. Now let me sit here before your golden glory. I want to save Zeeb, Lord — my love's child, the child we raised together, Sibyl and I — to keep faith with my love.

And I can't. All I can do is watch.

Yet I can watch, not shut my eyes to my mind's eye.

Watch with me, Sakyamuni, be with me as I watch the young king, my Zeeb, pass through this time of the loss of language. Let my hovering love have been sufficient through the days of his youth to gird him now, let love be enough to encompass his dark passage.

1

Friday

They'd asphalted the second line since Zeeb was last up to old Paddy's hobby farm, and asphalt was certainly better than gravel when you were biking, but heat-wise it was unbearable. Even the roadkill — raccoons, porcupines, a kitten, no, two kittens — all the corpses were so dried out and flat there weren't even maggots in them, no crows chortling over their bones, no stink even of rotting flesh.

He licked salt from the corner of his mouth, ran the back of his hand over his itching eyes, pumped on.

It was evident the world was disintegrating around him,

not just his own personal world. Where were the overarching maples? Where were the little shady ditches and the green and bubbly puddles? Where were the birds?

In his pack the PowerBook computer, which had to make (or break) him this week — but it had to make him, it just had to — and the battery charger, they pressed down on the small of his back, the weight of them and the spare battery dragged at his shoulders. Why hadn't he balanced the pack better, padded the PowerBook stuff with more than just his extra jeans? But then again, maybe it was just as well that he feel that spur — the pea in the pilgrim's shoe.

His face ached from squinting against sun and dust. His hands were sliding on the handlebars as if they were greased. From the skunk areas — armpits, groin — rose the stench of a gym bag.

First thing he got to the farm, when he'd coasted down the drive and around the pond and to the cabin, he'd strip right there on the little beach Paddy made, and just walk into the pond. Maybe the raft would be out, moored in the middle to the flotsam buoy he and Polly had scavenged that long-ago bleak vacation in Cape Breton when he was fifteen, after Sibyl died. Sibyl. His mother; Polly's lover. Different griefs. Two grieving people with different griefs.

Pump.

Pump.

No but he'd swim out through the algae to the raft. There'd still be algae, the pond wouldn't be the pond without algae, big corruptions of it blooming in the shallows and drifting towards the downpipe, acid green as Emily Carr forests, flies and dragonflies and beetles copulating on them. The water in the pond was so alive that if you boiled it, it cooked, turned brown from green.

But now there was a well, Polly said, a generator, a shower even. All the comforts of home.

Sweat pricked him all over — and frustrated impatience with the slow passage of time. Pump, pump, fucking pump.

Focus on the raft then. Swim out. Think of getting chilled through.

That's the way it had always been. You'd be swimming along, you'd hit a cold spot, get shivery. Trout thrive there, in the cold spots, Paddy's precious trout. That's where you lay your fly, Paddy taught him years ago. Like a grandfather, Paddy taught him things like a grandfather. He didn't have a grandfather, didn't really have a father. Long McAdam — his dad was an absentee. But he'd always had Paddy, Polly's Uncle Paddy. With Polly came Paddy and Paddy's farm. Even kids who had a father didn't have that.

He'd swim out into the pond through the soupy surface, the cold spots, haul up on the raft, getting splinters from its cedar logs, disturbing cellophane-winged dragonflies. He'd stretch out, dripping a streaky silhouette into the grey plywood deck. He'd close his eyes and let the wind swing him. Eyes closed, you know what direction you're pointing by sounds. Soughing is pines around the drive. Jays shrieking is the cedars behind the cabin. Redwing blackbirds burbling is the swamp.

We are interactive watchers of nature, Sakyamuni — my country men and women. The forest path, the humble home, the lonely pond with its magnificent belt of dark pines sighing in the breeze, the cedar-swamp, the rugged snake fence, tormenting mosquitoes, blackflies, intense heat — if you cut to our hearts, you'll find these words written there.

He'd feel heat and anger and bewilderment drain from him. He'd be a new person tomorrow when he hit the PowerBook. Clear.

Pump, pump, pump, pumpety, pump.

He tried to give his thighs some relief by changing his pedal action. He sat back, pressed his heels down, stretched his calves. He had to pay attention to the right knee that wanted to swivel in from some bruising from some old game of touch. Things weren't made any easier by the toe clip on the right pedal having broken. The left leg got all the relief of lift as well as push.

And now, in the distance, there, at the last crossroads before the cabin — what the fuck was that? A *Globe & Mail* box?

What did you have to do to get away from civilization these days? First, concrete spaghetti engulfed you at the end of the subway. Then tanker trucks forced you into the gravel on Steeles. Then some idiot white Renault played chicken with him on the bike halfway up the line before speeding into a dip and out of sight. Down the line he had passed a Canadian Tire warehouse in what had been a marsh with birds singing last time he was up, and after the warehouse there had been an Industrial Park, every unit empty still and for rent. And then a Banquet Hall, ta da! — white curtains in two-storey windows awaiting wedding receptions.

Leslie.

He shivered through heat. A month ago she was his, Leslie, she was in his arms, and now — gone, over, finished, everything down the drain. For nothing, nothing — different standards, a brief loss of control, a streak of silver blood in the moonlight, he'd said a million times he was sorry.

He felt as if he were twisted in two, like someone trying to split an apple with their bare hands. He leaned forward and charged past the *Globe & Mail* box. No cars were coming so he stood up and coasted through the crossroads.

"Leslie!" he hollered. "Leslie!"

The wind whipped her name from his lips.

He slid back down into the seat and pumped and pumped on. What had looked from a distance like a pink and green monster house in a farmer's field was turning out to be a school. Saint Somebody's.

A school. A school, for fuck's sake. The place where you begin your entrapment in the coils of adult life, planted in a farmer's hay field, giant rolls of hay lying all around. Little did they know, the kids who went to that school, where it was all taking them. Not for a roll in the hay, that's for sure.

Leslie's grin when he punned.

Pump, pump, fucking pump.

At last the road hit a maple grove and for a few minutes he travelled through puffs of cool moisture-laden air, but then the road came out from under the trees again and began to get serious about the hill ahead. He geared down and made his legs spin faster. The hill rose before him. Like the curved belly of Leslie, yes, like his fucking faithless lady's curved sexy belly the hill rose before him. He put his head down and came at her jousting.

They think with their dicks, young men. You find me coarse, Prince of the Sakyas? Spiteful? Petty? These are the words women keen in, Prince. Long McAdam, Zeeb's father, he thought with his dick, that's why there is a Zeeb. My Uncle Paddy too probably, though he's old now. And Michael Randolph Hughes, ahead there at the farm — he thinks with his dick.

The hill rose before him.

Do her. Do Leslie.

The hill grew steeper, more resistant. Forward his legs spun. Get her.

Not fast enough. Not fierce enough. He was losing ground.

He stood up on the pedals. He pressed his arms down taut on the handlebars. The muscles in his thighs hardened to rocks.

And so, metres before he reached the crest and the mindless coast down towards the cabin and the pond, his right thigh cramped, knotted like a padlock, and he crashed down into the gravel at the side of the road.

His breath jerked. Stones pierced his cheek and palms. He could taste blood. His legs were tangled in the bike frame. The PowerBook equipment was pressing him down. Grunting through his nose, he made himself twist round, pulled his legs free. He fell back against his pack, fuck the PowerBook, tried only to breathe.

Close your eyes. Breathe. Breathe.

Open your eyes.

The road he had come on extended before him away in the distance, a black thread back to the hazy city. From here the CN Tower was no more than a silver centimetre on the flat horizon. Cars beetled along the road. Two, one after the other, disappeared into the maple grove below, sped towards him up the hill, whizzed past, hot and huge. He squinted into the distance. Like a spider on a web, a yellow pickup truck was bustling up the thread of the road.

Breathe, breathe.

He strained at the siren pull of the pond. He could almost smell his yearned-for destination. In the old days they would walk down this road, him and Sibyl and Polly, to pick daisies. Sibyl would be coughing away as she always did when she exerted herself, long juicy revvings of her engine, nothing to get excited about, he thought then, just Ma coughing, though Polly would curse and hide her cigarettes. He would run ahead and crouch behind a clump of grass and then leap out and yell, Hey, Ma! She would scream and put her hand to her heart. Then she and Polly would pick him up between them and swing him to where the daisies grew in the sandy roadside and they would tug at the ropy stems. Polly would weave crowns from grass and stud them with daisies and clover and they'd wear them back to the cabin, and then they'd hang them on nails in the screened-in porch, where they glowed and gleamed for a while, then dried out and died, and someone chucked them onto the compost heap. One time, just him and Sibyl, mother and son alone for once, they trekked off through the bush to the Big House which Paddy was then a-building.

The farm is a square hundred acres on a southeast corner of intersecting concession roads. You can get from cabin to Big House by road. You go west out the cabin drive and turn north at the mailbox, go up to the crossroads, then turn east along to the Big House mailbox. There you turn south down that drive.

They liked to avoid the road, though. They moved between

cabin and Big House by the trail Paddy made through the bush. You angle north from the cabin into sunless bush, cross the stream, skirt swamp, brush, deadfall on moss, fallen logs, ferns, emerge at last into light at the bottom of the Big House pasture, where spiked black locust trees tower. You climb the slope through the black locusts till the Big House itself appears, a red brick bag lady squatted on a hillside.

This one time when he and Sibyl went to the Big House alone, Paddy was getting ready to put in the well and the well-digger had said he wouldn't dig it without first it was divined. Sibyl was there when Paddy had interviewed the diviner. She'd gone ape over his black fingernails and so she came back to watch the divining, bringing Zeeb. They stood in the grassy pasture and watched the diviner going back and forth, back and forth, double-fisted with his stick. Sibyl gripped her right elbow with her left hand, the way she always did to smoke her cigarette. She eyed the diviner . . .

She was a devil woman, my love, my Sibyl, my own.

. . . smiling so her crooked front teeth showed. Then Polly came up out of the woods and into the pasture. As usual, she was wearing one of her Uncle Paddy's cast-off white shirts, sleeves rolled up, her shorn head bristling. She got technical with the diviner about willow twigs. She said she knew of a Bell lineman who divined for underground cables with a piece of copper wire. Would you believe it? the diviner said. Met a fella oncet could do it with his elbow, his blamed elbow. And so the well got sited, and Paddy later caused it to be dug and water flowed. And Polly took Sibyl back through the bush to the cabin and stretched her out oilily on the deck and gave her a massage, untying the knots in her brown skinny limbs, while he and Paddy caught trout for dinner.

Tears, idle tears. Salty. Soaking my cheeks, dripping onto my shirt.

pressed his foot down. The cramp eased.

The guy was a head taller than him. He walked the bike with one hand, holding out his other arm for him to lean on while he limped along. The truck had SAM THE MAN on the side, and a city phone number. Sam swung the bike and then the pack into the back beside a chain saw, some concrete blocks and some two-by-fours.

Zeeb eased his bum backwards up onto the seat, levering with his one good leg, stretched his other leg under the dash, and then they were moving.

Turned out Sam was up here on a job, renovating the A-frame at the southwest corner of the crossroads. The A-frame belonged to a city slicker called Roy Taylor. Taylor was always getting bright ideas and having his A-frame remodelled. One year it was skylights, and then they leaked, so the next year it was cedar shingles.

Quite soon they got to the gate with Polly's name almost obliterated from the mailbox where Zeeb had painted it years ago, window-frame green on the blue-painted metal. The cramp had let go of his thigh. Sam lifted down the bike and helped him into his pack.

"Hey, Sam. Thanks." He gripped the hard dry hand. "See you round?"

"Sure."

The yellow truck headed up the line in a cloud.

☙

The gate was open, but grasses had matted around the mailbox post. Daisies furred the crease of gravel and pines rose on either side like a woman's welcoming thighs. He started into it, erect and proud . . .

The image disturbs your golden silence, teacher? But this is the young king, coming home.

. . . walking his bike into the shade of the pines. Birds flurried up before him, a big one surprising him, a hawk he thought, and little ones, robins. He pressed on. The wind whispered high in the thirty-foot pine tops. He could hear his heart. He rounded the curve of the drive on springy slippery pine needle duff, started down the hill, slipping, going faster, in spite of himself, pulled by the bike, squeaking because of the pack and his leg. He slid out from under the pines and halted. There was the pond gleaming, across it the old brown-stained, green-trimmed cabin.

And Paddy, sitting in a lawn chair in front of the cabin, same as always, smoking his pipe, his Labrador bitch, Marmalade, by his feet, knees crossed in the old way, blue plastic cooler beside him — beer in it, no doubt, if Zeeb knew his Paddy. Paddy's fly rod in its case leaned against his chair. You could see the white of his little car, parked where Polly had always parked too, between a row of cedars and the pond.

Zeeb felt this big dumb smile on his face, he couldn't help it. Some archetypal homecoming this was. Ulysses. The hired man. Lassie even.

He kept on the grassy median, walking his bike in the gravel rut, down the hill, round the curve the drive makes to circle the pond, still smiling. Paddy hadn't seen him yet. He was just sitting there, smoking, looking at his trees and his pond and his fish leaping. Marmalade pricked up her ears though, but she didn't rise and wag her tail. She was Paddy's dog. Now Paddy was out of sight, the cedars beside the pond had grown that much, and an elm, and some cherry and birches. Now he rounded the curve of the drive and came onto the dam, and again Paddy was in view.

He whistled. There was an old whistle call Polly used to gather them together, the song sparrow's song. He whistled the call, a little wavery because he was hot and dry and his lips wouldn't pucker, but Paddy nonetheless raised his head, held his pipe in his hand, listened.

He kept on, off the dam now, around the end of the pond.

He laid his bike under the willow, eased out of his pack, shook his arms, hobbled the last bit.

Then Paddy saw him. "What the Sam Hill!" He pushed himself out of the chair onto his old man legs.

The dumb smile wouldn't leave Zeeb's face. He hauled himself up the bank. Paddy was just standing there, staring at him. "Zebu!"

Jeez. Nobody called him that any more. Nobody. Dad never. Even Polly never used his real name. The smile wiggled. His vision smeared. He opened his arms, stepped forward, said, "Jesus, Paddy! It's good to see you!" He put his arms around the old man, him all hot and sweaty from the long road, Paddy cool and old-man soft in a faded red plaid shirt, chin bristly, unshaven.

"What brings you here, son?" Paddy was thumping his back and pushing him away to look at him.

His face that close to Paddy's he couldn't think. You. He gripped the old man's arms. The slings and arrows of outrageous fortune, he could say that. He wanted to tell Paddy about Leslie. He wanted to ask him about women, why they exaggerated and had moods. Or smog, concrete, he could say. He wiped his hand across mouth and eyes. "I've got one week to key in my thesis corrections." It was like shouting in a dream. "One fucking week. Polly said I could use the cabin. Didn't she phone you? I need space. I've got to get ready to defend. Polly said she would phone and tell you."

Paddy turned away. "Mike!" His old man voice cracked.

At the end of the pond there was a guy in white chinos and a straw hat and a tucked-in long-sleeved shirt. Zeeb ran his fingers through his hair. The guy was flinging a silver lure out over the water.

The girl, Jade, later will have a lure like that as an earring, and another in her other bloody ear.

Put your golden arm around me, Sakyamuni. Can't stop shivering.

The girl. Jade. Will have an earring like that lure later. And another in her other bloody ear.

Paddy cleared his throat and hollered again. "Mike!" The sound got lost in the wind and birdcalls.

"Why don't you whistle? I'll whistle." Zeeb did Polly's call again, stronger. Flush him, friend or foe.

Paddy snorted. "Doesn't know that. Kid's from the city. Ah, what the hell, let him fish. You must be thirsty, old son. Wait. How'd you get here. Where's your car? You got a car? What you need is a nice cold beer." Paddy reached a beer out of the plastic cooler. He unscrewed it with a flourish.

Zeeb lowered himself to the grass.

Home.

Home.

But there should be two perfect rings of yellow irises around the pond, not just one. You should see the real one and also a reflected one, in the water. You would too, if it weren't for that lure flying out and plopping into the middle of the pond, shaking up bits of yellow. Why wasn't this Mike person laying flies? That was Paddy's rule, you fly-fish the pond, or at least it used to be. Paddy used to file the barbs off the hooks so he could play with the fish. Catch 'em, put 'em back, catch 'em again another day when they're bigger. Even after Mike reeled in, hefted a plastic pail from the edge of the pond and came towards them, ripples threw the reflection of the yellow irises up and down.

"Come on over here, Mike," Paddy called. "Come meet Zeeb."

"One moment." Mike veered to the water's edge with his plastic pail. You could see him reach into his back pocket and get out a knife as he came down on one knee. He worked away there, dipping fish out of the pail, knifing them open.

Zeeb pulled on his beer. Paddy's pipe was dead.

Mike spilled water out of the pail into the silvered pond. Sometimes the pond would be so still you'd think there were two worlds. You could turn the picture upside down and it would be the same. Maybe even clearer.

Not now.

Mike washed his hands, dried them on a red handkerchief from his pocket. He got up, picked up his pail, came up to them. "There's your dinner, Paddy."

Paddy looked into the pail, looked away. He pointed his pipe stem at Mike. "Well, kid. This is Zeeb. Zeeb Porteus. Friend of the family. My niece has lent him the cabin for a while so we're going to have a neighbour. Did she phone? Did I get a call from Polly? Did I mention it to you? Well, anyway, you come over here fishing, you better let him know. What you do is you honk at the top of the hill. Zeeb old son, this is Michael Randolph Hughes."

Zeeb reached up his hand, but Mike didn't come forward. Zeeb got up and moved towards him, to make him shake his hand.

He felt dark and hulking. He was taller than Mike, his arms thick beside Mike's arms. Mike had creamy soft girl's skin under the brim of his straw hat, patches of shade and freckles. His hand was like a cat, the way they'll curl their pads and claws around your finger if you offer it to them, holding the end of your finger in an embrace, pulsing their claws, as if they were contemplating you as a mouse. Zeeb thought of how the dog he'd had as a boy had taught himself to kill mice and chipmunks and squirrels, tossing stones up and catching them in his teeth and tossing them up again, to break their necks.

"Let's see what you got," he said. "Did you get rainbow or speckled?"

"I'm afraid I can't answer that question."

Inside the pail there was a plastic container and in that the fish were curled, headless, slit white bellies turned up so they looked like giant grubs. Zeeb was afraid he couldn't answer that question either. You couldn't see their backs, what colour they were.

"Nice," he said.

"Well, we do have to eat," Mike said.

"Fry 'em up in butter," Paddy said. "Yum, yum."

"Uh, uh, Paddy." Mike shook his finger and his head. "No butter for you. Remember your cholesterol, and your triglycerides." He put his hands on Paddy's shoulders and said to Zeeb, "Will you join us for dinner?"

Zeeb wanted to drag him into the pond and under water the way his dog used to drag Marmalade. The leg that had been cramped was shaking out of control.

"Later," he said.

Paddy pulled on his dead pipe.

∾

At last Paddy's car was ghosting up the drive out of sight away under the pines. Zeeb got the cabin key from its hiding place on a nail knocked into one of the struts which supported the deck. He carried his pack in, opened the doors, raised the windows. Spiders scuttled away bearing egg sacs. Flies roused and buzzed. Polly had partitioned off one end of the screened porch for a bathroom. There was even a shower in it. Unreal. Civilization? Here? In the toilet there was a drowned mouse. He took it out and laid it under a cedar and covered it with cedar duff. He brushed mouse droppings off the kitchen counter, opened the cupboards. Canned corn. Dried lentils in a bottle. Tea. A couple of cans of Carnation milk still, left over from Sibyl. That's how she had her coffee, with Carnation. The tops of the cans were rusted. There were sardines and vegetable oil.

He sat down at the table in the window corner and leaned on his elbows. You could see nothing but trees, water, sky, algae. The raft was still pulled up on the shore. Yellow coreopsis dropped petals. Phoebes intersected dragonfly trajectories, and phoebe babies got fed in their nest under the eaves of the screened porch. He pulled out the PowerBook, the extra battery, the charger, the rejected draft of his thesis, arranged them on the table. He carried the rest of his stuff into the bedroom.

He poked under the old rubber war surplus ponchos on hooks, where the axe lived and the shovel. There'd always been a fly rod there. Polly didn't fish. And Sibyl wouldn't even look at his catch, not till they were cooked. Yuck! Get that thing away from me! But some of their men fished.

Long McAdam did. Dad. He could just remember him prowling the bank with a fly rod.

Polly also kept a box of flies from the hardware store in the kitchen drawer. He took the box and rod out to the deck and sat, his legs dangling into the tall grass. He picked out a fly, began to tie it on.

Across the way Strickland was still turning over the shit in his shit farm. You could hear the backup beep of his front loader. Strickland would clean out septic tanks and ponds, and turn the cleanings into topsoil, then sell the topsoil back to the tank owners for their lawns. There were still cars going up Airport Road, Friday night, also escaping the city. You could hear them roar a concession away. Such was the stillness and the density of the atmosphere, you could hear Mike at the Big House call Paddy. Come on in now, Paddy, it's time for your dinner.

Zeeb spat into the grass beyond the deck. Little licking noises of the fish rose to the surface of the pond as evening bugs hatched, like handfuls of gravel, thrown, and thrown, and thrown into the water. He stripped, went naked with his rod down to the far end of the pond, waded into the shallows, began the long cool laying of the line across the water.

Whop.

Whop.

Whop.

High among the cedars. Let it out. Drop it. Pull it in. And again. You and the line with the fly at the end become one with the big one which would rise to your cast.

He slapped at mosquitoes on his shoulders, thighs. His feet in the blood-warm shallows were slowed right down. He anticipated the crackle of a fire in the fire pit and him crouched by it in the dusk frying up his big one, watched by coons, other night creatures, moths banging the cabin windows for the gold of the kerosene lamp.

Fuck his thesis.

Fuck bitching Leslie.

Fortune's fool he was to be up here alone in the womb of the world.

2

By nightfall it was still far too hot in the city. Lisa and Jade were in the kitchen.

"Now let me get this straight," Jade was saying. "You're going for a drive in the country tomorrow to visit a friend. Today it was thirty-three. With the humidex, forty-seven. Tomorrow's going to be even hotter. And you won't take me with you. Is that what you're telling me? You're going to leave me here to stifle?"

All the windows in their part of the house were open to the night sky, night noises. You could hear kids screaming from houses nearby. There was a party across the way. The girl next door was talking on the telephone, and on the next floor up in that house, under the impression that if they cranked up the bass they'd create white noise, the girl's roommate and her boyfriend were loudly screwing. Traffic sizzled up and down Bathurst Street. Boom boxes pounded in the park.

Jade took a strawberry from the green cardboard box on the kitchen table at her elbow.

Yes, that's what I'm telling you. Could say that, thought Lisa.

Gee, Jade, I'm sorry, how thoughtless of me, of course you must come along, how could I think of leaving you here to broil? She could say that. Sarcastic. Jade would droop her dirty blonde hair over her face, and shut up.

Those berries are washed, so get your dirty fingers out of them. That too.

But she didn't say anything. She just went on making cookies, beating eggs and sugar in her big blue bowl with her wooden spoon. She was going to add raisins. She'd gotten the packet out of the fridge. Now she snipped it open with the scissors, shook and squeezed some out into the glass measuring cup, and then sprinkled them into the bowl. She turned on the oven. She rattled the cookie sheets out of the cupboard under the sink and greased them with a wrapper she'd saved from the butter. Then she started stirring again.

"I can't tell you how much you remind me of my mother standing there stirring like that, your bum wiggling. She cooks and cooks and cooks, just like you. She's always stirring things. Soup. Barley and bones. Jam, strawberry jam."

Jade ate another berry.

Still Lisa said nothing.

"I can't imagine why you're making so many cookies. Just for a drive in the country."

With two teaspoons, Lisa pushed small mounds of cookie dough in even rows onto the cookie sheets. Jade scooped a taste off the edge of the bowl.

"The only difference is my mother would be talking. Jade darling, don't you think it would be a good idea to put your money into an RRSP? You won't need all this education when you're married."

What Momma would actually be saying was, Oh, Laverna, Laverna, why all this school business? Why do you want to stuff your head so full? Will this find a husband?

Sweat trickled between Jade's breasts, stained her tank top.

"On top of which you're heating up the place so it's going to be an oven. The least you could do, if you have to take cookies out into the country, is buy them."

She was reaching for another berry but Lisa, having slipped the cookie sheets into the oven, took the box and tucked clear plastic film around it and folded the ends under. She put it in the fridge beside the bottle of wine.

Jade moved her jade bangle up and down her upper arm. "Why won't you take me? Can't I come? Pretty please?"

When Jade was sitting and Lisa was standing, Lisa was the taller. Jade slouched even further. She wiggled her toes in their slave girl sandals and blinked her eyelashes up.

"You don't really want to come." Lisa dried her hands on a tea towel. "There's this new guy, you know? It's going to be just me and him."

Who first used words to wound? Eve, in converse with the snake? The snake, waylaying Eve? God, making the snake subtle? These two are cruel with each other, Sakyamuni, not loving. They give disaster permission.

3

"You quite comfy, Paddy?" Mike was standing in the bedroom doorway.

Paddy was lying in bed, in clean pyjamas, the back of his head propped on his hands.

It still took him aback every time the kid called him that. Paddy. Who told him he could? King? But no, he knew King, had begot King, taught him, watched him grow and go, and he knew that wasn't the kind of friendly detail his son, King, would ever have gotten into. King would have wanted to know two things and two things only. That the house was going to be safe from vandals, after all he would be going to sell it sometime and you didn't want it all patched up and with a bad reputation. And that someone was going to be there to pick his aged parent up if he should fall, that was the second thing King would want to know. You wouldn't want a death by misadventure on your record.

In Paddy's youth it would never have been Paddy. It wouldn't even have been Mr. Slater. It would have been Sir. Is there anything more I can do for you, Sir?

Paddy.

Maggie would have found it funny. She would have found some similarly fresh name for Mike, something that put him in his place, let him know he was Paddy's personal servant.

Batman.

Sure, that's it, why not? He, Captain Patrick Slater, was the officer in charge of the day. All Michael Randolph Hughes was was Captain Patrick Slater's batman.

He coughed. "That'll be all thanks. Batman."

Kid paused.

"I'm going down now, Paddy. Oh. I found your single malt in the liquor store in the city. I put it in the sideboard. Would you like a little snort right now?"

"No thanks. Dismissed. Batman."

Kid grew still, possibly paler. His green eyes became glass. Marmalade groaned on her blanket under the window.

"Nighty-night then, Paddy. Just shout at the top of the stairs, won't you, if there's anything you need."

"Very good. Good-night. Batman."

The way the kid looked at him Paddy thought for sure he was going to say something but he left instead. He was tweaking the copper coils at his nape.

That had fixed him. Batman.

Paddy clicked out the light. He tried to lie still between the clean white sheets, absorbing trout, steamed, without salt or butter, peeled boiled potatoes, frozen peas, Bird's custard. He gazed back. At this time of night he often saw his life as a series of bubbles which fortune had blown him through, one by one, side by each, over the years. He saw his mother in a slim coat with a huge fur collar, holding his hand as they walked down the wooden steps of the rose-covered cottage in Weston to Methodist Sunday School. He smelled pipe smoke, tasted beer — that was Varsity. He heard girls in stockings clacking type-writers, bachelor girls, hard-nosed secretarial types. He saw Maggie hiding the milk stains on her blue print dress with the frilled bib of her apron. He felt the red press mark on his fore-head from his Air Force blue hat; smelled Maggie's rose perfume and her cigarette smoke over the bridge table; heard the clunk of earth on the brown paper-covered box that held her ashes; found himself in the white kitchen again, Mike steaming trout.

But then there were other bubbles, the other kind of bubble, random escape hatches that weren't part of any series.

He used to like to go over to the cabin and drink beer when Polly and Sibyl were up with the boy. If it was dusk, Polly would sit cross-legged on the picnic table and watch him lay long lines across the cooling pond. The boy would crouch in the iris by the water's edge. Paddy would leave them some sweet little ones for breakfast. Then the boy grew bigger and fished too.

Now again there was the other kind of bubble, the boy arrived on his bike, grown.

Lord, the times they'd had. He remembered their dog. The boy and the dog were puppies together. He remembered the dog's game, how he'd take a stone in his mouth and throw it up with a toss of his head. If it had been a mouse, a squirrel, the toss would have broken its neck. The dog's game, how he taught himself to be a hunter when he was a pup. Zeeb's game, how Paddy taught him to be a fisherman.

Tomorrow, after dinner, he'd tell the kid he was going over to the pond to see the boy, leave him drying dishes. That's what he was paid for, after all, to keep house. Paddy would go over to the pond by himself. Drive himself over, surely he could still drive himself over to the pond. He'd drink some beer with the boy, chew the fat.

Damn twitching toes between clean white sheets.

He felt himself dragged back to the string of bubbles, the series, side by each. Now they were laid out in gooey strings, like frogs' eggs, him humping through them, one by one, over the years. Maggie with flour on her apron. His ears popping as the plane came down in Scotland. King hiring Mike Hughes.

Batman.

He felt himself relax into a smile.

He thought again about the other kind of bubble.

From Pacific time, from this red and gold space, I want to shout out a warning, shout out danger. Do not go so gentle, Paddy.

ᴄᴧᴐ

Standing on the desk chair before the three-way mirror in the privacy of the little basement bathroom, Michael Randolph Hughes paused in mid-pirouette. The mousetrap had snapped. Excellent.

He had put the trap at what he considered a likely rodent crossroads, at the bottom of the stairs in the corner angle of the doors to the furnace room and the garage, and he'd set it with a bit of Paddy's cheddar. He had felt quite confident he would catch a number of the little beasts there. He knew about mice, oh yes, the disgusting musty clutter under the kitchen sink in old liquor store bags and never used pots and aged cleanser left over from when Mother thought she'd teach herself to polish brass, the scurryings through the nibbled cereal boxes in the cupboard, stiff corpses in traps.

This was one enterprise this gentleman's estate was going to profit by, now he was in charge. Rodents would be removed, by mousetrap, or by poison bait if necessary. He went hot and cold when he thought of poison bait, the concept of even tiny animals increasingly disabled in their nests as their blood thinned until, ultimately, they bled to death, internally.

The trap stirred. Grated along the tiles.

The mouse was not dead then. It had managed to manoeuvre part of itself free of the spring. Possibly only its tail was caught, or its hindquarters, squashed and paralysed.

But caught it was, and that was one less nibbler and gnawer to deal with, a furthering of progress in a damask-damaged and tea towel-nested world, one less producer of little black pellets which rattled in fine bone china teacups and sterling silver teaspoons, generations of destruction eliminated. In a minute he would deal with mouse and trap. He refocused on the mirror and resumed his slow turning.

He loved these three views of himself. His skin glowed so rosy through the fine red nylon of the new pantyhose.

A cross-dresser. O serpent heart.

Yet, golden teacher, where is the crossover?

Your monk there, walking past again to get a good look at this big white round-eye who has washed up in his temple — his brown skirts swoosh along the red carpet like any belle dame in a ball gown.

And your noisy little devotée kneeling warmly at prayer beside me, waving her fistfuls of joss — her pyjamas were anathema to the Victorian ladies whose husbands imported her forebears.

And a woman who loved a woman and liked to wear her uncle's old cast-off shirts — isn't she also a cross-dresser?

Framed by the cut out crotch, his limp pink sex curled among the coiled red corkscrews of his coppery pubic hair. In the rear view, the red of the nylon set off the curve of his pale buttocks. He thought his calves might be a little over-muscled for pantyhose, so he kicked off the red satin mules with the malibu pompoms that pumped them up, and stood on the hard wooden chair in only his stockinged feet. That was more shapely, and that was the routine he would expect a girl to go through too. He wouldn't want her to extend herself on the bed with the mules still on.

Or would he? That might be an interesting scenario. His sex began to rise at the thought. He would push her in the mules, watch her fall, hear her say, No, no, no.

He had to laugh at himself a bit, quite an extraordinarily virile man, wearing women's red nylon pantyhose and getting turned on, and nary a femme in sight. He cuffed himself, semi-playfully the way he would cuff his puppy when it leapt into his face with moist tongue and nose, and he shrank back into himself. He got down off the chair and, with care, peeled off the tights. They shrank neatly back to size when he folded them, and settled nicely back into the pink tissue paper, and that neatly into the bottom of the glossy pink carrier bag with the two red hearts drawn on it.

The bag was a bonus. He hadn't expected a pretty bag when he went shopping in the city this afternoon for lingerie. The saleslady had drawn the two hearts, intertwined, and she had winked when she handed him the bag, pink tissue paper frothing out of it, handles tied together tight with a pink ribbon. That would have pleased his therapist, that interaction. First, Mike had smiled at the saleslady, the way he and the therapist had practised, and then the saleslady had not only smiled but winked at him. His heart had been beating quite hard, or he would have asked if she'd like to drive out with him to the country.

He pulled on his white jockey shorts and his chinos, tightened his belt, resumed his Birkenstocks.

The chair he toted back to the old man's former study, which he had requisitioned for himself as his bedroom. When King had shown him around the house he seemed to expect that Mike would take the room upstairs beside the old man's. But where would guests stay? was what Mike had countered with, where will you stay when you come to visit? although Mike certainly had no expectation that King would ever more than drop by. I'll be all right down here, he had told King.

He'd been right about King too. It was weeks since King had come out to the farm. Mike made regular telephone reports to him on the state of Paddy's health, unintonated and factual, with copious details about Paddy's bowel movements, and he made the calls to King's place of business, not his home.

But now there actually was an intruder. It made Mike almost nauseous and he did a little rapid breathing to get himself under control again. This Zeeb Porteus, a hunk on a bike with dark smooth arms. Familiar enough with the old man to be settling in over there in that mouldy dump by the pond.

How would he know if there had been a communication about him from the old bugger's niece? He'd been in town all day. Could he help it if Paddy didn't remember his phone calls?

Batman.

Holy senility, Robin.

He lit a cigarette and opened the combination lock on the old blue trunk which he sometimes called his hope chest. He arranged himself on his knees before his treasures. So much softness. So much restraint. He pulled out the black and red merry widow which he imagined her wearing with the red panty-hose. The satin waist of it was so soft, and it never suited him at all, he was too square, not like a girl. He snapped an elastic garter. He heard her squeal.

The mousetrap rattled again.

He should do something about that. He would do something about it in a minute.

His girl was going to be nothing like Maggie Slater. He talked to Maggie sometimes, particularly under cover of the vacuum cleaner. There were two pictures of Maggie, so he knew whom he was addressing.

He felt more comfortable with the picture in the bedroom on Paddy's dresser. It sat beside Paddy's own portrait in the air force officer's uniform, in front of the square wooden jewel box.

The key of the jewel box was kept in the lock. Mike had checked inside. Well, it was his duty to see that everything was clean, wasn't it? It was red velvet in there. There were drawers, even a secret drawer, though all the secret drawer had in it were a few old one-dollar bills. The box held Paddy's now never-used tiepins, cuff links, collar studs, an old thick gold signet ring, rings of keys whose uses puzzled Mike, two plastic pill bottles, one with matches, the other with pennies, a bullet.

The Maggie in this picture, beside the jewel box, was girl-ish and blonde and laughing. The picture was set in a little frame of enamel chips and tarnished silver, made in Italy. To this Maggie he said, What you knew about mice, my dear, would have fitted into a thimble. Do you realize that there are mouse droppings in every drawer, in every cupboard, on every shelf in your house? Rather, there *were* mouse droppings, for I, having taken on the responsibility of your husband, have not been lax in extending my duties to all matters affecting his well-being. Mice there will no longer be, while I dwell herein.

And he would give the finger to this young Maggie with her blonde curls and her smile and her blue frock with its white lace collar, and Maggie would have nothing to say, Made in Italy stamped into her soft back.

The other picture sat in the living room on a table, a white-haired lady looking sideways out of a silver frame, a frame Mike had polished till it gleamed. He believed about this Maggie that, as she might have proceeded across the living room broadloom to consult her engagement calendar about the date of the next meeting to organize the church picnic, she would simply have walked around him, the housekeeper, as if he weren't there. He would like to smash the glass over her stuck-up snoot as she studied the horizon, wreathed in smoke.

He held up from his trunk, as if for Maggie's inspection, the silver chain-link belt with dangling hearts, the scarves in rainbow colours with which he would bind his true love's hands, the frothy pink panties with white lace and bows. The dildo he had carved from an axe handle. A piece of pure white yachting rope. He watched Maggie focus, and drop her eyes.

It was too hot. Even in the green leafy country it was quite impossible this evening to have the doors and windows shut; you had to let as much coolness as possible sift in through the screened windows and circulate through open doors throughout the house. The problem with this method of dealing with the heat problem was the outside noises that also entered the house. The blackness of night in the country prevented a view of the sources of the noises. The light from the green-shaded banker's lamp on Paddy's former desk, the flare when he pulled on his cigarette — these stopped abruptly at the windows and screens. What was outside was wilderness, pure and simple: sniffings, whickering and rustling, intermittent squealings and hootings, steppings, whirrings, yippings. Something which mourned and mourned. A distant snorting.

There was also silence out there. By the pond you were always comforted by the constant civilized whine of traffic on Airport Road, but here at the Big House, under the bulk of the hill, the sounds of the bush crept in through the windows.

Even the mousetrap flapped and bumped less now and the smoke from his cigarette rose fairly peacefully, and drifted out the window.

The trunk had always travelled with him, from the time he'd been translated to the foster home at age thirteen. In it the detritus of his life had accumulated over time: winter woollies, old unfinished bottles of medication, dress shoes, an LP of Ian and Sylvia featuring "Four Strong Winds," and one of The Travellers doing, among other things, "Michael Row Your Boat Ashore" — a lady he once boarded with as an outpatient had lost those to him in unwitting payment for certain lawn mowings and dog groomings. His ashtray collection had gathered in the trunk: the bubbly gold glass tricorn with the pestle to stub your cigarettes that had been one of Mother's and Father's wedding gifts; the one from the King Edward Hotel, the one Father had thrown at him; the red glass one that, according to another lady he boarded with, was Venetian, her dearest possession, now Mike's possession; a curious beigey one from a concrete company that had been on the desk of one of the doctors — it had a lip on it to rest your pipe. Like the old bugger here, that doctor would lean back in his shirt sleeves behind his desk puffing on his pipe, watching. But not watching well enough, for Mike had the ashtray, didn't he? There was a cobalt blue one. He couldn't remember where he'd scoffed that. The pulsing three-dimensional shade of the blue nauseated him, like water dropping over Niagara Falls, or the pulsing yellow campfire at Children's Summer Bible Camp.

Gaiter, Children's Summer Bible Camp Director, thought Mike was going to grow up to be a preacher and so there was also, in the trunk, the bible he'd been awarded for diction, a white one. White bibles, he'd learned later from a drying out priest in his ward, were for weddings and confirmations. He wondered where Gaiter had acquired a collection of white wedding and confirmation bibles to distribute as prizes.

There was his father's kilt, unpressed, whisky stained, but

wrapped in an old flowered pillowslip with mothballs. There was the bottle of red nailpolish, dried up, that Mother had left on the steps when she went away.

The trap flapped again. He wondered why the mouse didn't squeak, and how long it was going to take it to die.

In the front of the white bible was written, Wash me thoroughly from my iniquity and cleanse me from my sins, in Gaiter's sprawly ballpoint. They used to sing it in parts around the campfire. Mike sang his part now, the tenor, making his ears ring, as he brushed ashes off his shirtfront. He laid the pink bag on top of the pillowslip. He closed his trunk.

Taking the ashtray with his ashes and his three butts — this ashtray belonged to the Slater household, a chipped little blue cloisonné thing, not worth acquiring — he rose to empty it upstairs. He hummed in his falsetto down the hall, and then he halted. Where he had stationed the mousetrap, at the foot of the stairs, the beige tiles shone empty.

Where could the trap have got to? He set the ashtray on the stairs. He looked and saw no small rodent lurking in the corner, masquerading as a dust ball. Nothing was down the hall the way he'd come. Under the stairs there was a box of newspapers waiting to be recycled. He lifted it quietly, so as not to rouse the old bugger upstairs, and probed with his toe, but there was no trace of mouse or trap there. He lowered the box gently. The door to the garage was locked. Nothing could have got through that.

But the door to the furnace room was open a tinch.

It didn't seem possible that a trap could have been dragged through there by a hobbled mouse, but where else could it have got to? Stealthily he pushed open the door and listened. Was that a grating sound? Over there? Under the workbench? He flicked on the light. The room leapt into objects and shadows: furnace, water heater, coiled wire and hoses on hooks, shelves of bottles, the workbench, the long wooden box of tools, the window reflecting back the room. He listened. Was that a stirring? He tiptoed to the workbench, and knelt at a distance.

Underneath, it was cobwebby, and dark. There was movement.

In the kitchen drawer, Maggie had kept a flashlight. He went upstairs for that.

The kitchen was white and peaceful. He emptied the ashtray into the old juice can, kept beside the kitchen sink, in which the household leavings were collected for disposal in the compost. He rinsed the ashtray, dried his hands on a paper towel, which he refolded for re-use. Then he found the flashlight. It worked, weakly. Like everything else in this house the batteries were run down, but at least it worked. He kept it on as he went back downstairs and into the furnace room, and knelt to probe the clutter under the workbench with the pale beam.

The animal he had trapped was not a mouse. It was a larger creature with a tawny body, virtually the size of a rat.

His breathing was quick as he stood up and contemplated his next move. You shouldn't reach in there, not with your bare hand. Trapped animals could be vicious. They'd been given instruction on animal bites at Children's Summer Bible Camp, about tetanus, rabies. A man in a brown uniform had lectured them with slides and a pointer, and a voice at least as military as his father's.

Again he went upstairs. Under the drawer used for the elastic bands, wax paper, tin foil and the flashlight, there was another drawer containing barbecue tools: skewers, spatulas, mitts and tongs. He selected a large sturdy pair of tongs, the kind you'd use to turn hamburgers. He went back downstairs but before he returned to the furnace room he went down the hall, past his own room, through the mud room and unlatched the exit to the well outdoors. Then he returned to the furnace room, crouched, and reached the tongs under the workbench. The trap grated. The animal was moving out of reach. He probed further and managed to clutch the creature in the tongs. The body was surprisingly soft. He drew it forth. It hung limply from the tongs as if dead, the trap dangling from a paw with its tiny hooks of nails: a shapely creature, cream stripes down its back inside black boundary stripes, set in beige; black eyeliner, though the lids were down. He knew its name, though it momentarily escaped him. Holding it before him he went down the hall and let himself outside.

The night was dark, as nights always were in the country, unless there was a moon. The stars were too distant to cast any illumination. Noises were magnified by the dewy atmosphere. Silences too — those also were magnified. Mosquitoes found him and he brushed at them on his face and neck and arms with the back of his one free hand.

The creature was a chipmunk. At Children's Summer Bible Camp they'd fed them peanuts, until they began to infest the cabins, running over your sleeping face. Nails on your skin in the dark.

He picked his way over the dark wet lawn towards the compost heap, the soft body limp in the tongs, the trap bobbing. A mosquito whined in his ear. The wet came over his Birkenstocks and through his socks. So, before he reached the compost, he simply unclutched the tongs and let trap and chipmunk fall, heard the thud in the wet grass. He hustled back indoors.

4

Some guys in a black Valiant with red interior were thundering down the second line, chucking beer cans out the windows and cranking up the sound.

A thumpa! thumpa! thumpa!

Zeeb rolled over and shouted, Hey! You guys! Turn it down!

But the noise did not go away. He twisted in soft sheets.

Oh. The cabin, he was in the cabin. You got swept up in dreams in the cabin, stuff left over from the old days with Polly and Sybil, summers at the farm.

My sweet Zeeb . . .

He went and poured himself a glass of water and took it over to the screen door to drink.

Then he just about had a heart attack because the guys of his dream were actually out there, sucking on their cigarettes in the dark. About a hundred of them. Surrounding the cabin. Standing out there watching him standing here by the screened door.

The guys were everywhere.

On the dam. Down by the pond. Along the drive. Even on the other side, across the pond. Everywhere.

They were walking around and talking in the gurgle of the

downpipe. In the dark the glowing ends of their cigarettes pulsed and waved.

He stood there at the screen, naked, and shouted at them. "Hey! What the fuck are you doing? Get out of here!"

But the motherfuckers didn't move. They did not move. They just went on smoking their fucking cigarettes, and watching the cabin, him in the cabin.

Heart thudding, he pulled the whiteness of his naked body inside, away from view. He put his glass down on the Franklin stove. They didn't keep the .22 rifle . . .

. . . don't play with guns, we always said. Don't play with guns.

. . . with the axe and the fishing rod. They kept it up in the loft. You didn't really want anyone to be able to get at it too easily. But this was no time to be moving the stepladder and hefting up the trapdoor to get into the loft.

Yes. No time for guns now.

Under cover of the door frame, hiding behind the curtain, he crept back to his vantage point. He looked out the window. Jeez.

He was an idiot. Those were not cigarettes, those lights out there. They were fireflies. Moist nights in June, July bring fireflies to life. That's when they breed. They turn on their lights to attract one another, and arc through the darkness, beckoning mates.

Shivering, he got his glass of water off the Franklin, and coiled back into the flannelette sheets. He heard noises in the pond, raccoon fishing probably.

Or a poplar toppling?

What if there were beaver again, wreaking havoc, slaughtering trees, damming the drainpipe?

Kill the buggers. Start with a clean slate. Let nothing disturb his concentration.

The thumpa that had wakened him, he realized, was the neighbours' boom box.

Put a bullet in its guts.

∽

Paddy heard trains from over by Alliston. Minded him of the time he and Maggie took a trip out West. They went over to Alliston and picked up the cross Canada there. Bill, the butcher, drove them over. They'd got chatting with Bill one day over the fillets, and they'd told him about their plans for the trip out West. Their idea then had been to drive into Toronto, leave their car at King's place, have an early dinner with him and Gloria, and then get them to take them down to Union Station, and board the train out West there.

But when Bill Van Dyken heard this he said, Hell, why go all the way into the city? That train goes through Alliston. Hell, it stops there. I know because when my wife's brother-in-law's sister Ida went out West to see her daughter Rose, the one that had the new baby in Winnipeg, why she caught the train there. Hell, I'll take you. You can catch the train an hour later and have your own dinner at home.

Poor Bill Van Dyken. Ended up like all the rest of them, pissing on the floor, tied to a chair. Poor old Bill Van Dyken.

At least Maggie kept her marbles.

He prayed he would keep his marbles.

∽

A quite extraordinarily loud noise awakened Mike. He thought about it for some time, but he could put no name to it. As he lay there, trying to get back to sleep, his mind roamed and he thought of Paddy's little white Renault. He quite liked it, a passable compact, except that its colour set it off from other cars on the road and in his opinion that was counterproductive. You didn't want to stand out from the crowd.

The noise came again, like a heartbeat.

He decided his room had been sufficiently cooled down. He got up, pulled on the banker's lamp on what had formerly been the old bugger's desk, and cranked the windows shut, both those facing the lawn and those over the desk that faced the exit well. He tugged at the drapes. Their wheels creaked along the tracks, and dust blew out, continuing confirmation of years of neglect. He pulled off the light.

As he lay awake, failing to identify the noise that woke him, he thought of how they say babies grow accustomed to the beat of their mothers' hearts in the womb. They say that's why those pouches are so effective. The child's mother continues in a supportive role simply by walking around with him strapped to her back. Or front. Some of the carriers kept the babies, particularly the newly born, strapped to the front in a position similar to the fetal position.

They neglected to say, however, what happened when the mother vanished. Her heart went on beating, but not for the abandoned child. In his opinion, the planet's mental health would be better served if children were removed from mothers at birth and fed in cots by bottle.

He got out of bed again, pulled the light back on, lifted open his trunk, and removed the pink carrier bag with the two hearts. He drew out the pantyhose, shook the folds out gently. He stroked the rough silk fabric down the underside of his forearm. It was not possible to keep a straight face because of the tickling. He returned the pantyhose to the bag and set the bag on top of the trunk, to greet his eyes first thing in the morning. He pulled off the light and slid back into bed.

Now, of course, fathers could carry babies in those pouches, and imprint them with the rhythm of their heartbeats.

Two

temple
not yet dawn

Must get to Paddy, send a card. Mouth like a sewer from
eating your rotten fruit offerings, Saky. Bones like bricks
from lying on this bench. Are you awake in this flicker-
ing golden darkness? Are you watching? Are you with me?

1

Saturday

Lisa woke up light and glad, thinking about taking off into the
country for the day and having some fun. But while she was
making her coffee she heard Jade upstairs talking to herself
again. Coming down heavy on her heels as she prowled around
her third floor loft and talking to herself.

Jade had elected to live in the loft, even though it was
under the eaves and she was the tall one, because of the deck.
Lisa got the room on the second floor with the air conditioner.

Mug in hand, she went to stick her head up the stairwell to
say hi.

☙

Dolly's pink dress was dirty. Jade undid the buttons and yanked her out of it.

Dolly was big and pink and soft. Uncle Freddy had given her to her when she wasn't yet Jade but was still only little Laverna, to hold in her arms to comfort her in bed at night. She kept her always.

But now dolly was dirty.

"Sometimes you get that way, you bad dolly, don't you? So I'm going to have to take off your pretty pink dress, yes, and your little white panties, yes, you bad naughty dolly. That's what happens to little dollies with pink pink bottoms. Unless they want to be spanked."

She pushed the doll, pink bottom upwards, on to the bed. The doll had on one white knitted knee sock and one black patent leather shoe. Her yellow hair fell either side of her head, obscuring her face which was pressed into the bedspread. Her other shoe lay beside her.

Jade poked her. "Lie still!"

She put the pink dress and white panties and the one sock, along with her sheets and her gym things, into the baggage buggy she and Lisa used to tote the laundry.

ᴄⱱᴆ

Lisa ducked her head back down into the stairwell. She tiptoed back down the stairs.

Not that she thought Jade would hear. It was almost as if it were some different person up there, not Jade at all, she was so weird with that doll. Episodes like this had happened before. Once she'd caught her rocking the doll and crying. Once she'd been spanking the doll softly and hissing strange words. But Jade never mentioned the doll, or anger, or misery, as if she didn't know she'd ever made her inner life visible.

Lisa thought bringing it up might be like waking someone sleepwalking on a tightrope. She wondered if she should tell someone. But who? Jade didn't seem to have any friends. Her family wasn't too far away — Peterborough, or was it Belleville — but Jade never went to see them, they never phoned. Jade had moved in with the help of a kid with a truck, whom she paid.

Lisa promised herself never again to pick up a roommate just because you joked together in the locker room. Jade had this zany sense of humour which made her look tough. She had admired the way Jade swaggered around and made assertions about life and men. But Jade had turned out to have this dark side to her personality. Lisa was very glad they'd only leased the house together for the summer.

She wanted to finish her ethics lesson plan for the summer engineering students Tuesday. It was the long weekend and she was anxious to take off with a clear conscience. So there she was, trying to concentrate, sitting at the kitchen table with her coffee and her books, when Jade came bumping the baggage buggy down the stairs.

Jade went into the bathroom and came out with her own towels and the bath mat. Then she went back in and came out with Lisa's towels too, she saw her jamming them into the baggage buggy.

She couldn't figure out how to stop Jade, she was on such a fuzzed out roll, even though those were her pink towels she'd just put out Thursday and she didn't think they needed washing yet. Then Jade came into the kitchen and took the tea towels, dishcloths and pot holders too, even though these were the ones Lisa had put out when she cleaned up after cooking last night.

ᲚᲧᲒ

Mel in the corner store liked the girl's red shorts.

He crinkled out a Craven Light from the pack he kept under the counter and flicked his Bic at it. The phone rang. "Speak," he said, and flipped over the sports page. "Three," he said. "No, no. I said three," and he put down the phone.

Morris shouldn't try to second-guess him.

You see a lot of women come in here, you know what kind of cigarettes Georgia wants before she asks, and how it takes Mrs. Steele fifteen minutes to buy one small bottle of juice because she can't make up her mind should it be Passion Fruit, should it be Cranapple.

But this was one of the new tenants at Sadie's, and he liked her red shorts, tight around her waist with a brown belt, and almost straight over her hips and her little ass . . .

Tell me, gold god on high, was it this you feared? This lusting after women? Your own lack of self-control? Was it this that spurred your enlightenment?

. . . but then flaring. He laid his cigarette by the cash register. The girl's thighs were thin and tanned and smooth. She shaved them. And her good calves — you could tell she walked. But not far, not in those sandals. Little straps laced over her ankles from thin flat leather soles. You wonder sometimes who they think they are, these girls. But a khaki shirt, like what a kid would wear in camp. And no makeup.

He put down his cigarette to make change for a woman buying yogurt.

What the girl bought was a *Globe*. And she picked up some Hall's Black Currant, and a little pack of tissues. She said she needed quarters in her change, for the laundromat. She didn't want a bag. She tucked the tissues and the Hall's in the left and right pockets of her shorts. But then the phone rang, and Mel couldn't see what page she opened the paper to.

"Mo says four," he said. "By me, three."

Not the sports page, that's for sure. Probably the horoscopes. Her neck was soft and white as she bowed her head over the paper and trundled her baggage buggy out the door, without even glancing at, let alone thanking, whoever was holding it open for her.

✺

The robins that nested under the deck off Jade's third floor bedroom were making a terrible ruckus in the landlady's garden, hopping back and forth, back and forth, from tree to fence, filling the air with alarmed cries. Jade reeled out the clothesline which was anchored from her deck to the ailanthus tree growing against the neighbour's fence. She always hung her clothes out to dry. The clothesline was one of the reasons for choosing the third floor. In summer, Momma always dried her clothes on a clothesline. Jade flapped out wet sheets and towels vigorously.

But the robins kept on screeching. She peered down the three storeys, past the sheets.

A white cat lay among the dry brown drift of ailanthus flowers on the landlady's deck, a baby robin between its paws. The three other babies were down there too, brown smudges huddled in the ailanthus debris.

✺

Lisa sent up prayers of thanks she wasn't going to live with Jade in this little frame house always, the way she thundered down the stairs and everything rattled and vibrated. She wiped up spilled coffee from the table and her notes.

"Oh, you poor little angels!" Jade was squeaking as she ran down their stairs, then down the stairs to the landlady's floor and out the side door. Lisa could hear her pounding round into the landlady's garden.

✺

Ailanthus stuff crunched under Jade's feet. "Shoo! Shoo! Bad pussycat! Bad momma! Bad poppa!"

She scooped up the three baby robins, dusty and trembling, light as spiders in her hand. Under the landlady's deck was garden equipment, including a toppled stack of green plastic flowerpots. She clattered one out, dirty and damp, and set the three baby robins in it. Above her, the parents screeched like smoke detectors.

The white cat had retreated under the cedar trees at the end of the landlady's garden, the fourth baby in its mouth. Jade crouched and crept, past forsythia and rock formations, closer and closer to the cat. The cat leapt, baby in mouth, to the top of the fence, and away. Jade pushed through the cedars but the fence was too high for her to see over. The parent robins dive-bombed her, screeching. The cat reappeared two fences down, then disappeared again.

Jade carried the three babies in the flowerpot through the house, up, out onto her deck. The nest was down there under the deck against a post. If she had a long pair of barbecue tongs she might be able to reach under and get them back in, but she didn't.

She set the pot on the deck in the shade close to the house. The baby robins reached out with their wobbly necks and open yellow mouths. She hung out the towels, her gym tights, the pink things, the pink things.

The parent robins circled, yelling.

Worms.

"That's what you'd like, isn't it, you silly wee minkies, isn't it? Long dangly pink juicy worms."

The landlady had a composter, black plastic, sold by the Ministry of the Environment at low cost to reduce garbage collections. Jade trudged back downstairs. She hauled the garden fork from under the deck and began to poke in the compost.

She didn't find any worms, but what she did find, among old ailanthus knuckles, prune pits, wine corks, plastic tags from bread wrappers, elastic bands, half eggshells, broccoli stems, squash skins, apple cores, banana peels and bread crusts, were a lot of many-legged bugs. She scooped up what she could into a plastic yogurt container, also from under the deck. Dirt came too, and stained her khaki shirt. On the way back to the deck she got Lisa's tweezers from the little leather zippered case in the bathroom. Up on the deck, the baby robins opened their mouths when she came at them with the tweezers and she was actually beginning to stuff some bugs down them.

Then Lisa hollered up to her from the foot of the stairs.

ᏬᏜᎧ

Really, if you came right down to it, Lisa thought later, you should go with your first . . . what she meant was, you shouldn't change your . . . if you'd decided to do something a certain way, you should do it that way.

But Jade had been so wired.

And also, if you came right down to it, this was a new guy, and he was way out in the country. She didn't really know him all that well yet at all. It was only at the party the Saturday before that they had met, and she had liked him enough — he was tall and he moved like a panther and he was going into law — that she gave him her number, and then, when he called, an expedition to the country at the end of a blistering week had sounded so great. But really you should have someone along, for backup. That was plain sense.

That's why she asked Jade to come into the country with her after all. It seemed like a good idea at the time.

2

Your teaching, Saky: birth is sorrowful; growth, decay, illness, death are all sorrowful; separation from objects we love, hating what cannot be avoided, craving what cannot be obtained are sorrowful.

Limes always rolled out of the compost heap when Mike turned it over, which, because the old bugger had barked at him so, he undertook every four weeks. He preferred to do the turning in the cool of the morning, like now, when the order of the day was to take out the odoriferous contents of the rusted juice can from beside the kitchen sink: the egg shells, orange skins and uneaten marmaladey toast left over from breakfast — Paddy's toast, it was; Mike's own appetite was just fine, thank you very much — and also last night's fish bones and potato peelings.

You had first to jerk the fork out of the ground beside the compost heap where it remained always, snow or sleet, rain or shine, leaning against the low walls of concrete blocks which framed three sides of a bin to contain the waste.

Or rather, to not contain the waste. The bin certainly did not contain the waste at this time of year. The seeds of melons and squashes stuck green leaves and tendrils out the holes in the concrete blocks. Potato sprouts lusted for life . . .

These, say you, Saky, are the causes of sorrow: the action of the outside world on the senses, exciting a craving thirst for something to satisfy them, or a delight in the objects presenting themselves, either of which is accompanied by a lust for life.

. . . sprouts lusted for life around the edges of the heavy gauge plastic sheet which was spread over the heap for cover. Oozings of damp black composted soil journeyed forth from the open side of the concrete bin to creep and crawl into the long grasses and then to the lawn and the daisies which flourished so lushly here where they found nourishment.

The old bugger mowed the lawn weekly. Sitting on his little tractor like a kid on a kiddy cart, he would bumpily circle the house in ever grander circles. Over the years he had encroached on pasture. The lawn had become an acre, two acres, bigger even than the pond. You could tell what areas were added because of the increased ratio of weeds to grass in them the farther you got from the house. These unfertilized outer reaches showed the effects of Paddy's assiduity in patches of brown dryness, even down to bare earth. But near the compost heap the lawn was always lush.

In order to deal correctly with the compost, you had to remove the pink and grey fieldstones which anchored the plastic cover. Flies circled the heap. Maggots matured in it. Earwigs tumbled. Spiders wove their traps between the concrete blocks and stones and plastic, and the blades of grass and weeds. But when you yanked back the cover and plunged in your fork, all insect life got ripped up.

The limes, however, had remained whole and still smelt limey, although they had to have been there over the winter, through frost and thaw. It was true that the compost heap generated a fair amount of heat and it was possible, therefore, that all that had happened to the limes was a process of drying out, or even of cooking, which had browned them but left them whole. It was curious, though, that there should be so many whole limes, little citrus corpses, mummified. He had to suppose it was further evidence of Maggie's profligacy.

Digging into the compost heap had revolted him enough at first that he had allowed himself to berate Paddy about the chore for, over months, even years of neglect, the compost had become compacted. The lower levels had got soggy and hard, matted with twigs and layers of leaves. He would turn up carelessly included bits of plastic in his digging, old elastic bands, beer bottle caps, triangles of asphalt roofing, cellophane cigarette wrappers, cedar chips, ivoried steak bones, along with the black and sodden sludge. The smell of rot, redolent of the outhouse at Children's Summer Bible Camp, blew around even now, the minute he removed the cover, and mingled with pollens and moulds.

You can see where thinking the girl would rot in the bush unnoticed came from, can't you, Saky? The fumes from her flesh just another strand in the bucolic bouquet.

He wore gloves to turn the compost, for otherwise the sight and smell of so much change and decay overwhelmed him. He had found a packet of disposable plastic painters' gloves in the bottom of the drawer with the tin foil. Yet, now that balmy weather was upon them, even in the cool of a morning like this he would roll up his sleeves and it was impossible that he should avoid dirtying himself. Nonetheless, under the streaks of decayed matter on his arms, at least his own blood continued to course healthy and normal, his cells to regenerate, the old to be swept away and evacuated to make way for the new. It thrilled him that even human waste is preserved in the country, first in the septic tank which lay under Paddy's lawn, then in the composting bins of Strickland who came and pumped out the tank, and then back on lawns next season, after conversion into topsoil by Strickland. Once a thing was dead and wanted no more in its present state, you were obliged to recycle it.

A lime lay on the lawn at the toe of his white socks in his brown Birkenstocks. He picked it up and heaved it into the sumacs beyond the clearing. He listened to it crash through branches. Something squealed. It was going to be a hot day. He banged the juice can to rid it of the last dreg and peel, and set off to collect the chipmunk.

His coordinates were the line of exit from the concrete well off his room and the easiest route across the grass to the compost heap, and there the trap lay in the grass where he had dropped it the night before.

But the chipmunk was not there.

No trace. Not even fur.

Only the trap. Sprung. Dewy. Getting a little rusted.

Rocks, grass, trees, sky shimmered as if about to change form, and come together, and engulf him, just the way the first day, when they locked him up on the psychiatric ward, everything had swum about, and he had fainted.

Had there ever been a chipmunk?

He found himself rubbing his forehead with the filthy plastic glove. He bent and picked up the trap and the can, and made his way out of the sun. Before he prepared the old man's lunch, he showered again. In the shower he saw that his body was being divided by this lifestyle into two parts, a clear distinction between white torso, legs and upper arms, and burned redness of hands and forearms.

They had used ashes in the outhouse at Children's Summer Bible Camp, he remembered over the cheese sandwiches, to promote decay and prevent odours. You didn't have to wait for God to work the changes of time. You could assist. The only ashes here at this time of year were in the barbecue, but he did believe that now there was also a product that you spread in composters to hasten decay. He believed he'd seen it in the village hardware. He'd make an expedition to the village hardware very soon.

That's quite some shop stall you have here, Saky. Beyond this wall though. I guess your gold eyes can't see it. Near the door, just before you get to the great glass contributions box on its sturdy pedestal on your way into your gold and red sanctuary.

They sell everything a person might want for worshipping there, and for soothsaying, and for remembering the dead — joss sticks, great bundles of them in long narrow cardboard boxes on top of a huge glass and wood showcase, plastic-wrapped packets of incense, pricey or cheap according to how it's made and what it's made of, and on the wall, behind the fat grinning stall custodian behind his creaking cash register, are scrolls — which I can't read — pictures of mountains with snowy peaks, pictures of you, statues of you, small and large, made out of everything from gold and red plastic to rosewood to marble, on the glass counter, inside the case, on shelves on the wall. There is a rotating rack of postcards.

On the postcards the temple yard is in a state of extreme cleanliness, extreme neatness, not a leaf in the statue garden, not a matchstick on the courtyard paving stones. The postcards illustrating the inside show only your golden statues — not a worshipper in sight, not one plate of rotting oranges before a picture of an ancestor, no cooling soup, no drying rice cakes, no stubs of burnt joss sticks.

The postcard I got for Paddy is the one of the dragons. They sell stamps too. They send mail. Soon the dragons will sit on the table in the Big House hall where Michael Randolph Hughes always puts the mail.

How can I warn Paddy? Here be dragons? Take care?

3

Jade and Lisa, driving out of Toronto past the airport and on up Airport Road, marvelled at the short bright leaves of new corn, two-by-two in undulating rows, emerald against the black earth; the swoop over the road of flocks of grey and beige doves with white arrow tails; the frantic green of forests in the distance.

It's June, becoming July, Saky. How can everything not be concerned with begetting and the begotten, not lust for life? It's the nature of the beast.

∾

As Zeeb prowled around outside the cabin, he banged against the thick green seed pods that topped the daffodils Polly had planted by the steps long ago. He watched muskrats swim sails of green fodder across the pond to feed the kits in their dens. Phoebe nestlings squeaked under the eaves of the screened porch.

Yet the complete conquest over and destruction of this eager thirst, this lust for life, is how sorrow ceases. Your teaching, teacher.

You met an old man, a sick man, a decaying corpse, a hermit. The details of your comfortable domestic dailiness became insupportable. The life of a monk seemed a haven of peace. You turned your back on thirst and lust, and became the Buddha.

Can you teach me to turn my back on those I call family? Not to thirst for Zeeb's salvation? Not to lust for his life?

Before he settled down to work, he had to get rid of the phoebe nest under the porch eaves. The phoebes always nested under the eaves, dipping in, come spring, with mud and peat moss to build their fortresses on top of the two-by-four that framed the screened porch. After one disastrous hot summer long ago, one of the family — Polly, he, even Sibyl got sufficiently energized by vengeance sometimes to help out with this task — one of them would knock their nests down.

He could still get a little hot retelling himself the story of the disaster, the cause of it all, Sibyl, no underpants on, bending over to peer at her tilted-up crotch and shrieking at it, "Where have you been?" Red welts shone through her pubes, like a boy's acne. "They itch like crazy! It's creatures, Polly! You can see them on the toilet paper!"

She had liked to smoke on the chaise longue in the corner of the screened porch, in her nothings as often as it was hot enough. From that vantage she could watch the ducks on the pond, and listen to the phoebe babies greet their parents, and read her book. She had a big brown pottery ashtray with a fish on it that was really Paddy's, for his pipes. She would rest it on a wooden chair by the chaise longue and wave her ashes over it. Long after his friends' mothers would rush to cover up their nakedness, Sibyl maintained her aloof do-whatever-the-hell-you-want attitude. The corner of the porch was the breeziest shadiest place in the cabin on a hot day, so there she would lounge, in her nothings. At the time she got bitten she hadn't begun yet to get thin, her body was still long and curved and white, and her cough only interesting. Afterwards, when they had diagnosed and dosed the problem with the phoebes, Polly put a piece of typewriter paper on the chaise longue. Within minutes it was crawling with minute transparent bugs. The insect book called them biting lice.

Leslie knew all about them. She was a biologist. "They're endemic," she said. "All birds have them. A nestling is infested within seconds of hatching. Your poor mom."

"They're breeding in my bottom," Sibyl had cried and even the nestlings hadn't been able to endure the situation that summer. Maybe the mites were worse than usual because of exceptional heat. Anyway, first the little naked birds hopped out of the nest and onto the two-by-four on which the nest was built, and the parents fed them there. But that perch must have got infested too. So then, not quite fledged enough to fly, they dive-bombed to the deck and tried to propel themselves with bare beating wings along the hot boards and over the edge into the cool bushes, but they got caught in the spaces between the boards and, one by one, gaping silent beaks, they dehydrated and died. The parents darted back and forth in fruitless journeys to the empty nest screeching, Phoebe! Phoebe!

You had to go fifteen miles into a drugstore in Bolton to get lice shampoo in those days. Ever after, they knocked down the phoebe nests each weekend, all spring, until the parents gave up. Bits of mud and dried moss would litter the bottom of the screen and hang from the two-by-four as the phoebes attempted again and again to breed. Bits of yolk and shell decayed on the deck. Bird eggs never became wonderful and mysterious to him as they were to other kids in his class. He never went through a period of collecting them.

He strode into the cabin. He put on the jeans that had no holes in them and socks and one of Polly's long-sleeved shirts, before that Paddy's. He unlocked the tool shed and disentangled the rake from the hoe and the big yellow roll of binder twine. He strode back round the cabin and halted on the deck thus armed, looking up at the nest, reviewing his strategy.

The twittering parent phoebes carried on as usual without

a suspicion of the ethnic cleansing to come, though this dispossession happened every year. They were bobbing down by the pond on the wild purple flags, mouths dangling, out of one a butterfly, out of the other a dragonfly, like gum wrappers, waiting for him to get out of the way so they could fly back to their squeaking babes and satisfy their growing needs.

He raised the rake and scraped along the two-by-four. The nest loosened, tumbled, hit the deck, hit the stairs, and landed upside down on the ground. In the grass beside it one nestling opened and shut a yellow beak. The nest itself, grey and fragile, undulated slowly, the other babies trapped beneath.

You hadn't been able to see how nearly bird-like they had got when you reached up with the rake.

He threw down the rake and plunged down to the pond and in, clothes and all. Dripping, with fingers that fumbled, he unfastened wet buttons and zipper, pulled off clinging clothes, flung them on the beach. He cleaved the icy water, scrubbing and scrubbing at the possibility of lice, the tug of life and death, the thrill of power, in scalp, armpits, crotch.

When he surfaced he saw the pair of mallards watching him from the silt basin at the far end of the pond.

～

Jade insisted on painting her nails in the car. It made Lisa nervous. On top of having to figure out where they were going, she now also had to worry about Jade spilling red nailpolish all over her interior. On top of that, the traffic was horrendous.

"Jerks!" she breathed, and braked hard.

A red car with two big guys in it had zoomed past and then had not been able to make it beyond the car she was following before getting crowded out by a car heading towards them. With a cloud of smoke, the red car had swerved into line directly in front of her and Jade.

Jade cranked open the window. "Toadstools!" she yelled.

She wound the window up again.

"Toadstools?" Lisa was relieved to see Jade back in form. "Now that's a new one."

"Stick around, girl, and you'll hear lots of new ones." Jade stuck her feet up on the dashboard and put the hand she was painting on her thigh, the bottle of polish supported in a crease in her shorts. "Know what else I call those creatures? Those asinine fools who don't know how to drive?"

"Asinine fools."

"Generically though," said Jade.

"Assholes."

"No. Scromen."

"Scromen?"

"A woman is a man with a womb. A scroman is a man with a scrotum. Those creatures in front of us are two dumb scromen."

"And women's histories are herstories, I suppose."

"Something wrong with that?" Jade dipped the brush into the polish.

"It's not a word."

"What's not?"

"Herstories. And woman means wife slash man. A person who is a wife. Read the dictionary."

"I see," said Jade. "So. We're not women. We're maidens."

"Speak for yourself."

Jade jabbed on the cap of the nailpolish so violently she smudged red polish on her thighs. "Shouldn't we get some wine," she said, looking around, out the windows, ahead, "some more wine? There must be a wine store in one of those villages. Stop at the wine store and I'll buy a bottle of wine. You got red, didn't you? Well then, I should get a bottle of white. We can chill it in the wine store, in . . .

Jade/Laverna will turn out not to be the heroine of her own life. She cannot tell her story. She babbles. Words fail her. She cannot connect.

She is the victim.

The piles of fruit, the bowls of food, I have found, are not for you, Prince of the Sakyas. They are for the worshippers' ancestors, to console their loneliness.

What will I be able to offer Jade/Laverna's hungry ghost?

. . . that chiller thing they have in wine stores. Should I get bubbly maybe? Or would you like me to get you a bottle of vodka? That's white."

When Lisa had broken down and changed her mind and invited her to come with her into the country after all, Jade hadn't wasted a second. The robins could have been a problem, but then a light snapped, and she put the plug in the bathtub, and dumped in the bugs, and settled the ugly little creatures there with their floppy little wings, and shut the bathroom door. Lisa wouldn't like it. You don't put birds in the bathtub, Jade. But Lisa would never know. She would whip them out the instant they got back. She hadn't even changed her clothes. She wasn't going to keep Lisa waiting, give her time to change her mind again. She just jammed the nailpolish and her lipstick and her wallet into her little shoulder bag, and went.

"And let me get some cold cuts," she embroidered. "Is there a deli somewhere do you think?" She looked out on an apple orchard. You could hardly distinguish the apples from the leaves. "Pemale."

"What's that mean?" said Lisa.

"Well, Lisa, if you won't let me say scroman, will you at least let me say pemale? Those people in front of us are two hairy pemales."

The red car again pulled out to pass, and made it this time, spilling forward in a roar and a cloud of black smoke. Soon Jade and Lisa could see it climbing the hill ahead.

"Did you ever climb the ouch tower?" Lisa said. For her mother it had been the spire of Salisbury Cathedral. Ouch! She waited for Jade's response.

"The ouch tower?"

"The CN Tower." She could see it in the rearview mirror, at this distance a minute silvery rod. "Ouch."

Jade sat up straight. Uncle Freddy had a place in the country. The whole family used to go there for many many summer weekends. There were paths that went deep into the woods. Uncle Freddy would plant dimes on the paths. Little Laverna, in her little white shorts and little pink T, her feet in little white sandals, would follow the dimes down the woodsy path. She'd pick up the dimes, here, and there, and over there, all over the place, and put them into the little white pocket of her little white shorts as she went deeper and deeper into bristly darkness.

"Toadstools," Jade said.

"Okay, toadstools," said Lisa.

"Inverted toadstools," said Jade.

"Not when I see them, they're not inverted," said Lisa. "Not usually."

Jade covered her mouth. She crossed her legs.

∽

Zeeb had spent the first part of the morning looking beyond the PowerBook screen out the window at the duck and drake who were fooling around in the silt basin. They had upended by turns to feed. One would upend and feed for fifteen minutes or so and the other one would guard. And then they'd switch roles. Now, sated on water bugs and duckweed, they were sailing to the middle of the pond. They began to throw water all over themselves, diving under, standing on the water and flapping.

There were two of them, two ducks.

There were two phoebes trying to rebuild under the eaves oblivious to their dying young in the grass by the steps.

Two cardinals, red male, olive female, darted among the cedars.

Dragonflies in twos everywhere flew and poised on leaves and grasses, locked in the pulsations of mating.

He tried to focus the computer screen.

Leslie on her island would be focusing her microscope. He could see her fingers moving the slide, turning the knob, he could feel her fingers.

He sat erect and frowned at the screen. His thesis supervisor had found two errors in the calculations by which he was deconstructing the essays and sermons of Ralph Waldo Emerson. The consequence was that he had to run all the numbers through the calculator again and check all the graphs.

Very mechanical.

Very accurate this time.

Maybe he should have gone by recurrent etymologies instead of meaning derived from the recurrences of words and images. Maybe he should have run his formula through that way.

Leave well enough alone.

If it ain't broke, don't fix it.

You could see why they say duck. The ducks ducked under the water, first one, then the other. Each swam about two metres right under the water before bobbing up again. A trout leaped up to see what on earth was going on.

The shower at their apartment — his and Leslie's, until a month ago — the water there was always hot and steamy, and Leslie's body under his soapy hands was square and efficient and speedy and silk. The showers on Leslie's island — the island where she went every summer to examine the sea and its creatures — those showers were communal, unisex, men and women together. The guy on the stool beside her in the lab would stand beside her in the shower sharing her soap. Gull cries and salt wind and seas crashing — that was Leslie's island. Ten miles out. He had been there. The isolation was complete.

The ducks were now flapping across the pond, flying off. They were never more than three metres apart.

A letter from Leslie. There could be one. One could have been delivered before he got up here. She could have recanted.

It was possible, reasonable really. He hadn't looked in the mailbox in all the commotion with Sam. Why not take ten now, head up the drive and see if there was a letter from Leslie in the mailbox?

He took the Swing King with him.

The Swing King was a lethal instrument of vegetable destruction given Polly by Paddy — or it was on permanent loan. That's the way they did things between them. Years ago Paddy had given Polly the Swing King and then, when he came over to fish, he would come into the cabin for a beer after and lay down his catch, little beauties threaded on a cedar branch through gills to mouth, plunk them on the table, and look around, and see the Swing King still leaning in the corner by the ice box, and he would say, See you still got the Swing King. Still work? And what this meant was, was Polly still patrolling the drive for thistles? And Polly would say, Yup, still works. And Paddy and Polly would both feel good.

The Swing King was hooked like a shepherd's crook, except that the crook was a double-edged blade. You could stand among tall grasses and slash high and wide like a golfer — only you'd be swinging both ways — and grass, and pink and white clover, and purple vetch, and ox-eyed daisies — everything would go flying. You could face a six-foot thistle in the eye and say, Die! and snap its wrist-thick stem at double arm's length and never meet a prickle.

He dawdled across the dam, the Swing King on his shoulder, looking over the steep jungly precipice of the down side of the dam to where the water poured out the drainpipe. Thistles were hard to see yet, it being only June. They weren't yet in bloom; their green merged with everything else. He waded into the patch of green on the flat place beside the drive where it curved round the pond to the cabin and the dam. He was looking for young thistles among the tall stalks that would bloom as goldenrod in August and also he was looking to visit Polly's yucca.

The yucca was a desert cactus plant. Polly had rescued it from the demolition of somebody's rock garden for sentimental reasons to do with the antiwar songs she and Sibyl and their friends used to sing sitting around with the hash pipe and the guitar.

We sang against the dark. The power of words to show our hearts was lost then too. We spoke in riddles.

Mid the yuccas and the thistles
I'll watch those guided missiles
While the old F.B.I. watches me.
I'll have on my sombrero
And of course I'll wear a pair o'
Levis over my lead B.V.D.'s.

Your monk is frowning, Saky. I guess he doesn't like me singing. If he says anything I'll say it's a middle-aged form of round-eye worship.

The old house on Huron Street descended on Zeeb with a rush, where he and Polly and Sibyl had the second floor when he was a kid. The Indian print bedspreads. Him leaving his little room in the night and peering into the big room at Sibyl sitting cross-legged on the bed on an Indian print bedspread, twanging her guitar and smoking while Polly and the rest of them sang songs, runaways from the U.S. and tough dropouts and people with long hair. Long McAdam would be hunched there too sometimes. Even after he'd gone on to better things he would be back with them sometimes singing to Sibyl's guitar, uncomfortable but defiant in a velvet shirt, ochre, that Sibyl had thought he would look good in.

It was hard at school for him to explain his family, hard ever to explain it to anyone. I live with my mother and my stepmother was an almost impossible thing to say. But, inasmuch as Polly and Sibyl were together and Long had left them all for law school, Polly was his stepmother.

He slashed through the green stems of goldenrods-to-be. The female cardinal was clucking a warning at him from the cedars lining the pond. There was no sign of the yucca. Polly used to be so proud of its tall stem of white blooms.

I live with my mother and my stepmother.

The only person who had ever understood without long detailed explanations was Leslie. "Polly and your father both loved Sibyl," Leslie said. "Makes sense to me."

Leslie, too, would sit on the bed cross-legged; but they never had an Indian print bedspread, they had a paisley duvet cover made for them by her mother. And Leslie didn't play guitar and she didn't smoke. They had both their computers in their bedroom because the apartment was too small to put them anywhere else. All was for the best in this best of all possible worlds when they were working there, back to back, she on her graphs, he on his. Their bikes had hung on hooks from the living room ceiling, three of them, his, hers, and a collapsible bicycle-built-for-two they had found in a secondhand shop. They used that one for Sunday rides by the river.

No more. Broken up. Empty. Everything jammed away in boxes. His stored with his friends, hers with hers.

He sliced back to the drive, chanting, his voice husky, "There are four men mowing down by the Isar; I can hear the swish of the scythe-strokes, four Sharp breaths taken; yea, and I Am sorry for what's in store."

In the poplar copse he saw a fresh-chewed stump, and a green-leafed little poplar tumbled.

So. There really was a beaver.

He swung at a thistle under the pines, soft and green from living in the shade, so soft the force of his stroke uprooted it. He dumped it from his blade onto the drive to shrivel and die. The surface of the pond was unruffled. It disclosed nothing, like a woman in a raincoat. He pushed away from it on up the drive.

The raspberries were not yet ripe either, like the thistles and, looking at the hard little green seed cases in brown calyxes, he doubted they were going to amount to much this year. Too dry. Too hot. The male cardinal was following him down the drive, issuing the long descending notes of his territorial affirmative from tree tops. Even the blackberries weren't going to amount to much this year. The berries had arranged themselves on the brambly branches in unripe succession, the least unripe tinged faintly with scarlet and quite large and then they got greener and smaller down to little pinheads.

Leslie, cleaning an old boiling fowl to make chicken soup, had pulled out eggs, complete ones, yolk and all except for the shell, and then just small yolks and then smaller, finally gradating down to tiny knobs on twig-like structures. "That's what's in me," she said, "just so many eggs, just so many opportunities to reproduce and then finis to perpetuating the race." Her hands had been bloody to the wrists with chicken goo as she hauled out strips of guts and the gizzard. She cut the gizzard open to show him the stones. The chicken guts had emitted a sulphur smell and there was a streak of chicken blood on her forehead under her bangs where she'd pushed them back with the back of her hand.

Leslie had wanted to marry him.

Leslie had wanted his babies.

Leslie had wanted to make him a home.

Before.

He sliced a daisy.

He had moved out of Polly's house when he was sixteen. Polly had been trying to turn him into a Sibyl, a constant companion for going to the movies on Friday nights, with dinner always at 6:00 and summer weekends always at the farm. They had shouted at one another in the kitchen and he, hot and swollen, had flung out and found a haven in the sixth floor of a warehouse with a floating population.

There was an Indian bedspread on the couch there too, and a view of the lake out the loading door. That was where he first smoked dope. They never let him when Sibyl was alive, and Polly stopped after Sibyl died. Smoking dope that first time he had seen the outline of the loading door become hard and clear with streetlights and little chugging airplanes from the island airport framed in it. He had never felt so sick in his life. He had been sitting on the floor. He had moved so he was backed up against the couch. Time had eventually passed.

That was also the last time he smoked dope. He got a job waiting tables. Long brought him home once to meet his half-brothers with their white shirts hanging out over their belts and their school ties undone. Later he got a job hefting boxes at a Brewers' Retail. When he was nineteen he had gone back to school and met Leslie.

He creaked open the mailbox. All that was there was a flyer about a cleaning service and a real estate brochure. He jammed them into his back pocket, clanked the blue lid back down and swung the Swing King up onto his shoulder like a rifle, stood tall.

Jeez.

A woman was retreating down the road. He hadn't seen her but there she was, pushing a squeaky stroller. A little boy scurried along beside her under a sun hat. She was wearing shorts and a shiny belt. The muscles on her calves bulged with speed.

With more than speed. She'd seen him and turned. She was running away from him.

Why? Why? Why? What the fuck was the matter with women? This was what he and Leslie had fought over, this ridiculous female paranoia. Why, he had screamed, why do I have to cross to the other side of the street just because some stupid cunt thinks I'm following her? I'm not following her. I wouldn't follow a woman on the street for a million dollars.

Because, she had screamed back at him, you're a man. That's why. How does she know you're not a rapist!

I'm not a rapist!

We can't tell by looking!

And she wouldn't shut up. She wouldn't give him credit for any sense at all and she would not shut up, she kept on and on at him. And so . . . in the silver moonlight . . . And so . . .

Yet who would have thought her to have had so much blood in her? He wiped his nose and eyes with the back of his hand. He stood tall. He stuck his thumb in his mouth and pumped up his bicep, huge and veined and shading dark under the sun.

∽

"There's a prepossessing specimen of hemale humanity," said Jade. "See? There. Coming up on the right. Beside that blue mailbox. Look at him scan the sky and suck his thumb. Your prototypical hick consulting the sky for the weather. Let's ask him for directions. My, they do breed them big and brown in the country, don't they? Is your friend as workmanlike as that? Muscles in all the right sizes and places? He probably won't know what's meant by a deli, but he will know where there's beer, and where there's beer there's got to be wine and at least a lead to a deli. Stop, Lisa, stop. Excuse me, excuse me. Hey! You in the jeans. Drive right up beside him, Lisa. He's not paying attention. Hello! Could you tell us where there's a beer store around here?"

Zeeb drew his thumb out of his mouth. He bent down, leaned his arms on the window frame and looked into the car. Bare legs, two pairs, one pair with smudges of red on the thighs. He didn't think it was blood. He looked at the one who was driving. She had good tits. Back to the dirty blonde. Back to the driver.

"Griselda was the lady's name all right," he said, "and on my word in all of Albion's city was none so fair, surpassing every wight. So angelic was her native beauty that like a thing immortal appeared she, as doth a heavenly perfect creature, who was sent down in scorn of nature."

"Chaucer," said Lisa. "Eh? Chaucer?"

"Hey!" He looked her over. "You got it. Chaucer, through Concord, Mass."

"Concord?" How brown his face was. His body smelled, not of sweat, but of the brown, and also of green. "Mass?"

"Concord, Massachusetts. Ralph Waldo Emerson. My thesis topic. Internal patterns of connotative and denotative logic in Emerson's transcendentalism. I'm working it out with a calculator."

"A calculator?"

The voices of Lisa and this improbable hick/poet merged into incomprehensibility and their outlines went blurry. Jade drew her feet up on the seat, put her arms around her legs, dropped her head to her knees. She understood nothing. She never understood anything and never understood why.

When she was still little Laverna she would say that when she grew up she was going to play basketball and cream the Harlem Globe Trotters and Poppa would shout at her. Not for wanting to cream the Harlem Globe Trotters. Poppa wanted to cream the Harlem Globe Trotters himself, and a few other sports players who, he thought, monopolized games and kept him and his like out. Poppa would shout at little Laverna for being unladylike. Or she'd scoop baked beans out of the can with her fingers and Momma would slap her wrist. For having no manners. Though Momma often told stories of hunger and famine in the perilous escape from the old land. Uncle Freddy, though, would always smile down at little Laverna with his wet petunia eyes.

Uncle Freddy loved little Laverna, of that you could be sure. He interposed himself between her and the cruel world at every possible step. Why, it was Uncle Freddy who took little Laverna to Eaton's to buy an Easter bonnet. They got on the bus to go downtown and they sat behind the driver. Little Laverna's legs would always feel as if they wanted to twinkle and flip when she was with Uncle Freddy. They'd want to race around in circles all on their own and do the things legs do in handstands.

Uncle Freddy kept a smiling eye on what little Laverna's legs were doing as they sat on the seat behind the bus driver. Little Laverna's black shoes twinkled and danced and Uncle

Freddy laid the cool tips of his fingers on her bare legs. She could feel little shivers turn her tummy to jelly. She smiled up at Uncle Freddy and his wet petunia eyes.

I want the prettiest Easter bonnet in the store, Uncle Freddy had said to the saleslady, for my pretty little niece.

Little Laverna's face grew lines so deep she could feel them corroding from eyes to chin as she grinned up at Uncle Freddy who clasped her hot hand in his cool spongy one.

You would always look up at Uncle Freddy and smile till you could feel the lines on your face. Then Uncle Freddy's eyes wouldn't actually see you. They would see something else. You always grinned so Uncle Freddy wouldn't see you when he looked down with his wet petunia eyes.

"Sam the Man?" the hick/poet/whatever was saying. "That's the guy you're going to visit? Well, you can't miss him. He's working on the white A-frame at the corner up that way. But to get to the beer store you have to go back the other way, the way you came, and take the first right and then the first right again. Then you can just keep going round the concession to get back to the A-frame."

Jade ran her fingers down the lines on her cheeks. The guy was looking at her fingers. Polish had bled into the cuticles. She sat on her hands.

Zeeb looked away from the girl's blank eyes. "Hey," he said, "Why don't you all come over and fish. Or swim. You could come over and swim. Tell Sam Polly's place, he'll know. Remind him the fishing's good."

See? he wanted to shout at Leslie. See? he wanted to tell the woman with the stroller and the kid. Where's the rapist? Only a screwball would fucking worry.

But the girl was winding up the window. He had to jerk his arms out of the way. The other girl gunned the engine and waved. The car made a three point turn and took off.

⌇

Now that they'd turned back towards Toronto, Jade could see the CN Tower, a centimetre of silver spume breaking away from the distant horizon. She looked back to where they'd just been. That hairy hemale had been erased by a rise. The line of blue hills in the far distance, back there beyond where he had been, they looked like storm clouds, though they weren't. But still, sometimes, on a perfectly beautiful day like today, a day when the best idea in the world was to leave the city and go for a walk in the woods, sometimes, from nowhere, one, then two, then many bristly clouds would appear, and they would darken, and the skies would open, and in no time at all you would be flooded and drowning. She felt twitchy, as if they should just head right on back home. She pressed her knees together. Silence must be kept at bay.

"When my Uncle Freddy died," she said, "it was really hard to believe he wasn't there any more. At his funeral I kept thinking he must be there, just around the corner, in the front room, standing in front of the TV, blocking it like always, with his cigarette drooping from his fingers. Or else he had to be around the corner sitting at the table, eating, talking."

Lisa wished Jade would be quiet for a minute, but then she saw a rusty *Globe & Mail* box at the corner and that made her feel more oriented, closer to civilization. She turned right. Jade was picking at the excess polish around the moon of her ring finger. He had said the next right. The next right led into a cul de sac. Now what?

"Eating with Uncle Freddy was like eating with God," Jade said. "When Uncle Freddy talked, everybody listened. He'd begin a sentence. We'd all be sitting around the table putting stuff on our plates and passing bowls and cutting, you'd hear the sounds of the knives and forks on the plates and water pouring, and Uncle Freddy would start talking: This was a so interesting man that worked with me, a medical doctor who had so many degrees, very well educated, very well educated, and one day he brought in a coin. Then Uncle Freddy pops a forkful of food in his mouth and starts to chew. It's like there's a war on his face.

The food has to go down. But the words still want to come up. And his face is struggling with his thoughts, his eyes looking inside at them, and his wet bristly moustache is working at what shapes the words will have when they do come up and also covering the teeth that are chewing the food." She pressed up and down on her thighs with her inflamed fingers. "These grunts come up through the strain on Uncle Freddy's face. You have to watch his face in silence waiting for him to work it out and finish. You have to smile. If you speak or sigh Uncle Freddy will give you this black look and start in all over again."

"What about the medical doctor?" They were approaching the traffic lights at last. At last, the second corner.

"What medical doctor?" Jade scraped at the red stains on her thighs with her red fingers. "Uncle Freddy had this place in the country. We'd take walks in the woods." Her knees pressed together and opened, pressed together and opened. "Wet, bristly, dark."

"The woods?" Jade said the weirdest things. "Wet? Bristly?"

"My God, Lisa." Jade waved her fingers out the window. "See that white car? See? Heading up the hill? That's the car that was parked in front of our house all day yesterday . . ."

These doublings and coincidences, Saky — the essence of life, the essence of karma. Yes?

"Remember? Don't you hate it when they do that? These dorks from the boonies drive in and park on our street and play around town all day and leave their cars in our parking space. Doesn't it just make you sick?"

"Oh, come on." Lisa wheeled into the parking lot between the liquor store and the deli and got out. The sun shone down from a large blue sky. You could hear birds. "You don't know it's the same car, and anyway, what's it to you? I'm the one who drives and I'm not upset."

"Well, you should be." Jade got out and gave the disappearing car the finger. "Stupid hemale! Look, Lisa, there's a deli!"

What Lisa then thought was that if, or really since, they wouldn't be able to use all the food Jade decided to buy, what they'd do was they'd take most of it back home to the city, although at home the shelves were already overladen with delicacies and luxuries from Jade's bouts of shopping. She didn't mind the canned provisions because cans keep. Hams, olives, sardines, smoked oysters, mandarin orange sections, hot eggplant antipasto, baked beans. Nor did she mind the dried stuff, the rice cakes, the digestive biscuits. Rice cakes and digestive biscuits are always useful.

That's what she was thinking as Jade loaded everything onto the glass deli counter. Today they could eat the sliced black forest ham and the swiss cheese, packed in their neat brown paper packages. They'd eat them with the fresh baked buns. The cheese and meat would fit in nicely with her cookies and the berries, and the devilled eggs. They'd drink one of Jade's bottles of wine, plus hers, and a bit of the sherry, and then they'd take the rest of the food home. Maybe Jade would want to open the antipasto or something, but they'd be taking most of the food home. That's what she was planning.

Deep down she was hoping Jade would pig out on all the goodies and fall asleep. That would leave her at least semi-alone to get a sense of Sam.

But that was all she was hoping would happen to Jade.

Of course, when she finally did leave to go back to the city she went in such a hurry that all that food got left behind.

And now, whatever was she going to do with all the cans, and boxes, and packets, and parcels at home? What did you do with miso?

4

Zeeb attacked the gravel drive like a drill sergeant, Swing King at arms. He barked orders.

"Sound off!"

Sound off.

"Sound off!"

Sound off.

"One. Two. Three. Four. One. Two." He marked time hard with his bare feet in the gravel. "Three, four!" He came to attention.

"I had a good home and I left."

Your right.

The drive closed in behind him. He re-entered the cool privacy of his fortifications, pines overarching, road sounds disappearing. He marched briskly, focusing his mind on the beaver.

One evening they'd got up to the cabin — he must have been about ten — to find the pond surface blanketed with green debris: stripped poplar boughs and leaves, reeds, pollen, rafts of algae, all moored in great logjams against the downpipe. The dimple of the downpipe was almost obliterated, the water level raised by six inches. The copse of little poplar trees by the drive was so thinned, fresh stumps showing, trunks jutting low, that you could see the cabin between the trees. The feet of the irises were drowning and the little beach Paddy had made with a truckload of sand at the drive end of the pond was awash with gently surging muck.

Polly had stripped right there beside the car and swum out and put her arms around the downpipe under the water and lifted the jammed branches. They jerked loose and began to skid down the pipe. Gallons of water, six inches of it raised across the acre wide surface of the pond, thundered down the pipe with such a strong pull that Polly said she could feel it tugging at her as she swam back to shore. He and Sibyl watched over the down side of the dam and marvelled at this miniature Niagara tumbling out of their pond.

While they ate dinner they could see the beaver, two of them, swimming in the pond, the vees of snouts, heads, ears arcing through the inexorable pull of leaves, branches, pollen, making a wake. One beaver climbed slowly out of the water and up the far bank. As the brown body emerged it showed its immensity and you could see, trailing after it, its broad tail.

"Ca-na-da!" sang Sibyl.

When they had washed the dishes, Polly had set off on the trail through the bush to the Big House to consult with Paddy, and Zeeb and Sibyl got on the raft to investigate. The beaver had excavated underwater into the far bank, dumping yellow dirt in pyramids on the bottom. Zeeb leaned over the edge of the raft and pushed the rafting pole through the water into the excavation as far as it would go to measure how deep the beaver had dug, but he couldn't touch the end. Humongous. Over the entrance, just above the surface of the water, the beaver had laid a sheltering roof of peeled poplar branches in straight rows and covered them with mud.

"Would you believe it?" said Sibyl. "Can you imagine animals being so smart?"

He ferried her around the verge of the pond. They saw the mud pads where the beaver had pounded a platform and the cherry trees gnawed off at the far end and the trail through the brush and over the dam which the beaver came and went by and the thinning of the poplars.

"Imagine all that happening while we're away," Sibyl said.

The next week when they drove down the drive the pond was clear. No debris. But a terrible stench assailed them through the car window as they rounded the curve of the drive.

"Ugh!" said Sibyl.

Hands over noses, they went to investigate. Two beaver corpses lay under the decimated poplars, bloated, crawling with maggots.

"Who?" cried Sibyl.

Polly explained about Paddy's trapper.

"He killed them!" said Sibyl. "He didn't have to kill them! He could have taken them to Algonquin! He could have put them in a zoo!"

Sibyl would not listen while Polly explained and explained that there was a crisis of beaver overpopulation, that the beavers, by means of their engineering, could plug the down-pipe totally and then the pond would overflow and the rush of water over the dam, which was only earth after all, would erode it and wash it away. They could lose the pond.

But the beaver, Sibyl cried. You killed them. In the night she had sobbed and wouldn't let Polly rock her.

The drive was coming out from under the pines. Zeeb lowered the Swing King and held it at the ready. He crouched and approached.

There was indeed a beaver down there, arcing through the pond. In spite of his stealthy approach, it caught sight of his reflection. It slapped the pond with a hard crash and vanished. He crouched by the poplars. After a while the beaver surfaced and began again to circle. Zeeb dashed low and soundless over the dam towards the cabin.

Inside, he erected the stepladder under the trapdoor to the loft. He climbed, pushed up the door, raised his head into the murkiness. It was hot up there. It smelled of old canvas tents. There were wasps. King's precious fly rod was there in its canvas case beside the green plastic bundle of the rifle. When King got out there with his fly rod, you weren't allowed to fish too, its cast was that long. He didn't want to hook you, that's what he said.

Zeeb backed down the stepladder with the rifle. Behind the door, out of sight of the pond, he unwrapped it. First the green plastic garbage bag. Then the linen pillow slip. Sitting there on the floor, he methodically cleaned it . . .

Always keep your powder dry — Paddy's teaching, Saky.
Never take life unnecessarily — yours.

. . . running the pull-through, a strip of rag tied in the middle of a fish line and weighted with a lead sinker, one of Paddy's inventions, back and forth, back and forth down the barrel. He sighted down it. Nothing. Smooth.

He went silently out the screen door, crept down the stairs, through the weeds to behind the cedars. Now he could slip under cover of reeds and tall grasses to the edge of the pond. The beaver was swimming unalarmed. Silently he fitted a shell into the rifle, cocked it, laid his cheek against the wood and metal. Squeezed the trigger.

The shot echoed against the pines. The beaver swam towards him. Jeez. Maybe it was rabid. He shot again, trying to remember the skew of the sights. But the fucking beaver kept coming. He shot a third time, hit. The beaver flurried up a little struggle of waves under the surface. A few silver bubbles rose. But she did not come up again.

When Zeeb could breathe he leapt back into the cabin. Quickly he cleaned the rifle. Wrapped it — the pillow slip, the plastic bag. Stowed it back up in the loft. Stowed the stepladder. He had to get over to the Big House, debrief to Paddy. Out the back door. Down the grassy path. Into the darkness under the cedars. But, halt. Where was the trail? All in shadows here was changed. He ran his forefinger back and forth along the bullet casings in his pocket.

Which way?

5

A place for everything and everything in its place, they'd taught Mike at the training school, and the place of the whetstone in this household, the old bugger insisted, was in a plastic bag inside a loaf pan in the cupboard which also housed Maggie's old Mixmaster. The whetstone came out sticky with oil and smelling rancid. He laid it on its bag on the kitchen table, opened his knife, and began to stroke it back and forth, back and forth along the gritty stone. He ran his thumb lightly along the edge, stroked it on the stone again, back and forth, back and forth.

It wasn't really his knife. It was the old bugger's from the workshop. He'd taken it, appropriated it. Why not? He lived here now, didn't he? But Paddy hadn't said anything, maybe hadn't recognized it.

The edge was fine now, razor-sharp. If any enemy impeded him he could draw blood.

He pulled out a chair and sat, began to carve at his fingernails. Little moons of nail accumulated on the table. The left hand was difficult to control but you had to master that weakness. Your punishment for lapses in steadiness was the sight of your own blood dripping. He liked his fingernails to be even with his fingertips but there was a fine line between too long and bloody injury.

When he had finished, he spread his hands on the table. There was dirt under his nails still from the compost. He ran the point of the knife under his nails, stropped the dirt off on his chinos.

He took off his Birks and his socks, cocked one foot up on the seat of his chair, and let toenail parings fall as they willed. The baby toe wanted to slip in behind the others and he lashed it over the fourth toe to make it behave.

When he had his socks and Birks back on he whetted the blade again. He left the knife open on the table, put the stone away, washed his hands, and went into the living room where the old bugger was playing with his pipe.

"Come into the kitchen, Paddy," he said, "and I'll cut your nails."

6

There was the white A-frame, Lisa saw, overhung by trees, just off the road down a churned-up muddy drive and, as she was bumping to a stop, there was Sam coming out the door. Her heart flipped. His dark face and arms and jeans were powdered with white plaster dust. He was carrying a load of plastery newspapers. When he heaved the load up and over into the blue Dumpster, his naked upper body curved like a discus thrower. Lust prickled in her armpits. She got out of the car and moved close to him and touched his arm and he grinned down at her. There didn't seem to be any need to speak.

Then Jade got out of the car and stood rigid against the open door looking at Sam. "Heighdey hi," she said, "if it ain't Aunt Jemima." She turned and slammed the door. She leaned over to where the bags were in the backseat.

Jade's shorts were far far too short to be bending over like that, far too revealing, she was doing it out of hostility. Lisa could smell herself now, not just the prickling of lust in her armpits but a skunky smell too, the way animals give warning signs in danger.

Sam turned away from the sight of Jade and began to pick up pieces of paper that had slipped from his load to the muddy drive. He tossed them up into the Dumpster, picked up more pieces, moving farther away from her and Jade.

She wanted to just shove Jade into the backseat and slam the door on her. Now Jade was backing out of the car with the deli bag and her purse. "Get the liquor store bag, will you," she called over her shoulder to Sam. "And there's a cooler and a basket in the back. Cute place," she said to Lisa as she passed. She walked into the A-frame.

It was at the party Saturday night that this way Sam had of gazing down his nose — not snootily, but while thinking — had got Lisa spinning. He was looking that way after Jade.

"My roommate," she said.

He turned the gaze on her.

She gave a tiny shrug. "It was hot in the city." The heat in the city couldn't possibly have got as bad as this scalding stinking flush she was experiencing. What could she say? There was nothing to say. "Sorry."

She picked up the cooler fast so he wouldn't take it from her. He swung up the basket on a finger, toted the liquor store bag. She followed him into the A-frame.

All the floors were stripped and partly covered with newspaper. The insides of the outside walls were clad with new drywall, the tape partly sanded. He put the basket on the dusty kitchen table.

She put the cooler there too. "Bathroom upstairs?"

He gave her a sort of smile.

One thing her mother had taught her was that if all else failed, soap and water were as good, temporarily at any rate, as any deodorant.

The staircase was spiral, simply half logs for stairs stuck into a tree trunk. "This is weird," she called down. "What do you hold onto? Is there going to be a railing?"

"All in good time."

His voice was just like her dad's. Close your eyes and you'd think it was her dad even to the bywords. All in good time.

Out the bathroom window, because you were up on the second floor now, you could see the tiny CN Tower again, clean and sunny in the distance. There was one big bath towel and a roll of paper towels. She was going to use the paper towels but then she thought of Sam reaching up to the Dumpster. She buried her face in the bath towel — soap, and the gentle smell of a man. She stroked her armpits dry with the bath towel. When she came back down Sam had gone back to his sanding.

Jade was peering into the bags of food. "Whose place is this anyway?" she said. "You better tell him to stop sanding. We're never going to be able to eat in here."

"Whose place is this?" Lisa called to Sam.

"Taylor's," said Sam. He started to put his tools away.

"Sam Taylor's?" said Jade.

"No, no." Lisa attempted a laugh. "This is Sam. Sam Yerby. Sam, this is Jade. Jade Hagner."

"Happy to know you," Sam said and he too went up the spiral staircase.

"Let's eat outdoors," said Lisa. "Let's eat out there at that picnic table. It's too great a day to be indoors. Is that a pond?" She was babbling, she couldn't help it. "We can look at the pond while we eat. Let's just take the cooler and the basket and the bags out there. I've got plastic plates and glasses."

Jade had her mouth pressed together.

"Okay, Jade?" She wanted to take Jade by the shoulders and shake her.

"That's Sam?"

"Yes. I told you. He's renovating this place in the country."

"You didn't tell me he was black."

"What's with you, Jade?"

"Imagine dating a black guy."

Then Jade shut up because Sam was coming back down the spiral staircase. At least she had the decency to do that. At lunch she said she was allergic to the pine of the picnic table and stacked a plate of food and took it off to the edge of the brick deck where she sat swinging her legs and throwing cucumber rinds and the casings of cold cuts into the grass.

After lunch Lisa said to Sam, "Can we go walk around that pond?"

There were yellow irises. Frogs plopped out of the way in front of them as they strolled. After a while he took her hand. She could feel softness in the air.

When they got back to the A-frame Jade was gone.

For a walk?

For a nap under the trees?

Who gave a shit?

Lisa didn't find the note till later. The sweet afternoon began to unfold as if Jade had never been.

7

Jade strode away from the A-frame, down the drive, her little cloth shoulder bag firm on her shoulder. It made her sick, their hands. Marble cake. Your sweat would mingle. Momma and Poppa never held hands, she hadn't seen them hold hands once in her entire twenty-four years, they had separate lives, separate bedrooms, Momma and Poppa. But they completed each other's sentences. Poppa: You're not going to school today, Laverna? Momma: All right then, no dinner tonight, Laverna. Momma: Is that boy staying here tonight? Poppa: He will sleep with Uncle Frederick in the basement. You sleep in your room where Momma can see you. Momma: You leave your door open tonight, Laverna, no kidding, don't forget. Duet: You're leaving? You're not going to live with us this summer? Okay, Laverna, but don't come home when you have no money in the fall.

Little did Momma and Poppa know that she was never ever coming home again. Little did they know that little Laverna was a person of the past. She was Jade now. She had a good summer job. She was working in a bank. She was handling other people's money for them.

It was just a short distance from the drive of the A-frame to a crossroads and there the pavement ended. Black asphalt became dusty gravel in three directions. Which way to go? Where would the most traffic be to hitch a ride back to the city? In fact, which way was the city? She couldn't see the tower to orient herself. Which way had they come?

Down that way the road went rippling over hills between grassy fields like in some school hall painting. There'd be little farmhouses and cows. There'd never been farmhouses and cows on the way up, there'd been traffic. They'd passed news-paper boxes and mailboxes, yes, and you couldn't see boxes of any kind down that road. Left, the road vanished under over-arching trees. Ahead it climbed a hill. Back towards the A-frame was asphalt. Had they travelled on asphalt?

Her legs did a little dance trying to make up their minds which way to go and her sandal caught in a pothole in the gravel just over the lip from the asphalt, her foot wrenched sideways and she crashed down, breath frozen, knees burning, pain knif-ing to her groin. Her breath came out in a horrible whine. Uncle Freddy loomed over her, she felt his soft sweating palms and she held herself rigid, throat rigid. You don't scream just because something hurts, little Laverna. I want the prettiest dolly in the whole store for my pretty little niece. She will not cry.

She pushed against the gravel till she was sitting. Her knees were beading blood, her dangling sandal tugged at her ankle, she gagged, dragged herself over the gravel to the grass at the side of the road biting her lip, she could taste blood. She slid her feet down the cool grass into the ditch. Her ankle caught on a twig, she heard a muffled squeal, squeezed her eyes shut, opened them wide. No tears, little Laverna, no tears.

Across the ditch thistles grew huge and glossy. Get up from there, Laverna, you will be eaten by bugs. She bent her knee to right her sandal. Little yips burst out of her like a puppy at bay. She could hardly find the sandal laces.

Ayuga, ayuga.

A black Valiant, two male silhouettes in the front seat, was dragging towards her, stereo thumping, blasting its horn.

She locked her jaw and forced herself erect, made herself tall. The Valiant thundered honking up the rise and out of sight.

She must find a mailbox, a respectable mailbox at the head of a respectable driveway, and ask for help from respectable people in a respectable house.

∽∾

Mike had gone down to the headquarters of the entertainment weekly in person to put in the ads. He didn't want to use the phone. He didn't want to chance Paddy listening in while he made his desires known.

He had placed one ad in each of the two different Companions Wanted sections of the paper to run indefinitely, bill him monthly, would you? The ad in Personals — the section intended to attract tender interest, people looking for love — read thus:

You know life is a jungle. But you also know love comes when stars cross. I am looking for a wife.

The second ad, in the section which disclaimed any interest but sex, he contrived thus:

Not the $. Not love but could be. It's the bond that turns you on. SWM seeks SF.

The ads had different box numbers. What he was waiting for was two letters from the same girl, one in response to each ad. Someone marriage-minded, yes, but just that little bit kinky. Someone who thought she could get away with things. Who could be punished. That girl would be his.

It wasn't just the certainty of weekly mail in a plain brown envelope that endeared this placing of classifieds to him. Unlike the Valentine's Day box at school, this was a love lottery over which you had some control. There was, of course, some degree of certainty about the valentines at school. The teacher always gave you one as she gave one to everybody else. There was also the certainty that for him there would be no others.

One year he bought one of those books where you punch out cartoon valentines. He signed them all with a question mark and licked all the little white envelopes and stuck them down and addressed one to each member of the class, including the smelly little girl with the wires of yellow unwashed hair who lived above a store on Yonge Street, and also including the teacher. Shivering with cold and excitement in line in the school yard he mentioned loudly and often to no one in particular that he'd bought the book. Everybody would know they could expect a valentine from him. He made a disgusted face over the taste of the glue.

Again the teacher alone gave him a card.

Another year in a new school he fell in love. In the back row there sat a goddess with golden arms and grasshopper thighs, who could get the ball in the basket every time. He stood on the sidelines of the gym, a funny little guy, short by comparison even then, in a T-shirt in February, dancing and clutching his arms across his chest as his Amazon idol chased the ball.

He raided Father's bottom drawer for Mother's old red satin panties. He and Father had moved — the first time? was it the second time? the third? Who knew which time? Mother had left, that was the main fact. That winter? The previous winter? Neither he nor the therapist had ever made complete sense of all his and his father's peregrinations. But back that year of his idolization of the golden grasshopper-thighed basketball player, he also found a linen doily in the box of things packed from when Mother had set a fancy table for festive meals, when they still had a dining room and a dining room table. With the red satin panties and the white linen doily he made his creation. This homemade card, gorgeous to him in its ribbons and laces, was his gift of love.

Again that year there was no card for him except the teacher's in the Valentine's Day box.

৵৵

Paddy had always liked to fetch the mail, the routine of it, rain or shine. Maggie would be sleeping still, in later years anyway, when her cough wouldn't go away. He would put on a second pot of coffee. He'd go down to the mud room and put on his rubber boots and his windbreaker or parka, depending on the weather. Then he would trudge out to the mailbox and get the paper and the mail. Then he could take a tray in to Maggie and sit with her while she had her first cigarette, and he'd read her the hatched, matched and dispatched. They usually knew someone in at least one of the columns, even if it was only someone's grandchild drawn into production.

Supposing it was spring and it was time to get the mail. He would set about his morning routines. Rinse his bacon and egg plate and let it soak. Tap the barometer. Fill the humidifier. Go down to the mud room to change into his boots and parka.

Now summer.

Maggie dead.

The kid got the mail now.

But still, he liked to change into his boots, go down to the mud room every morning and put on his boots, and toddle out with old Marmalade and the kid to get the mail.

You could see the kid's layout as you passed the open door, the way he had rearranged his study. Kid's big blue trunk, padlocked, now stood under the window where he, Paddy, used to keep his easy chair, where he used to sit, cross-legged, smoking his pipe, reading the business section of the paper. Kid had strongly resisted storing his trunk in the furnace room along with all the family trunks. Got rid of the easy chair instead.

Paddy drifted into his old study. He pulled out the desk chair and sat down at his old desk, laying his arms along the wooden arms of the chair, curling his ankles around the legs to keep it from rolling. The concrete wall of the well to the outside stared at him as he stared at it out the little window, just as it always had when he used to sit here.

Here he would sit writing cheques. Here he would balance his and Maggie's cheque books. He would address Christmas cards to the boys back in the office sitting here. And then at their homes, when they too had taken the golden handshake, like him. Sometimes his cards came back. Moved. Address unknown. Sometimes there was a note from the wife. Just me now, alas, Harold passed away, passed over, passed on. At this desk he would go over his will, check insurance policies. Here he had sat when he phoned King when Maggie wasn't going to be coming home from the hospital any more. Old man tears ran down his cheeks. He snivelled and reached in his back pocket for his handkerchief.

Which wasn't there.

Kid preferred paper tissues. Less washing. Less ironing.

On his desk, not now his desk, was a TV set, where his gold clock given upon retirement used to stand.

Where was his clock? Where had they moved it to?

Beside the TV set was a box of tissues, a wishy washy design of pastel tulips with the leaves of morning glories, for God's sake.

He wiped his nose on his sleeve. He pressed his face dry on the insides of his cuffs. He opened the big left-hand file drawer of his desk.

Socks?

White ribbed socks. Grey wool work socks. Black dress socks. Goddamn file drawer full of rolled-up socks.

Where were his files? Battalions of file folders neatly labelled in his precise engineer's hand. Where had they gone? His clock, his easy chair, his files. Where had they all gone?

You used to be able to slide open the drawer, easy as butter, pull out your file, the one you wanted, the one on the pond say, and there it would be at your disposal, labelled in his neat slanted printing, black ink from his good old Waterman. Pond. Inside would be the bills from when Wilf Bowles dug it, miring — Paddy had to chuckle — miring three bulldozers in the process, having to use a chain and a truck with a winch to get them out. And the permit from the government for building it. And a record of all the times he had stocked it, and with what, rainbow or speckled, from 1962 till now.

Well, not exactly till now. Till whenever he had last stocked it. Which he couldn't find out because there were goddamn socks in his file drawer. He felt as if his feet and hands were coming off, not being able to think when he had last stocked the pond, not being able to find out because his desk wasn't his desk any more and there were socks in his file drawer.

But. King must know. King stocked the pond now. Didn't he? Or did he?

Maybe he didn't. Maybe King didn't care. That was a possibility, that the pond was no longer anyone's priority. That the fish he ate for dinner last night were among the last of a dwindling race.

His own wishes. Sidelined, out of control, sent to the showers, not wanted on the voyage. King paid the bills now.

Didn't he?

He knuckled his eyes. Could you be sure of anything? Anything at all? He stood up and started stalking around the room. He kicked the intruding blue trunk. He had an urge to grab the curtains and yank them down, rip them up, tear them into great weeping cloths.

"Oh, oh!" he shouted. "Oh!"

And then he came to a halt.

What if the kid were to hear him? What if he were to hear him, and come down, and find him invading his privacy?

There was a horrible danger that someone who didn't know him, the kid for instance, could see grief and think only that he had lost his marbles, see him stomping around the housekeeper's private room and howling, and think he had gone loony. It was dangerous to be old. Kid could tell King. He had heard him talking to King, all right, telling him intimate details about his poo, things people didn't talk about if they were polite. Oh yes, he had heard Mike talking to King.

He scooted into the hall, scooted into the mud room and

stood there looking at rows of shoes and boots.

Maggie's boots.

Why hadn't King disposed of Maggie's boots? Why hadn't he and Gloria got them into the green garbage bags along with everything else of Maggie's to take down to the Sally Ann? If they had decided to run things, to take away file folders, move the easy chair, forget to stock the pond, why did they have to be so goddamn half-assed about it?

Paddy picked up Maggie's boots. He sat down on the little cedar bench. He bent over, bending his face into the old rubbery furry sweaty smell of Maggie's boots. He shook with sobs.

Oxygen was the fruit of life. No, that wasn't it. Oh two plus cee two made. He couldn't remember. He couldn't remember the formula. Him an engineer and he couldn't remember formulae.

Maggie. Concentrate on Maggie. Sentences would form in his mind and mouth if he concentrated on Maggie.

Oxygen was what you needed to make everything else go, yes, and Maggie hadn't been able to get enough of it any more. He giggled into the boots remembering how they'd thought that fresh lime juice in hot toddy would be just the ticket to restore her, before they knew, when they still thought all she had was a bad cold. What fools they were, playing in the sand while death rolled in upon them. Maggie's lungs. Her lungs. Corroded. Collapsed. Eroded. Eaten away. Maggie's lungs done in by sixty years of smoking. And so she lay in a hospital bed, bruises on her arms, tubes up her nose, dirtying herself because those useless nurses didn't come when she called and he couldn't lift her any more.

Her voice a whisper. Her skinny chest pulsing four to the second like a dying kitten.

But her breasts. Maggie's breasts were still beautiful on her deathbed, on the white hospital deathbed. How could that be, that in all that decay, Maggie still had beautiful breasts?

Which grew cold under his hands as he sat alone with her, after.

Large. And full. And cold.

That was how he finally accepted it. Maggie's breasts grew still, and cold.

Dead.

He whimpered into the boots.

He had never imagined such loneliness in his life, to be nothing, alone, without kith or kin to touch, to speak to.

Under the jurisdiction of a sassy stranger brat who kept socks in his file drawer and wouldn't wash his pocket handkerchiefs and cut his nails with a pocketknife. Who got regular mail while he Paddy got nary a postcard.

Suddenly he hushed. He was not alone though. The boy, Zebu, was over at the pond this very minute. How could he have forgotten something so important as the boy settling in over at the pond? Well, that cast another light on it.

What was he doing here moping? Silly old man. Enough slobbering over stinky boots. Put on your own shiny new rubber boots from the village. Yes, and your jacket. But no. It was July. Put on, put on. Bug stuff! Yes. That was it. From the shelf by his head beside his yellow hard hat. Slather it on ears and neck and bald spot. Head off now. Sneak out the door. Escape, and don't tell the file folder thief, the paper laundryman, the fingernail toenail surgeon where he was going.

Go see the boy. Take the trail through the bush. Go visit the boy by the pond.

∞

Jade gripped the mailbox. She was sweating and dizzy but she had made it over the little hill and down to a little valley. She had actually seen a mailbox, got to the mailbox. She had tried to walk erect. If she strode erect, her backbone must pull her tendons in place like a puppet. Her ankle would see it was not possible to be injured and act normal. But it hadn't happened that way. At every step jabs of pain made her sick and then her ankle collapsed and she'd had to hop the last steps, springing ahead with little tiny pushes of her hurt foot, whimpering.

The mailbox was cool on her cheek. In the distance you could hear the rumblings and backup bells of heavy machinery. Cows bent over grass on a hill to the left. Birds flew in and out of the forest wall to her right. Perhaps she should pick up a stone and bang the mailbox till Paddy Slater, whoever he was, came to see what was the matter.

Jade has walked to her doom. I twist speechless here on this bench.

I want to call out, Stop! Go back. Go home. Ahead lies disaster.

Sure.

Call out stop to the river, stop to the earthquake, stop to war, love, Eve eating the apple.

We are not shapers, we who see, only narrators. Alone in the dark, we sing against night vision — like when we were kids.

Oh dear, what can the matter be?
Three old ladies locked in the lavatory.
They were there from Monday to Saturday
Nobody knew they were there.
Oh, Lord, he's coming, your monk. I'll close my eyes.

I'm chanting. I'm in prayer.

Far overhead in the blue dome a jet trail materialized, travelling and vanishing. The cows moved farther up the grassy hill. And Jade turned to look along the long treed driveway of Paddy Slater, down which now rumbled a golden rush of fur and a guy.

∽

It was shivery, mosquitoey in the bush and Zeeb was ploughing through he didn't know where, no trail. He thought he should maybe go back and get a shirt and shoes but he'd got this far and he wanted Paddy badly, needed to see the light in his old blue eyes harden and grow stiff as he listened to what had happened with the beaver.

He cracked past grey dead cedar branches, snapped them down. Angry birds flitted and twitted above him. The bridge he had built with Polly over the gully beside the spring, hammering their fury at dead Sibyl into it, it slid under his bare feet. His leg wasn't too good yet, still tight. Raspberry canes grabbed his jeans, bloodied his hands. The bridge across the stream had lost so many of its split log steps he could slip, end face down in the swift icy water.

He leapt off the bridge and landed in sinking moss, pushed on through ferns that bruised acrid.

A fallen rotten trunk forced him to halt. Fungi fed on it. Puncture marks of woodpeckers streaked the sides, claw marks, bears maybe, hungry for grubs. Beyond, in what might have once been the path, lay, any which way, broken fingers of three-foot sawn cedar logs, tumbled corduroy old enough the bark had rotted off, as if the old man had started to make trail from deadfall across a swampy stretch, had trimmed the trees, sawn the logs, hauled them, and then not been able to see why.

Paddy would have straightened up, he could see it. He would have blinked at sun dapple through the wings of cedar overhead, got dizzy, just as he himself now looked ahead, swayed.

He could not see where to go. The PowerBook was his antagonist. The trail was lost. His feet were black with swamp muck and he didn't have a hatchet.

It used to be a breeze to get through the bush from cabin to Big House, even for the little kid he was then, because of the trail, because they used it all the time, because they kept it clear. Paddy had blazed the trail, chipped creamy patches out of the living cedars so he could make his way over to visit alone.

Paddy said the best time to clear trail was winter. Then you were raised by snow so you could hack away at upper branches. He would go with him sometimes when they were up for a day in the winter. Sometimes the old man took the chain saw but most often it was just the Swede saw and hatchet. Paddy would be in his yellow hard hat and his leather mitts, his steel-toed boots dinting a trail through the snow, and he would follow, trying to match the big stride, carrying the hatchet, hacking furiously at twigs.

He thought of the soft penetrable flesh of the old man, his wrists and neck. He thought of his rubber boots, how they'd be covered with green leaves, or pond muck sometimes, sometimes snow.

Paddy had authorized the deaths of the other beaver.

He looked up to see where the sun was, took bearings, plunged on, careless of gripping branches. He ducked under where raccoon trail led, dipped into deer paths, continuously sought the sun.

The Big House was that way.

Wasn't it? Wasn't it?

Who could say for sure? Paddy's blazes had ceased to be.

King had got ambitious once and cleared a circular trail around the farm for cross-country skiing. You traversed the stream on a log bridge, herringboned through bush up past the deadfall where deer tracks trailed in and out, glided by the end of the pond over dead stalks of goldenrod and loosestrife up to the pines where you'd slide past an animal anthology in the snow — mice and grouse tracks, fur from a fight between owl and hare — and then you'd run clear back through bush again, down the old loggers' trail, across the stream again on a bridge made of poles, and up through the slashing, and then around to meet your tracks below the Big House. A two hour trail.

Now also fallen, he supposed.

He beat back branches, a dull ache inside him.

He didn't know the noises here. He could identify an alarmed robin, mosquitoes. But what was that screeching? That rustling? Pounding?

He was used to the pond. That's where he had spent his

young years. Silent as a stump himself he would crouch to watch the grey heron stalk frogs and fish on silent legs, an elevated lizard, watch it, too, convert to a stump in the shallows, pterodactyl off low when light finally vanished. He'd swing with the swallows as they swooped to the evening hatch of bugs, meeting trout leaping to eat through the silvery surface from below. And then the bats would come as sky darkened. As territory calls of catbird, cardinal, phoebe ceased, and light was no longer sufficient for his eyes, splashings were raccoons hunting beetles and crayfish. Mornings there'd be floating reeds whose tender stems were gnawed by muskrat. There was the morning there were the duckling feathers.

Once he smelled cat, a pungent sting as he pushed up the headwater past deer cover stalking his territory. Cougars' territory could be hundreds of kilometres from their dens. Snarling yellow-toothed cougar. Best, then, if your own territory ended where you stopped seeing the pond.

Yet still you'd encounter signs of civilization. Fisher people trespassed. You'd find their lines caught in branches. You'd find old beer bottles downstream where no foot apparently had ever trod.

Once, after a cloudburst and flash flood that put mud two metres up the slope of the dock, he'd found, in a backwater of the stream you could only crawl to, a child's big rubber ball. Sun glinted on it, a shape too regular to be wild. He'd crept, not snapping branches, squeezing past powdery trunks of cedars, stretched a hand past the white dainty crowfoot blooming in the shade, and scooped it up. It was in the cabin still, a red, black and silver rubber ball. He and Polly would hammer that ball at each other. When one of them missed and the ball went astray and floated on the pond, they'd race to strip and dive in through algae and weeds, be first to retrieve it.

He stopped, stymied.

No shadows, no sunlight.

No lawn mower roar, no gurgle of water, nary the slam of a door.

Lost. How in his own backyard could he so lose his way?

When he was young this bush was softer. Shorter. More intervaled. He could track the stream, leap from bank to mossy bank, bound through bush and through bush and through bush, rebound, not slip into icy water. He would crouch under branches, swing around a rough spot hand on a cedar.

Yet even then you could get totally turned round, sucked into mire, lose a shoe, skirt deadfalls till east was west, both unknowable in shaky swamp. You could slap bugs and sweat and get winded and beaten by branches till you wanted to cry.

He did once. He ran away from them at the cabin, Sibyl and Polly, still taller than him, although, he squealed to himself as he ran, he was a man now, thirteen, and they were only women. He didn't mean to get lost. He was filled like a plum with fury and he would go. He would seek his fortune. Find treasure beyond the wall of their clearing. Embrace bears. And then he was just tired and worn through and, though stung with cuts, running shoe gone on one foot, enraged by droopy gentle ferns overhanging the stream over him, he did have the smarts to follow the stream (which knew where it was going even if Paddy's fence was lost) down through miles and miles to the concession road.

He had heaved away his orphaned shoe, plodded dust barefoot — the line, the sideroad, the two sides of the concession — till he hit the drive of the Big House, unfamiliar from this angle but he had recognized the rows of black walnuts down it.

Paddy had leaned over the veranda off the living room and laughed as this ragamuffin adventurer crossed his lawn, and he wouldn't speak to the old galunk mocking him from on high. He had stumbled down pasture through black locusts and into bush along trail — still fresh blazed then and corduroyed and cleared — to the pond and just fallen in.

What he must do now, what his goal must be, what would give him direction and clear his mind, would be to think of getting that pale soft Mike over to the pond, make him fly

cast, show him how, make him clean the little beauties deli-
cately, thread them on a cedar branch as the old man had
taught him years ago. Make him forswear lures, make him
want to walk over through the bush, not drive over like a
wimp, make him want to help clear the jungly trail, make him
be friends.

You went uphill to get to the Big House, yes. Forge forward
with that, that direction. Mike was going to have to like him.
It didn't work up here in halves. The way it worked up here
was good trails make good neighbours. Ahead was light, a
glimpse through fortifications of Paddy's mown path. He
breathed out, considered his surroundings.

A maple had crashed here just inside the bush, its death tes-
tified above by neighbour trees' splintered branches. Wind
seethes, winter rages pull, whistle, an old tree gives over, drags
up roots, roars, thrashes. The earth would thunder with its fall.
And now, here, its corpse extended fifteen metres into the bush,
and here before him rose a three metre wall of root pad, barbed
interweavings of pebbles and silt, vegetal ganglia dangling, and
here at his feet opened a wet black depression.

> *A ready grave — the girl in her grave — though I close
> my eyes I see her — bound, speechless, helpless — breath-
> ing? just — in this her grave.*
> *Yet I'll not weep. I'll not cloud my eyes.*
> *But oh, Saky — I may go mad.*

Once he had thought such root holes were bear holes.

Mosquitoes had got him all over. Hot — he could smell
himself. Running his fingers through his hair, his hands came
away with twigs, duff. Silt was drying grey on his feet. He
looked back, half expecting spoor like blood or mud spiralling
in water, exhaust from a spitfire.

∽

Mike saw someone standing at the mailbox, a girl. She began to hop towards him and Marmalade. One foot she only let touch the ground barely. Her dull blonde hair swung as she hopped and the muscles moved on her long brown lean legs.

Marmalade rumbled forward and stuck her nose in the girl's crotch. She squealed and fell.

He walked up to her, looked down. She clutched at him and his pant leg rucked up.

"Oh, God. I'm so glad to find someone."

Her hand was on him.

"Help me."

When her hand had made contact with his skin, blood had thrust through him, engorged him. He did not wrap his windbreaker round him, to conceal him.

She had red nails. It was pathetic how she hadn't been able to stay between the lines. He could imagine that as a little girl she would constantly have been reprimanded by her teacher for slipping off the lines when she was trying to write.

"Are you injured?"

Her eyes were roving and swollen. He recognized the look. His cool nerve ends felt her lean sweaty hand with its crassly daubed red nails.

"Are you Paddy Slater?"

It would have suited him to say yes. Simply to relegate the old bugger gagged and bound to a closet for twenty-four hours and give her licence to pursue whatever route would follow naturally from the touch of her hand on his skin.

"I'm trying to get home." She pulled on him. "I'm trying to get back to the city. I tripped. I fell. I twisted my ankle."

Currents thrust from her hand through his skin to his nipples, hair follicles, scrotum.

She tightened her grip. "I can't walk."

He thought how grotesque it was that his body should be reaching for her while his mind made complete sentences. He thought of trout springing from the pond at dusk to reach for dragonflies, utterly helpless to will themselves separate from the food chain. He encouraged his mouth to shape the words of a gentleman.

"Possibly I could give you a lift somewhere."

He put out his hand to help her up and cuffed Marmalade, who slunk back and waddled behind them, tail and head down, as he led her along the drive. The therapist had said that it was unhealthy to fail to recognize the needs and conversations of the body. The girl was taller than he. He wondered how the act itself would be managed. He would have to force her to kneel. Her weight on his arm was heavy.

"Doesn't it just make your skin crawl?"

"Skin?"

"Yes. You know. Their skin. Next to your skin. People with different colour skin smell different from us, you know." She leaned on his shoulder.

At least she wasn't talking about his skin. He had forgotten to look in the mailbox. Not good to get unsettled like this, not good at all.

"Do you think you'd have anything to drink at your house?"

Once, before Mother had left them, when Father was doing repairs one time, laying a new board across the stairs that went down from the front porch to the cement walk and the grassy front yard, cigarette dangling from lips, beer bottle at the ready, hammering away while squinting through smoke, and he stood inside, pressed against the screen door watching, Father had hit his left index finger with the hammer.

"Damn! Oh Jesus Christ God damn!"

Clutching his finger Father rose and headed towards the screen door.

"Medicine! Open the door, you idiot child! Carol! Medicine!"

Mother ran from the kitchen, wiping her hands down her slacks. "Oh, Jimmy."

"Get that idiot child to open the door."

Mother opened the door. Father thundered in. Father kicked out in passing at the idiot child, little Mikey. Mother ran to the kitchen, ran back with the rye bottle, a juice glass. She pressed the bottle against her bosom while with trembling red-nailed fingers she unscrewed the top, attempted to pour rye into the juice glass.

"Give me that, you fool."

Father grabbed the bottle and chugalugged, holding his finger in his armpit. He lowered the bottle.

"Oh my God, will you look at that? Look at the blood on my finger. Look at my blood coming up there, under the nail. I'm going to lose it. I'm going to lose my bloody fingernail."

Mother reached for it.

"Leave it alone, you fool." Again Father raised the bottle. "You better come upstairs with me, Carol. You must be my angel of mercy. I need some real medicine."

From the stairs Mother glanced back at the idiot child, her little Mikey, his bare legs stuck out straight in front of him, his back against the wall, and went on up.

After a while Mike had gone out and got the unfinished bottle of beer from the porch and had drunk it, belching and coughing, and lost consciousness on the sofa. In the night he woke hearing Mother crying.

No, no, Jimmy. Please stop. Enough medicine.

A full bottle of Paddy's single malt sat in the sideboard of the Big House.

"Medicine, yes."

"Oh, goody good. Medicine."

They rounded the curve of the drive.

c\o

"Paddy! Paddy!" Zeeb called.

His voice echoed in the pasture. The old man snapped up his head, raised the rock he was holding.

"Hey! It's me!"

"Who?"

The old man was perched in the huge rock pile that terminated the southward circle of his ever-expanding lawn mowing. You could be a bird in your own little nest in among those rocks when you were a kid. You could build fortresses, hover, concealed from grown-ups. The old man raised the rock he was holding high over his head. He was scowling, his chin jutted forward.

"Paddy!"

The old man lowered the rock. "Zebu? What happened to you? What's the matter?"

"Nothing's the matter." Everything's the matter.

He was on the old man now. Paddy had his boots on the wrong feet.

"Your hair, it's full of wild things," the old man snorted, "and look at your feet. You get lost, black foot?" He dropped the rock which clattered, echoed. The rock pile shifted under his mismatched boots.

Zeeb held out a hand and Paddy held it to come down to the grass. "The trail's what's lost," Zeeb said. "I didn't get lost. Do you want to change your boots?"

"What for?"

"You've got them on the wrong feet. Don't they hurt?"

The old man was squinting at the wall of bush from which Zeeb had emerged.

"I'll hold you while you shift," Zeeb said.

"Whaddya mean the trail's lost. Why, I was over that way just the other day."

Zeeb found himself stuttering towards the Big House with little slow steps beside the old man who seemed to want to shuffle. The grey fuzz on the back of Paddy's neck was too long and the collar of his red plaid shirt had frayed through to white. He wanted to scream at him. How can you not know what's happening in your own bush? How can you be so neglectful?

The old man took hold of his arm, leaned on it like a cane. How could he pull out the bullet casings and exhibit them for inspection with Paddy clinging like that? How could he talk?

"Maggie's dead." There were tears running down the old man's cheeks.

People do die, dear.

That's what Maggie said when Sibyl died. Zeeb had wanted to slug her, arrogant old witch with her silver hair circled by her silver smoke. She had no right to live, old, smoking still, while Sibyl wasted and went.

Women's deaths, departures. What drove them to it? Power plays against those who love them. Dissatisfaction with your every effort. Screwed-up values. Polly could never be Long McAdam, and Long McAdam would never be Polly, and he was only a kid.

Sibyl died too. He could say that to Paddy.

And in this mood Paddy might say, Who's Sibyl when she's at home?

Maggie's long dead, old man, time you got on to other things. He could say that.

But what other things could such an old man get on to? Sore disappointment caressed his gut. He wanted to be holding on to Paddy's arm, not Paddy holding on to his. There was no way the next sentence in this dialogue could be, I killed a beaver.

The old man's strides lengthened as they got near the house. "Good Lord," he said. "My boots are on the wrong feet. Here, boy, hold my hand while I change them."

The sky was inscrutable.

What if he were up here to say, Leslie's dead? What if Leslie had taken off up there into the ineffable blue to join dead Sibyl and dead Maggie, instead of just taking off?

What if?

He felt cold. Paddy had his boots organized now and was charging ahead around the corner of the house to where the picnic table sat under a Chinese elm with the lawn chairs and the barbecue.

Me and you can cut trail like the old days, that's what he wanted to say to Paddy.

Then he heard Paddy say, "Well, hello. What have we got here?" in a flirtatious voice he remembered him using with Sibyl sometimes. He rounded the corner and saw sitting there with Mike the blonde with the red nails from the car this morning. They had two of Maggie's crystal sherry glasses and a bottle of Mortlach. She was laughing at Paddy and holding out one of her red-tipped hands. One of her feet was up on a little folding table. There was a dripping tea towel on her ankle which had swelled like a melon. Her knees glistened with dried blood. When she looked up and saw him she screamed.

8

Mike held out a scuffed pair of Birkenstocks to Zeeb. "These might fit you."

There was a pink bag on the blue trunk under the window with two hearts drawn on it. So Mike had a woman to give presents to, as well as the girl outside. Zeeb pressed back against the edge of the bed. It wasn't a real bed. It had been the daybed in Paddy's study. But it was Mike's bed now.

"They're a bit old," Mike went on.

"Thanks," Zeeb said. He took the Birks, laid them on the floor by his feet. He had scrubbed his feet, shaken the things out of his hair into the toilet, sluiced his head. He had on one of Paddy's old shirts again.

"Excuse me a sec." Mike went into the john.

Zeeb padded across the tiles to the trunk under the window. He picked up the pink bag, opened it, peeled back the tissue and saw red nylon — red nylon what? red . . . he pulled out red nylons.

Red nylon pantyhose.

Slit at the crotch.

The john flushed. Zeeb jabbed the pantyhose back into the bag and put the bag back and turned to face the door as Mike came in. "Nope. They don't fit. I'll be okay. I'll go bare. Grass feels good on your bare feet. You should try it."

9

"I don't get it," said Jade.

"I could help you with that." Mike was wiggling his pale eyebrows at the girl and blinking his eyes, and she was pressing her glass to her cheek and singing out a little scale of laughter.

Zeeb sat up very straight on the picnic bench. Paddy was staring at the girl too, clearing his throat. Paddy had gotten into telling jokes, his pewter beer mug on the grass beside his lawn chair, his pipe on the table within easy reach.

"What part don't you get?" Zeeb said. He couldn't see yet how he was going to get the old man off alone and focused enough to talk. They were all getting silly, drinking, and the girl was like a campfire. They were all turned towards her.

"Dory?" she said. "Is that something like sorry?" She giggled again.

Zeeb couldn't stand it. Paddy was drivelling on and they were laughing at him. "Anybody knows that," he burst in. "It's a long boat, a Newfoundland fisherman's boat like a rowboat. See, when the reporter said have you ever been bedridden, the old woman thought, well you know." Paddy was still leering over his beer at the girl even while he was trying to save him from their ridicule. His words began to fumble. "The old woman thought he meant, you know, screwed in bed, so she said yes, she had, and she was boasting, see, so she said she'd done it twice in a dory too."

Paddy snorted into his beer.

"How unpleasant." Mike ran his tongue around the rim of his empty glass. "You'd be sliming on fish intestines. There'd be fish scales and fish bones bristling into your knees."

The girl let out a little squeak.

Paddy held his beer mug loosely in his two hands. "Well now young lady, did you ever hear the one about the two eels? There was a man had an electric eel in a fish tank and one day he saw it moping, and he said why, and the eel said he was lonely, and the man went to a pet store and bought a lady electric eel. To keep it company, don't you know."

Jade creased her lips into their Uncle Freddy smile. This old guy was winking at her, grinning and winking, but he was just a soft little old man, none of Uncle Freddy's panache, and besides her saviour was sitting beside her.

On the other side the hick/poet — Zebu, Zebu? what kind of a crazy name was that? they called him Zeeb — he got up as if to stretch, reaching high so his shirt pulled out of his jeans. She could see where the little ruff of hair began to run colour down his belly under his belt. Her skin stung. She grew hot. But then he sat down again with his back to her and her saviour, and let his bare foot stretch out so it pressed against the old guy's rubber boot.

"Remember the goat keeper, Paddy?" he said.

"Eh?"

"You know. When you'd drive up. South there. The old brick house with the lilacs and the goats in the yard. The hermit with the long beard."

The old guy gave the hick/poet's foot a little shove. "Where's your shoes?"

"But the joke," Jade said. "You better finish it. What happened?"

"He brought the female electric eel home, remember?" the hick/poet said to the old guy. "He put her in the fish tank with the male electric eel."

The old guy snorted. "Oh, yes."

Her whole leg felt numb now, not just her ankle. Her mouth was sticky. Her saviour got up, headed for the house with their empty glasses. You could almost see the hollows in his buttocks, his chinos were that smooth. She leaned forward so her bra released her nipples.

Poppa would never have tolerated the state of this old guy's lawn. You could see down to bare earth and some of the grass was even brown. There were plantains and dandelions and crabgrass growing between the clumps. By the trunk of the tree they sat under, where the wooden tray of wild bird seed lay on the ground, the grey and black husks of sunflower seeds spread in all directions, and corn kernels too, and wheat. Whir of birds' wings flew in and out of the tree as if by their buzzing they could scare the people away and get back to the serious business of eating.

It suddenly struck her she hadn't put out any water for the baby robins.

"So?" She shifted her weight, lifting her bum up by the arms of the chair and trying to settle. "What happened?"

The old guy was staring at her again. She crossed her arms over her breasts.

"Wait'll the kid comes back." He knocked his pipe against the picnic table. Black ash fell into the grass. He got out his pipe tool and tried to pry it open with his ridged yellow thumbnail, tried and tried. Finally the blade came up. He scratched away at the inside of his pipe bowl with deliberate strokes. The aluminum screen door opened and closed, and there was her saviour again, with a bottle of wine now, and clean glasses, and a corkscrew.

"Now I misremember." The old guy laid his pipe and pipe tool on the table. "Where was I?"

"He brought home the lady eel," this Zeeb was saying.

"Oh, yes." The old guy snickered.

Her saviour was picking at the lead on the bottle with the point of the corkscrew. He looked up and caught her eyes with his. He touched the point of the corkscrew to the soft part of her hand where the thumb joined, pressed slowly, his eyes holding hers.

At first she couldn't believe what he was doing. Then it began to hurt. "No. No," she whispered.

He smiled. He dropped the corkscrew, picked up her hand. "Let me kiss it better," he whispered back.

He pressed his mouth to her skin. She felt his tongue come out between his lips. Warm. Wet. She tried to pull away but he held on tight. She let her hand go limp, and he went back to the corkscrew and the lead around the cork.

"He brought her home," the old guy was saying, "and he went over to the fish tank, and he lifted the lid."

"A lid on a fish tank!" Mike had stabbed through to the cork. He held the corkscrew steady against the neck of the bottle, began to turn. The wet bottle between his knees spread dark patches on his chinos. A jay whistled by, black against the blue above.

"What's that, young fellow?"

"Fish tanks don't have lids."

"They do so. There's one in the workshop still I believe. A glass lid. A light fixture. Belonged to my son, King. Did you never have fish?"

"One place."

Goldfish it was, two feathery gobbling wisps of light. You fed them from a little can, shook stuff out and they came swimming up at your command. He had them in his room as a special treat one July first weekend, while the foster mother attended some workshop, or went shopping, or drinking, and what he did was he gave them their total allotment of food Friday night, and then he took off for the rest of the weekend too, two whole days out in the hot city streets, and then he woke up Monday morning to such a stench. He couldn't imagine how he hadn't noticed it Sunday night when he crashed, except that's what he had done, crashed. Some kind of high, he couldn't recall precisely what. There was no lid on that fish tank. Monday morning was goldies floating in the tank, tank water a nauseating cloud of dissolved food they couldn't eat.

"He put the lady electric eel in with the gentleman electric eel, and oh! you've never seen such an explosion! Sparks, and sand and water flying. Then, everything settled down, don't you see? All quiet, the lady eel in her corner, the gentleman in his, still sulking."

"Post coitus omnes tristes sunt." The hick/poet was standing up again and stretching.

The prick on the back of her hand vibrated. A bead of blood was rising. She gazed around at the three, the old guy nestled into his beer, the hick/poet with no shoes, Mike pouring out more wine.

How hot it was getting. Even in the shade of the tree it was hot. "Is there a bus near here?" she said. "Can I get a bus? If you could drive me to the bus stop, then I could get home. Could one of you drive me to the bus stop?"

The old guy probably couldn't drive. Zeeb had been barefoot, had come up out of the forest like an animal.

"Let's walk over to the pond," he was saying. "Paddy?"

Mike's hands were on her shoulder, pressing her down. "I have to get things ready for supper," he said. "Why don't you stay for supper?"

She turned to Zeeb. "Pond? Where the fish are? Where there's swimming?"

"So the man said, what's the matter?" The old guy snorted. "And the eel said, don't you see? She's AC and I'm DC."

10

Paddy plonked himself in his lawn chair in front of the cabin with his half drunk beer he'd brought over in the car and stared out at the pond, waiting. Zebu had turned his back on them when they'd decided to drive over for a swim, said he'd make his way back through the bush, not sissy frowst in some hot pollution generator. He disliked the boy sulking like that. And now that girl was squealing inside the cabin. What the hell was the kid doing to her? Damn the young people. He pursed his lips and squinted.

What feckless neighbours he had. Strickland whipping the holiday air with his machines. And Taylor. He had always known that Taylor's A-frame wasn't going to last long, the way that idiot had laid it out. Plywood interiors simulating oak panels. Stairs warped and rotted by misadventures with the leaky skylights. He'd always said it'd have to be redone some-time. Lately he'd had occasion to reiterate his prophecy every time he and the kid drove by on errands to the village or trips over to the pond and he'd see the blue Dumpster. He wanted to make the kid stop and they'd go in and see what that car-penter was up to. Sam the Man. The names kids thought up these days. He'd be able to give him a tip or two.

But this time, when they drove past the A-frame, the girl — she was in the front seat beside Mike, kid had tucked her in

there, in his, Paddy's, rightful place, some excuse about her
ankle — she had waved her wine bottle out the window and
screamed, "Prost!" Her voice had echoed over the trees.
"Prost!" she had called.

Now why in the name of all that's holy would she do a fool
thing like that?

"Careful, careful," Mike had said. "Don't drop the bottle.
Then you'd have to crawl after it, and that would hurt your
ankle, wouldn't it?"

Paddy sucked on his beer.

The girl's underarm, where it came out of the khaki shirt,
had been pearly. You could see wiry golden armpit hairs.

How long was it since anyone had gone skinny-dipping in
the pond? King's lady wife? Ever? Not that he knew. He
believed that if Gloria had ever gone into the pond at all, which
he didn't believe she'd ever done, or maybe once, when she and
King were courting, but that was eons ago, when Maggie in her
black nylon skintight suit still strode about with legs that held
his eyes, Gloria was then still just an unformed girl. He seemed to
remember her covered from thigh to neck in purple and orange
flowers. Gloria's daughters-in-law? The pond had never been a
temptation to them. Might muss their hair.

Or maybe, secretively, on vacant Saturday afternoons.
When his grandsons were courting. He'd once found a used
blue safe sitting in the sun on a rock in the pine woods.

Could be vandals left it though, could be intruders.

Polly now. That was something else. Clean dive like a pink
otter off the dock to split the green water. And Sibyl. Sibyl's
breasts floated.

Well then, maybe this girl's breasts would float too.

Mike had honked at the top of the hill. "Just like you said,
Paddy." Then he had made a great show of waiting, the way
you'd wait if you rang someone's doorbell, and you expected
them to fix themselves up before you walked in. But Zebu
wouldn't be there yet, would he? Fool kid. Showing off for the
girl.

After the kid had parked the car, he had washed his hands of all their arrangements and made his way to his chair and settled down to wait. But the girl had hobbled into the cabin leaning on the kid's shoulder. Little Miss Priss. He had anticipated her stripping there beside the car, no fooling around with conventions, the cabin, towels, if your leg hurt. Well, it was none of his business. He was here for the scenery. He could wait.

He couldn't make out what was the matter with the boy. Peevishness didn't become him. Why not get a lift back to the cabin if the trail was in as bad a shape as he said? Now wasn't the moment to embark on major trail clearing. Why, was there even gas for the chain saw? The boy seemed not to realize that any major enterprise like that took planning.

He wondered if there was beer in the cabin, if Polly had left a cache of beer in the cabin. And then he caught himself yawning and thought he didn't want to miss anything and he'd better just nurse this one. He got out his pipe and tobacco and matches.

When he heard the cabin door slam behind him and Mike uttering warnings about the stairs down from the deck, and the girl squealing once more, his pipe was finally going. Pond, pines, sky lay before him, waiting for the show to begin, as if he and God between them had set the stage.

But what a disappointment. The girl was in her underwear. She was going in in her underwear. And what underwear. He bit his pipe. Droopy cotton drawers. You couldn't see the muscles moving. White brassière as sturdy as a nursing bra.

Squealing still, holding on to Mike, she got down to the beach, and the kid left her there leaning on the rake they used for removing algae. She was as he thought she'd be, full-chested. He should have been sitting here admiring the curving fall of loosened breasts, the slope of flesh around belly into groin.

He felt weary. He called to see if the kid could rustle him up another beer. The girl was arcing her foot through the water like a child.

11

When Zeeb finally made it through the bush once more and back to the cabin, the girl in her white underwear was already ankle deep in the water off the beach. She was leaning on the rake they used to comb up algae, swinging her swollen foot in little ripples.

He'd ripped Paddy's shirt. His feet were black again. He felt as if he were coming on the place backwards in shadow time, exactly the inverse of yesterday's homecoming. It was the back view of the old man he saw, sitting in his chair, staring. But not staring up the drive this time, nor at his fish. At the girl. He was pulling on his pipe, his beer, hunched and squinting at the girl. Zeeb wanted to whistle again like yesterday but he didn't have the heart.

It was also the back of the cabin he was approaching. He could get inside without anyone seeing him. Thus it was the back view of Mike he caught, holding the wine bottle by the neck, trying to open his PowerBook. Zeeb slammed the door.

Mike turned slowly, holding out the PowerBook. "What's this?"

My fucking identity. "My work, my thesis."

"Thesis? Thesis? You're still at school?" Though Mike was so short, his body was lean and broad-shouldered and erect. He had red wires of chest hairs. His shiny bikini was striped green and yellow and blue. He had tipped up the wine bottle and spoke out of the corner of his mouth.

What the fuck had made him ask them over? The insult of Paddy going in the car with Mike, and not through the bush with him, still burned in his chest. Mike had been ordering the girl to take care of the wine bottle and levering her into the front seat. Paddy had swung up a fresh beer from the refrigerator and gone down to climb in the backseat. And now their clothes were all over the floor.

He took the PowerBook, stuck it in his backpack and buckled that shut. He strode out. The front screen door squeaked behind him. He strode past Paddy down to the edge of the pond to the raft, stripped, folded shirt, jeans, laid them beside the cedar. He never wore underwear up here and now he was exposed naked. They were all looking at him, the girl on the beach pushing her jade bangle up and down her arm and staring, Paddy blinking, Mike behind Paddy picking his nose.

Zeeb hunkered to pick at the frayed plastic rope which moored the raft to the concrete block. Polly's reef knot finally loosened. He tried to shove the raft out into the water but it wouldn't budge. He had to stand on it, where he would be seen, and leap up and down. His weight should tip it free. Water did come up over the end and embrace his feet, his penis was flopping, but still the raft was not moving. It was embedded in the thick weeds and the soft spongy shore. He hated to walk out through water and weeds, feet sinking into algae and mud, ragged leaf edges rasping his thighs, the possibility of leeches, of the stinging bites of great diving beetles. But he hated them staring more. He leapt on the bank and plunged in through the weeds.

The water was still and soupy here. The smell of decay rose with bubbles. He began to shove at the raft, grunting. It moved a bit and then at last it slithered free. He pushed into the water after it, grabbed the end of one of the undergirding logs, flutterkicked himself and it over the weeds out to where the water was cold. Here he could swim free. The raft glided ahead of him past islands of algae. At the buoy he wound the faded yellow buoy rope around the log he'd been holding. The raft floated, secured.

He wished they'd all go. There was no place for him to escape to. That way was the girl on the beach staring. Over there Mike stood staring behind Paddy. That other way the beaver would be staring up at him through the water with dead reproving eyes. He heaved onto the raft.

∽

Jade blinked as the raft came into being in the middle of the pond with the poet dripping on it. He leaned on his elbows, stared into the water. All she could see now was his curvy bum. But she'd seen his toadstool, a simple pink piece of flesh. She stumbled towards him into the water, leaning on her rake, gasping as her sore foot came down. The water was cold as you got deeper.

Then a high voice came from behind her. "Last one in's a rotten egg!"

Mike whooshed by her, whipping her rake-crutch out from under her. She squealed and fell, and was under, came up gasping. Mike was churning towards the raft. She gave herself a push that carried her over the tall waving weeds and stroked after him, a one-legged frog.

"I'll get you, screwman!"

There was another littler splash. Zeeb had slipped off the raft. There were the two of them in the water now, Mike and Zeeb. But what would she say to Zeeb? She'd go breathless close to him, she knew she would. She'd want to reach out to him under the water, touch him.

His toadstool.

She went, burbling screams, after Mike, to drown him.

✧

"Paddy, you know the .22."

"What the hell are those two doing out there?"

This should have been the time, sitting here drying off in the sun beside the old man. He could have said. But out there it looked as if Mike was pulling the girl under. Of course he wasn't, but you couldn't really see there was such a commotion.

"Horseplay."

Paddy uncrossed his knees and leaned forward and pointed with his pipe. "Well, you go and tell them to cut it out. You don't play around in water. Someone could get hurt."

He wrapped his towel around his waist and plodded down to the shore.

"Hey!"

He'd like to wring both their necks, the long white neck of that girl, Jade. It was her, turning everybody's heads so he couldn't speak to Paddy.

"Paddy says to tell you two to quit horsing around!"

✧

Mike glided as close as he could to the girl. "Stop floundering," he said softly. "I can help you."

She sank and came up again, big-eyed and gasping.

"I'm serious," he whispered. "I mean it."

He came up under her.

"I'll take you to shore. Relax."

He put his hands around her, not under her arms as they'd been instructed at CSBC, under her brassière. Close. Except for her head, which she held rigid, watching him over her shoulder, she stayed limp as he stroked towards shore. Her weight glided. Her breasts bobbed inside the wet cloth. The difference in height between him and her was not an issue.

∽

"Six o'clock for supper," called Mike out the car window, and spun gravel up the drive.

Sure, thought Zeeb. But he wouldn't go. Paddy wasn't Paddy.

He let himself into the cabin. But here were the girl's cotton panties still, her big white bra puddling on the floor, pond sludgy. He pinched them up and went out back and flung them over the line.

12

When Lisa went out with an armful of drywall scraps to toss into the Dumpster she saw the little white Renault again, zipping up the road beyond the trees that overhung the A-frame. She shrugged, gazed at the trees. Jade was without doubt the weirdest person she'd ever met, saying trees were wet and bristly. You could see quite clearly on these trees here that tree bark is dry and flaky, and tree branches move slowly up and down, like Sam's arms sanding seams in drywall.

Where was Jade anyway? Quite some walk. Quite some nap. Whatever. Lisa couldn't really believe it was tact, not with Jade.

Then Sam came out with the last armful. He was almost marble, he was now so plastery. "That's enough for today," he said. "You want to shower first?"

Lisa looked down at herself. Yuck. Pillsbury dough girl. She ran her fingers through her hair. Stiff. Yuck. Still, "I was kind of wondering what had happened to Jade," she said.

Sam gazed down his nose at her, that way he had? Not really down his nose. More like contemplating?

"You know. My roommate? She's been gone an awfully long time."

Sam shrugged. "To each his own," he said. He went back into the A-frame.

His jeans rippled like panther skin over his bum. Lisa

laughed and ran after him. "I'll go first," she called. "You'll use up all the hot water. Have you got a shirt I could borrow?"

Sam's shampoo smelled of sandalwood. His soap smelled of pine. His toothbrush tasted minty. Lisa hoped he had another bath towel. This one was now sopping. A tiny strip of haze on the horizon obscured the CN Tower now, she could no longer really make it out. She found herself singing her father's fave under the cascading water. "To each his own, I've found my own, one and only you."

Three

Later, oh Sakyamuni, later, in the period of headlines after Mike disappears, when anyone who knows the least bit about him (and who will talk) will be interviewed — to keep the story hot, to keep the public informed — the television station will track down Mike's first foster parents.

First foster father, rather. Ted Scott is his name. Muriel Scott, Ted's wife, is dead. The cameraman will get a close-up of Muriel's engagement portrait which sits on the oak bookcase through whose glass doors you will be able to see the yellow backs of the National Geographic *collection. A Rita Hayworth beauty, the portrait shows Muriel Scott, the hair, the smile. A portrait of her face only, of course, the Scotts are respectable people, no legs. A bit down on their luck at the time Ted had his accident and Muriel began to take in kids, that's all.*

At the interview Ted Scott's grey-haired daughter will hover just outside camera range. Ted will tell the interviewer how the social worker always used to say she was so glad to come to their house because here she wasn't afraid to sit down. Well, Muriel was a lady.

Mike was Ted and Muriel's last charge. They thought they might be getting a bit old for kids. Ted's eyes will drift away from the interviewer, away from the camera, to the portrait of Muriel. He was always in some little scrape, that Mike. On this particular occasion they had got a call from the woman who ran the variety store over on Yonge Street. Going straight to hell he was, according to her. He had put a slug in a bubble gum machine.

Muriel said it must be a joke. A slug in a bubble gum machine? But still. Then Ted's annuity kicked in and they stopped taking in kids.

But you had to think. He'd seemed a likely lad and they'd let him peruse the magazines — Ted will indicate the precious repository of knowledge, the National Geographics *— he and Muriel had stayed up late one night putting paper clips around any articles with pictures they thought unsuitable, nudism, you know — Ted will look away — just as they had for their own children, but of course their own children . . . and at this point Ted's daughter will come in to ask if the TV crew liked cream or nondairy whitener in their coffee.*

1

In late afternoon light angles into Mike's basement lair but he had pulled the curtains this afternoon so the light was muted by the brown and yellow stripes of the Indian cotton bedspread Maggie had used to make the curtains, muted, and dusty from the curtains' long disuse, and Jade woke sneezing. Wha? Her head, her head. But, oh yes, she was sleeping it off, but now she must go, but, something, these weren't her clothes. Oh, yes. Her clothes had been grungy, he had taken them to wash, that was the sound of a drier upstairs, footsteps, him, maybe in the kitchen, maybe fixing steak and potatoes like he'd said, for a barbecue.

These clothes. Madonna. Her as Madonna.

He had driven the car right into the garage and lowered the garage door from inside the car with the switch. Oh yes, the

old man had lurched against the dog getting out and muttered
something about taking a nap and she had giggled and he had
squeezed her thigh and told her to stifle. She had been dizzy
and she had leaned on him and they had hip-hopped into the
house, into this basement. They had lockstepped down a hall
and then there was this bright room and she had collapsed in
the chair at the desk and it had gone whistling backwards and
that had got her hysterical again and then she had noticed her
shirt — mud, mustard. Pond muck streaked on her shorts. And
then she'd realized she'd left her underwear over there and he
had said, You left your panties in the cabin, didn't you, and
your tit sack? and tit sack had broken her up again and the
chair had rolled back and she tried to stop it but she had used
her twisted foot and that had sobered her up pretty fast. And
then he had opened that blue trunk under the window there
and said, Why don't you try on these? and he had handed her
a black satin corset and red tights and red satin slip-ons with
high heels and malibu pompoms and she had said, Are you kidding? and then she saw Madonna and thought, Why not? She
didn't even make him leave the room. She'd undressed right in
front of him.

The tights were torn. That's what she had thought as she
rolled them up to put on. She had showed him. But it turned out
. . . it turned out they were meant to be like that . . . slit . . . here.

He hadn't left when she changed at the cabin either, it was
all one room over there nearly and she had turned her back to
peel off her wet underwear and while she had no clothes on he
had laid the bottle of wine against her rear end and she had
jumped and he had caught her. That was when she had started
to get out of control and giggle.

She wanted a shirt. Not his shirt. It wouldn't be big
enough. Zeeb's shirt. She wanted Zeeb's shirt.

She tugged the bedspread out from where it was tucked
down against the wall and by the bookcases at the head and
foot and pulled it over her shoulders and legs . . . ein Apfel im
Schlafrock, that's what she looked like, that's what Momma

called it, pastry round an apple, an apple in a dressing gown, that's what Momma called it.

And then he had yanked the curtains shut and dust had flown and she had kicked off her sandal . . . only one . . . must have left the other in the car . . . she'd like to leave by that car right now, bonus would be to get in that car right now, walk, crawl, right now back down that hall to the garage and get in that car, find the key in the ignition, snap the switch, drive home.

She'd take the spread with her. Soft baked apple. Flaky pastry.

But she couldn't drive off, there was no way she could, she couldn't use her foot, she wouldn't be able to do it. But another door had faced them when they came together stepping, locked, down the hall, hadn't it? another way to the outside, to the bush, to the pond, to Zeeb . . . If she were to hop over to the window and open it, whip back the curtains on their noisy little tracks and open the window and holler, do you think he would hear her? Zeeb?

Then she had wiggled out of her shorts and pulled on the red tights and found the slit/torn crotch and he had turned to look at her chewing his lip. Open your legs, little Laverna. She could make a skirt out of the spread . . . she would have to hop . . . she'd trip on all that cloth. Come now, for Uncle Freddy. He had wanted to undo the buttons on her blouse but she had brushed his hand away and had undone them herself and she had had to shimmy out of the blouse with him looking on. Uncross your knees. Her breasts had been bare and she had whipped up the corset thing wondering when it was going to get funny again and he did up the hooks and eyes because she couldn't reach but the top ones wouldn't meet and she had said, Gross, and he had run his hand along her shoulder and her breasts had stung . . . like bruises, her breasts stung like bruises.

This corset thing had black garters, totally superfluous with these tights. It had red lace in a frill around her hips and above her breasts. Itchy. She felt compressed and pushed forward and swollen. How did Madonna dance, if she felt compressed and pushed forward and swollen? Maybe it was the itch. Maybe the itch made Madonna sing and dance.

Stand up, he had whispered and he had got hold of her hand and she had struggled up and he had kicked the malibu-decorated slip-ons towards her and she had begun to giggle a bit again and she had put her foot into one and teetered on it. I want you to spread your legs, he had whispered, and she had said, Dork, hardly recognizing her voice, on one foot? She could see pink scalp through his hair. Then he had pushed her and she had landed on the chair and it had spun backward again and she had said, I'm gonna puke, I gotta lie down, and he had said, Better get your act together, and he had picked up her clothes and left and she had heard him walking overhead and she had pushed herself up from the wobbly chair and hopped herself over to the bed and fallen on it and the room had spun.

She would phone Uncle Freddy.

Funny how she would phone Uncle Freddy.

If Uncle Freddy weren't dead. If she could get to a phone.

∾

The light in the drier had burned out. It was an odd size, the bulb. Like a Christmas tree ornament. You'd find a replacement in the hardware store in the village. But forget that now, there was always the flashlight with which to pursue lost socks, and meanwhile the girl awaited him in the basement. The dusters were stained pink from her red shorts and her shorts were fuzzed with white lint. The mustard hadn't completely come out of her shirt. He flapped and folded the dusters and, with his hand, he pressed flat the shirt and shorts, and folded them too, and put them away with the dusters on the shelf above the washer and drier, the place of the soaps and cleaning supplies, and the briquettes.

He had thawed the sirloin in the microwave and now it marinated on a blue and white platter in Kraft Italian to fat out the flesh. The potatoes were peeled and three of the four were sliced and layered with onions and butter and wrapped in tin foil. Paddy's was going to cook plain and he had indicated this fourth little tin foil envelope as different by folding the ends up instead of down. He'd cut his index finger slicing the onions and there was his blood in each package. He had kept thinking the bleeding would stop. He had ended tying his red handkerchief around it till it did.

He took down the bag of briquettes from the cleaning cupboard — they were the kind where you lay the bag on the barbecue and light the corners and come back in three-quarters of an hour and the coals are ready — and picked up the compost can full of potato peelings and onion skins and green bean tops and bottoms and the silken hair and stubby butts from the imported peaches-and-cream corncobs, and went out back. He left the briquettes by the door.

From the compost heap you could look back to the house and see the basement well and the windows of his room, curtains drawn secret and close over her. The sudden rush of blood made him sweat, the thought of the purplish flesh, pushed out by the red nylon, framed by blonde pubic hairs. The compost heap was dry on top. He'd left it exposed this morning. He'd forgotten to put back the plastic cover. He shook the can empty and went to whip up the cover but a mad chattering violated the smooth efficiency of his movement and he saw, just up the hill, on a portion of the old split cedar rail fence which still snaked here and there from hill to bush down through the meadow, the chipmunk — it must be the same chipmunk from last night, it drooped one paw — the chipmunk screamed at him. He threw the can at it. It skittered, on three legs, along the fence and vanished. The can clattered into the grass.

Forget the can. He was getting distracted. He strode across the lawn, down and around and through his basement well entrance . . .

Leaving the outside door, in his haste, a mite ajar.

. . . through his basement well entrance and through the mud room and into his room again, and shut his door. The girl had curled herself in his spread. A beam of light came through a crack in the curtain and hit the curve of her ass. He flicked the curtains tight shut. The rings screeched on their tracks, and she stirred. He yanked at the spread.

> *Here is where, oh Sakyamuni, teacher, happy blessed one, enlightened one, Gautama, Prince, if you weren't gold and male and immaterial, secure and lofty up there, surrounded by your candles, your incense, your devotées (a little grey woman has just left a bowl of rice and other little bowls which steam), if instead you were moving flesh, and bone, and blood, you might want to get out a paper clip, cordon off a few pages. You might choose to skip directly to the next appearance of the sun.*

"I have to go home now." Her ankle throbbed like a tooth but it hurt less now it was swollen, or maybe it was the beer. The skin was turning dark blue/red. She moved the cold anonymity of her bangle slowly up and down against her upper arm.

"I need my clothes." He'd rasped the spread off and out from under her and her rear end pulsed against the roughness of the wool blanket. She didn't think she'd ever felt so bare. "I have to go home."

"Oh no you don't," he said quietly, but he knew she could hear him all right. Her red-nailed fingers were moving slowly up and down her arm, up and down, running that bracelet up and down. Mother would wave her hands in the air like that, slowly, and blow on her nails, and wink slowly in the mirror at him watching her in the mirror. He'd be leaning against her dressing table where she would be sitting to make herself lovely. She'd reach over and reach up under his T-shirt and tickle his underarm and he'd pee his pants.

The girl's pinkie stood out. He pressed it down against her arm. "Now move it, nicely, up and down."

He was beginning to unbuckle his belt. Little Laverna knew if you scratch part of your body, like, say, this, your upper arm, irritate your upper arm long enough, it will tingle, and then it will go, eventually it will go, numb it will go, the way, if Uncle Freddy, if you were very good and quiet, would. And your mind would leave. And in the morning when you wake up you can't remember.

"I said move it."

She wished he wouldn't whisper. She couldn't hear for the buzz in her ears. He was taking off his pants. She wasn't going numb. She had stalled on her bangle, her jade talisman that when she came to Toronto she had bought since she had chosen rebirth as this name, Jade, since airbrush artwork emblazoned JADE in seven-foot full palette colour on all the concrete garage walls of the Annex like MADONNA. She felt she was screaming but she couldn't tell whether any sound had emerged.

He snorted, looking down, because look what the girl made him do, wet had seeped through the front of his jockey shorts. He pulled his belt out of the belt loops. His change clinked when he dropped his pants. He held the belt to swing the buckle at her. Then he thought she should see him, his glory. He pulled his shorts off. He swayed his hips to agitate his man, his sex, his servant, bursting almost his skin. "Move it," he whispered. "Move your hand up and down."

If she screamed the old man would see her bareness buttoned into Madonna clothes no innocent would ever don. "I'm just little and scared," lisped little Laverna.

"Move your hand up and down on your bangle."

"Bingle bangle." Little Laverna closed her eyes and opened her soft lips in an O. She made inviting little smacky kissy noises.

"Dirty bitch." He whipped the belt buckle at her face. "Stand up, bitch."

She clutched at the smart under her eye. He yanked her arm off her face and yanked her up, and she came down on her bad ankle. He pushed her arm around behind her and she spun and fell forward on the bed and then he pulled her other arm out from under her and pulled that back too. He was pressing her wrists together on her back, and he was wrapping his belt around them. She humped and flung herself at him. Something punched into where the tights were slit and she went rigid and then she really did scream.

ᴄᕲᴐ

Paddy in his chair upstairs in the living room, watched over by immobilized Maggie in her silver frame, dreamed of trains over by Alliston.

ᴄᕲᴐ

Knee on her back, he peeled off one of his socks and began to stuff it into her mouth. She bit his fingers. "Bitch," he hissed. He clamped his other fingers on her nose till she opened her mouth to breathe, and then he jammed the sock in past her slobber, with her gagging now, not bucking. He peeled off the other sock and forced it across her mouth. He pulled her jaw down on her neck and yanked at the ends so he could tie them at the back of her neck. He jerked the belt tight on her wrists, and tucked the end in and pulled up the slack and tucked it in again and pulled it. He was sorry things had gone so fast. This part was supposed to include the white yachting rope. There was a glistening slug trail of semen on the black satin of her merry widow. "Stand up."

She could do it, what he said, if she pressed her knee against the edge of the bed and levered herself up. If she didn't, he would hit her again. Her nose was snotting but she mustn't cry or she'd suffocate. She was upright at last. She tried to turn her head, to see him.

"Good," he was whispering. "Now put your one leg up on the bed so I can see how good you look."

She looked good? Tears stung her. She tried to get her ankle up, but it shot nauseating pain. She put her knee on the bed.

"Well, okay. Now I'm going to give your hands a real live toy to play with."

His whispery voice was breathing up to her ear. His hands grasped her waist. "You be nice now, be nice, be nice." She arched her hands away from wet nodding thrusts at her fingers. He whacked her and she could only grunt.

It wasn't just that she wouldn't cooperate. It was that she was too tall. He sat down on the chair and encouraged his erection with his own fingers while he thought. She dropped her foot and began to turn around. "Don't move."

What a real woman would do was she would, she would kick the man so hard, punch out so hard at him with her heel in his balls, he'd be paralysed. Sure, and here she'd be, arms twisted, hands tied behind her back, mouth stuffed with sock, till the old drunkard upstairs began to wonder where his dinner was and came down and saw what they'd been doing. Not to speak of the way the old man himself had been watching her. You don't cry just because something hurts.

Her red fingernails were twitching. "Bitch," he hissed. He got up and went over and pushed her. She staggered, blowing out through her nose. He pushed her again. He missed the sounds he'd imagined. No, no, no. But he daren't take off the gag. He pushed again and she fell, but not on the bed. She fell hard on the tiles, and she groaned.

She mustn't puke. She must not let tears come or she would die. There was blood in her mouth. She had bitten her cheek or her tongue. The floor was cold. By an effort of panicked concentration she made herself stay limp against the floor.

She was lying quite still now. Good. He opened his door. Not a peep. He was master of the silence as he paraded his

erection, his standard, before him, into the hall. By the door of
the mud room was his fishing rod and tackle box, and he got
those and brought them back to her. He sat on her back, facing her feet, his sex just touching her hands again. He arched
her one knee up along the floor so he could see the purplish
flesh. No, he would not go in there. You heard too much about
it, you got the real dope in the hospital, AIDS. He opened the
tackle box. But no, there was nothing better than his fishing
rod. He took the handle of his rod, and he pressed it against
her, and he pushed it against her, and into her. She was humping and bucking, cooing. He held steady, like driving a car over
ruts. The handle of his fishing rod was going into her. Muffled
twitterings were coming through the socks in her mouth. He
gave the rod some back and forth thrusts, just to make sure,
and then he counted the strokes softly for her, going backwards
from twenty. By zero the handle was in her as well as it ever
would be. The rod itself arched and trembled, a bit bloody
where it emerged from her. He'd forgotten there might be
blood. He hadn't contemplated that. But he should have
thought because his finger had bled on the potatoes. And the
prick on her hand he'd made with the corkscrew, that had bled.

The lures in his tackle box drew him, and he thought of her
ears. The lure that resembled a neon minnow, he chose that one.
And the other good one that looked like a little frog, he chose
that one too. There were tears running over the bridge of her
nose when he turned round. He bent and dipped his tongue in.
They were salty. He tried to ease the hook of the neon minnow
through the hole in her ear but it wouldn't go easily, there was
nothing for it, he had to jab. He liked that she was crying. He
wouldn't blindfold her. He lifted her head, and turned it, and
jabbed the frog through her other earlobe. She was bucking
again. He turned and sat on her backwards again and began
caressing her asshole with his thumb till she lay still. The throb-
bing in his sex, in his entire body was almost beyond control.

"You be good with your hands now."

He bent up her wrists, wrapped her painted fingers around

him, and they were soft and pliant now, and they held him, and
he began to rock and at last with his thumb to punch into
her asshole.

∽∾

Paddy sat up. There are no trains this time of day at Alliston.
But he could have sworn that one was coming right into the living room. The house was unbelievably quiet. He sat listening.
You could hear cars on the road somewhere, and the birds. He
was glad they were going to have a party for dinner. He better
rinse his mouth, sour, too much beer. He better shower. He
shoved at Marmalade who had come in and laid herself across
his feet. She nuzzled his shinbone.

∽∾

He lifted from the floor where he had collapsed forward
between her legs when he had spent himself. The bitch had
peed. His face was wet with her pee. He leapt up and kicked
her and went into the shower. Under the water he realized he
had forgotten to light the briquettes. The potatoes took an
hour. Dinner was going to be late.

∽∾

So the kid was having his shower. Well, if he used all the hot
water before his turn, he would have a word with him. He
banged the dottle out of his armchair pipe, and began to fill it,
poking the tobacco down, and poking it, and poking it.

∽∾

He realized he didn't have the use of his belt just now, it was on the girl. He had to hurry and he wasn't sure of her yet, he daren't release her till he was sure she was okay. He got the white rope from the trunk and threaded it through his belt loops. He let his T-shirt hang loose over it. It gave him an odd and daring kind of careless feeling.

The fishing rod was mostly out of her. He pulled it all the way out, quickly, the way Father trained him to tear off a bandage, ripping it up quick so you wouldn't notice the hurt. She arched her head off the floor soundlessly, eyes staring up at nothing like some kind of bird. He took the fishing rod to the bathroom and took a nail brush to it, and soap, and then he stashed it and the tackle box back by the mud room door. He paused at the door to his room. The lures looked good on her. He came in and covered her with the spread. "You rest now."

2

Meanwhile, on the pond side of the bush, it was just getting to the time of day when the sun . . .

> *The sun. Now, oh enlightened one, a mortal man or woman might be able to open his/her eyes, take his/her hands off his/her ears, come out from under the seat. Liberate the pages from the paper clip.*

. . . the sun, instead of bleaching the world from overhead, angles through the pines and cedars, and gilds the ripples on the pond, and lays gold dust on the planks of the deck — and the battery in Zeeb's PowerBook began to fail. He saved his work, shut down the system, took out the battery, set it into the charger and started the generator, which roared like a car with the choke on. It wasn't going to get quiet. So long as it was on it would keep right on roaring. But that meant the pump had come on too. He might as well shower off the stink of algae.

Shower water streamed over him. He lifted his face to it. Water poured down over his face, down into his mouth, warm salty water.

Leslie, on her unisex island.

The sea of Leslie's island roared in his imagination. The generator roared in fact.

He opened his mouth and roared back at them. He stuck his fingers in his ears and shouted Emerson. "Good-bye proud world! I'm going home. Thou art not my friend, and I'm not thine. Long through the weary crowds I roam, A river ark on the ocean brine. Long I've been tossed like the driven foam. But now, proud world! I'm going home."

Sibyl it was who had first turned them on to Emerson, who had started him down the path which led to the thesis he was writing now. There had always been an old maroon cloth-bound collected works of the sage of Concord up here, a discard, he supposed, from when Paddy and Maggie had moved up from the city, good enough for the guest cabin at least, if too shabby for the Big House. Sibyl, on her chaise longue on the screened porch, her knees up and the book propped against them, would wave her cigarette around and declaim, "But now, proud world! I'm going home." You always knew where the exclamation marks were because she shouted out the words. "Proud *world!*" By home she meant here, the cabin, the bush. She loved the way you could go natural up here, as they all did, all three. Sometimes they would stomp in down the drive, from a walk round the concession, shouting and marching in time, "Good-bye, proud *world!* I'm going home."

The water had grown cold and he shut it off. He combed his hair back and wrapped a towel around him. He pulled out the volume Sibyl had used. Must came out at him, and maybe his mother's cigarette smoke too. He went and sat at the table under the window.

Funny how he had strayed so far from the poetry. Learned papers rewritten and rewritten for submission to academic journals, footnotes, a supervisor who didn't really trust what he was doing, a life eked out with teaching assistant positions — these were Emerson to him now, and the generator out there roaring; microchips.

He pounded the table and read aloud to the beat of his hand. "'You ask,' he said, 'what guide Me through the track-less thickets led, Through thick-stemmed woodlands rough and wide. I found the water's bed. The water courses were my guide; I traveled grateful by their side.'" His childhood was in this poetry. This transcendent place could have been Emerson's inspiration, Emerson's poetry its best intellectualization. But now what was he doing about transcendence? Charting, on graphs, with the aid of a calculator, the structure of the master's essays, his sermons, his preachy prose. Not his poetry. He was recording on a computer a mechanical analysis of structure and meaning. How had he landed so far away from his promised seed bed?

He went out back with the book, brushed past the girl's underwear and stood beside the roaring generator and addressed it. "Hast thou named all the birds without a gun? Loved the wood-rose and left it on its stalk? At rich men's tables eaten bread and pulse? Unarmed, faced danger with a heart of trust?" It was no use. You couldn't hear the birds for the roar, let alone your own thoughts. He went in, reshelved Emerson and picked up the PowerBook manual. Recharging the battery, he discovered, was going to take six hours.

Despair clawed at his throat and stomach. What he was and what he wanted to be were not the same thing. And what he was becoming was again a third thing. In the roar of the generator he foresaw the house he and some Leslie look-alike would inhabit: a two-car garage, a basement bar, a gallery off the bedroom, white shag rugs. He saw himself, sticky in a tie, still in his office as evening fell, trying to prepare a faculty budget.

He flicked off the generator.

In the silence he heard the phoebes. Phoebe! Phoebe!

The ducks flew in and, angling back and forth over their wakes, aimed for the far end of the pond. They must have a nest.

He could recharge the battery at the Big House. Make it a routine. Wander over there every night with the battery. Wander over every morning to bring it back. He would clear the trail. In no time at all he'd be able to run it. His feet would learn the way.

He girded himself in jeans and a shirt and boots, took the axe and the Swede saw, and headed into the bush.

We never recited the last two verses of that Emersonian juvenilia. The rhythm changes. You can't march and shout them the way we did that first verse, Proud world! I'm going home! They're not defiant, those last verses. More spiritual.

We could have dwelt on them though. We could have provided our child with spiritual girding, provided ourselves with spiritual girding. We should have, those last verses, whispered them as a prayer.

O, when I am safe in my sylvan home,
I tread on the pride of Greece and Rome;
And when I am stretched beneath the pines,
Where the evening star so holy shines,
I laugh at the lore and the pride of man,
At the sophist schools and the learned clan,
For what are they all, in their high conceit,
When man in the bush with God may meet?

3

Generations back, at the beginning of the nineteenth century, settlers cleared the hilly acres hereabouts of bush and rocks. They burned the bush and massed the rocks in piles to clear the fields so they could till and mow them. But these, their allotted reserves, turned out not to be arable: there was cedar swamp, or the gravel of glacial moraine fit only for sheep pasture — or as it now turned out, the retirement estates of late twentieth-century gentlemen like Paddy.

Some of the rocks the settlers confronted were monumental; far too firmly planted to move with no tools but their hands and a stone boat, or maybe a horse, a pair of oxen; boulders as monumental and immovable as the granite hunk rooted in Taylor's hillside upon which Sam and Lisa sat, gazing over the little pond.

"I want to hold you," Sam said. His white T-shirt tapered to the tight waistband of his clean jeans.

Lisa went hot under the loose blue shirt she'd borrowed. His eyelashes curled on his cheek. His thumb was smoothing and smoothing at the granite, running over and over its flecks of quartz and streaks of basalt.

"I want to touch you." He looked up over the pond.

Sun caught gold fibres in the irises of his eyes. If he were to look at her, Lisa thought, he would see her scarlet.

"But first I want to tell you." He slipped off the boulder and picked up a handful of stones. "I want to let you know." He flung a stone. "I don't know what words to use."

The flung stone overreached the pond, crashed in the mud on the far side. He made a piece of sandstone skip across the smooth green surface. The frogs went still.

"This boulder," he said, climbing back up. "Who knows how it got here. A glacier retreated eons ago, melting, and dropping the chunks of mountains and lake beds it had picked up. This granite, this rock, this boulder, it boiled up from the hot crust under the earth somewhere and froze, and the glacier sliced it off and picked it up and trundled it along and dropped it here. But who knows its history." His legs hung over the edge. "My family is like this boulder."

∞

Mrs. Hagner didn't often phone her wayward daughter, Laverna. All she got out of her most of the time was monosyllables, and she would end up shouting. But today, Saturday, she had started marinating sauerbraten for dinner tomorrow, and then Joseph had reminded her that tomorrow night the marching band he belonged to was in a parade in Owen Sound and the bus probably wouldn't be home till midnight. So she thought that if she could lure Laverna home to help eat the sauerbraten, then she would also make strudel.

∞

"Who knows what forces carried my family north across the border, dropped us up there by Lake Simcoe, one black family in a sea of white? 1813. We would have come up the supply route that began during the War of 1812. But who knows where from? Who am I? Where did we come from?"

❧

Mrs. Hagner perched on the edge of the bed. She kept Laverna's phone number in her address book in the drawer of her bedside table. Laverna could come on the GO train. She imagined herself and Laverna eating the strudel, drinking coffee and a glass of wine in the sunlight on the back porch. They might talk of weddings, hope chests. Her heart gave a little thump. Wie geht's denn, mein Herzchen?

❧

"My great-grandfather used to make axe handles. An axe handle is a magic thing. Every piece of wood is different. If you make your axe handle on a machine, it doesn't balance right. Ever try a Canadian Tire axe handle? You have to make an axe handle by hand, so well balanced that when you raise it, and swing it down on your mark, your motion is effortless. My great-grandfather would take a hunk of wood and — I don't know what he did — but there, after a while, there'd be an axe handle, a perfect axe handle. Where did he learn to do that? Where did the mind learn to hold the tools and the hands learn to know the wood? If you follow back the trail of axe handles, where do you get to? Where, across the ocean, do you get to?"

He'll leave, Lisa thought. He'll never be still. Never satisfied.

❧

Mrs. Hagner dialled.

❧

"There's strawberries in the cooler," said Lisa. "I'm going to get the strawberries." She fled up the hill. He'll have a law practice and six three-piece suits in his closet and a Saab, and his mind will still always be across the ocean on the lineage of axe handles.

In the cooler she found Jade's note on a paper towel folded in four, "Lisa" written on the outside and underlined, and under that "Only Lisa" underlined twice.

> Dear Lisa,
> I think it was inconsiderate of you to not explain the whole situation with Sam Yerby. I certainly wouldn't have dreamed of intruding on your affair if I'd known. I promise to keep your secret but I can't stay here. Miscegenation is wrong, as you must know. I can hitch home.
> Your real friend,
> Jade.

Flaming, Lisa ripped the towel into little pieces and jammed them in the bottom of the cooler.

☙

Mrs. Hagner held the phone to her ear and listened to the bell ring on and on in Laverna's place. She stretched her hands out before her and considered her nailpolish. A red like strawberries. Newest thing. Look good on Laverna too, with her fair hair. They could give each other manicures, she and Laverna.

☙

Fury made Lisa punctilious. She picked up the phone and called Jade just to make sure she'd made it home. Fortunately a busy line answered her question without her having actually to check things out with Jade person-to-person. She didn't trust herself. She might say something she'd regret. She strode back down to Sam and sat on the rock beside him and put a strawberry in his mouth. "Pull," she said. She flicked the stem over the side of the rock and put a strawberry in her own mouth. Through tangy juices she said, "And what about you? Can you carve axe handles?" Rolling stone, or migrant bird — not the gates of hell would shut her out.

⌀⃥

Mrs. Hagner squinted. She brought her hand up closer to her face. Chipped. Cheap polish. Pretty colour but cheap. Laverna wasn't answering. She put down the phone and went to get the polish remover.

4

The robins were flapping around in the bathtub, caught in the light which angled in past the neighbour's roof at this time of day and set the white enamel gleaming. They made slippery little runs with beating wings, and then one by one they took off.

5

I read recently where a woman thought the ends of movies were mutable. Things might turn out differently this time. The end might change. Even though she'd seen the movie five times, she still thought that. She could make the ends of movies change.

Do you think the end of this movie will change? Try it, Saky. Be Jade now, bound and gagged, imprisoned. Slither along the floor shedding the spread as a snake sheds a skin. Inch along Mike's tiles, the sock . . .

Paddy in his chair, smoking, daydreamed of Maggie, how she used to wax floors and polish them with his old wool socks. He dreamed of the smell of floor wax.

. . . the sock bound over Jade's cheek buffs the floor tiles. Her forehead grits on the floor tiles. She makes no noise.

See her push with her good foot at the wooden corner of the daybed to get forward. See her nudge the door to Mike's room, try to nudge it open with her head. Hold your breath, Saky. See Jade triumph. Not nudge the door shut. Nudge it open. See her hump into the hallway, hump into the mud room, rasp on concrete, her face, her shoulders rasping raw on concrete.

Twist your arms behind your back, great gold statue, and imagine your wrists lashed one over the other with a belt. Hands sticky. Tuck your chin to your neck, mouth open. Hold your jaw there. Imagine a sock pulled across your tongue and against the corners of your mouth. The sock has been there an hour now. You have been drooling and gagging on it for an hour now. Are you on the floor? Lie down on the floor and hump yourself towards the door to the outside. Ready?

Roll over. You must toss back and forth on your shoulders to roll over. Keep your hands crossed behind you at the wrists. Feel your shoulders crunch, your skin scrape concrete as you toss. Toss. TOSS. Are you rolled over? Good. Now brace your one good foot against the wall, and sit up. Sit up. SIT UP!

Do not cry. No tears down your gold cheeks. You will choke. Put a toe in the crack there where the door to the outside is open. Yes? Now lever. Lever the door open. Smell. Can you smell? Smell grass. Brace your back on the shoe bench. Now stand. STAND.

Hop. Hop through the open door.

You are outside. You are moving along the cellar well. You can see the green bush in the distance, where the path leads. Forget the blood (gold dust) leaving a trail as your arm rasps along the wall of the cellar well.

∾

She would not cry. She would think of her shadow on the grass, the smell of garden rot, the bush, the pond. Blood dries, washes. Bruises go their course, like menses, swell, crescendo, fade.

And then she heard him. His footsteps. Inside the house. Above. And words, muffled. "You can take your shower now, Paddy." And footsteps again.

Forward. Slide along the grass, the only way to get there. Fall, the only way to get down. Fall forward on the grass. Slide like a snake on your belly.

🙞🙜

Paddy looked out the bedroom window across the lawn towards the bush while he unbuttoned his shirt, and stepped out of his trews . . .

> *Trews. From the Irish for trousers. It's not for nothing Paddy is Patrick Slater.*

. . . but his sight is failing, and he was looking where the black locusts had grown so much you couldn't see the CN Tower any more. He was thinking about cutting down the black locusts, him and Mike logging. He was thinking about the chain saw. Who did sharpening in the village these days?

🙞🙜

The briquettes were a perfect ashen colour at last. Mike tucked the foil-wrapped potatoes in among the coals and lifted some over the potatoes with the tongs. The picnic table was set for . . .

> *If Mike were Superman he would see Jade inchworming across the lawn the other side of the house. But he isn't Superman. He doesn't have X-ray vision. The house comes between them.*

. . . four, horn-handled steak knives, forks, butter for the corn, salad in the big brown salad bowl with the people-handled salad servers, and the dressing on the side in the cut glass vinegar jug with the stopper. He went inside to the kitchen. He flipped the steak in the marinade one more time. What was the old bugger muttering about there in the bathroom, grunting, slipping around under the shower? Thought he was the centre of the universe.

He poured a jigger of scotch into each of two clean highball glasses. He added ice and soda. Then he added another dollop of scotch to the girl's glass. The tinkling of the ice in the glasses as he headed down the stairs to his room reminded him of Father's rye. When Father lurched away from the table, little Mikey would linger and drink the watery dregs. The door to the cellar well was open. He kicked it shut and went into his room.

⌀

Plantains, satiny. Stubs of grass, stiff stubs scraping. The corset working off her breasts, her nipples dragging over stiff stubs, smooth plantains.

⌀

The room swirled. Windows, desk, chair pulsed, and haloed. Mike staggered, thought he would fall. Had there ever been a girl? Then ice tinkled, and he began to refocus. He held two drinks in his hands. The spread with which he had left her covered lay husked on the floor. Her shorts and shirt were upstairs in with the dusters, he could verify that. Her one sandal lay over there. His trunk was open and the merry widow was gone, the red tights. She had not been a dream, no, and the cellar well door had been open. He had kicked it shut. He set the glasses on the desk and scurried back to it, flung out to the front of the house.

⌀

His footsteps on gravel, on the drive — she could hear him, looking for her. Get off the lawn then, get onto the path through the meadow. The path — it was mowed. It went downhill. You could roll down it, you could fling yourself forward, roll, roll, and the world would turn, it was turning. That squealing — who was making that squealing? The walls of her nose were vibrating. Was that squealing something she herself was doing behind the sock?

⟳

At the curve of the drive he halted. There was a clear view of the drive before him, the pastures on either side, the mail box, the road, and there was nothing to see. Nothing. The smell of fire starter drifted down over the lawn, and towards the bush. He looked that way, towards the path, the bush.

⟳

Him? On the lawn? His footsteps? Was that him coming? Shelter, take shelter, roll off the path into shelter. Into the weeds. Curl. Close your eyes.

⟳

Females. He began to nose down the path. One moment they were there, the next not. Mother had sat on the steps, painting her nails, waiting in her coat with the fur collar and a hat. A hat? Where had Mother got a hat? A gift from the new man? And then, while little Mikey went to pee, too bloody tense, too bloody tense, she had vanished, without kissing him, without saying a word of good-bye.

The path ended at the edge of the bush and he came to a halt. Butterflies floated round him. The sound of sawing drifted over from the direction of the pond, and he hit his head. Of course. She'd been rescued by that turd by the pond. He had to get to the pond and forestall any misunderstandings.

∾

His footsteps faded back up the path and she began again to make herself roll down through the grass. Ahead, the bush echoed with sawing.

The other, Zeeb, existed.

And therefore she would roll through raspberry canes. She would heave herself past the dried lower branches of cedars at the edge of the bush. She would roll past a wall of dark roots dangling. She would roll on. She would . . . but she had rolled over the edge, into a pit, not able to stop, face down, crumpled into cold mud.

6

Water gleamed in the toilet bowl. The robins fluttered down to the toilet seat, slipped on slippery white, fell into the bowl of water one by one, fluttered stormily, more slowly, were still, floated, limp.

7

Paddy paints the handles of his tools orange. Just as well because Zeeb had reached the point of exhaustion where he wouldn't have been able to see where he had laid the axe if sun fingers sinking through the trees hadn't picked up the fierce orange colour of the handle among moss, swamp muck, cedar duff. He looked through the forbidding tangle towards where he wanted to be.

Clearing trail was like making computer graphs in that there were logical procedures to follow. These brittle branches here to crack off before you could reach that fallen tree beyond. That top end to saw through before you tackled the main trunk. But trail clearing was not like computer graphing in that the energy came, not from a battery, not from a wall plug, but from your own muscles.

He was shaking. His gut was growling. It would be way after 6:00 by now. Should he have wanted, by any chance, to go, he would have missed dinner at the Big House.

ᴄⱴᴐ

Breathing in shallow gasps, Mike hurtled the Renault along the ruts through the pines, down the hill, round the pond, to a thudding halt below the cabin. Sunlight slanted through the windshield right into his eyes, blinding, nauseating him. He put his hands over his ears and made his breath slow. When the quick rush of blood to his gut had subsided, when the need to crap had passed with air, he opened his eyes and saw the still water of the pond. Shading his eyes, he looked round the valley.

Silence.

But the girl's sandal — one of them was on the floor of the passenger seat there where she'd dropped it on the way back to the house. Quick, he stuffed it under his shirt, half down his chinos. He slammed the car door so anybody would know he was here. He strode towards the cabin whistling. Standing in the grass he hollered at the door, the windows, "Hi! Anybody home?"

Nothing moved inside the cabin.

He ran up onto the deck the way Father would when someone was watching, a politician glad-handing onto a stage. He flung open the door, went in.

Nothing moved.

His eyes shut. He would never let them put him away again. They had restrained him, tied his wrists to the sides of the bed. He had struggled. He had imagined he could break the metal bed. Thrashed, screamed. They came at him with a needle, flipped him, jammed it into him, and he had arched and squealed. When he awoke, he had smiled at them therefore, sadly, wisely. He had spoken to them, weakly. Weakly, he had murmured the correct words. Where am I? And so they had released his wrists. But the door to the ward had still been locked.

"Hey!" he shouted. What were they called? "Zebu!" Ridiculous name. And the girl's name. Her name. Her name was. Something equally idiotic. He went through the cabin, out the back door.

Again his breath froze. That was her underwear, there, hanging dripping from the clothesline. Ah, but the underwear was dripping pond dirt, this was where she had left it, she was known to have forgotten it here. Everybody knew she had for-gotten her underwear here.

Zeeb's bike was leaning against the end of the screened porch. They'd stolen bikes, at one foster home. A gang had. You sold them. There was a dealer. When the bikes were too securely locked to liberate, front wheels removed and attached with the frames to iron fences, he used to let the air out of the tires. He pictured the girl on the crossbar, elegant in black satin, red lace, Zeeb tooling her off. He felt for his knife.

Zeeb couldn't figure out what Mike was up to. Something was different. He didn't have his windbreaker on for one thing and he looked suddenly as if he needed a haircut. When they were living on Huron Street, when he was still a kid, he'd had a bow and arrow set with suction cups instead of arrowheads. A sur-face had to be very smooth for the arrows to stick, like the big front-room window or the tiles around the fireplace or parked cars. He would have sworn, up to this minute, that Mike was the kind of smoothie that fake arrows would stick to.

"What's up?" he said, walking into the light.

Mike peered past him into the bush. "Where is she?"

"She?" Zeeb's heart opened. Had he told Mike about Leslie? "Here?"

Mike began to laugh. There were twigs in the egghead's hair again. He squealed a panting laugh. "She'd get runs in her nylons." He bent over, folding his arms over his gut, rocking.

Mike's red nylons swam into Zeeb's mind, Leslie swam towards him in red nylons with a slit crotch. A rush of blood raised him. He hunched away to the tool shed to stash the axe and saw. His hands shook as he locked the shed.

Mike was smoothing his hair down when Zeeb was able to come back and face him. "You're late for dinner," Mike said. "I came to get you before I put the steak on. Paddy's waiting for you."

8

"That girl get off?" said Paddy. The picnic table vibrated as he sawed through his steak. He dipped the pink morsel in the bloody juices on his plate and popped it into his mouth and chewed.

Zeeb let red wine drift over his tongue.

"Oh yes." Mike slathered butter on a cob of corn with the fourth horn-handled steak knife, the one the girl would have used, except she wasn't here, and handed it to the old man. "Of course. She decided she had to be on her way. La donna e mobile, n'est ce pas? I had to drive her to the end of the subway. That's why dinner was so late."

"I can butter my own corn, young man," said Paddy. He tried not to smack his lips too obviously. The kid seemed to have forgotten all about his cholesterol and triglycerides. "Thank you all the same."

❧

Moths were drowning themselves in the wax that dripped down the sides of the candles on the picnic table. Zeeb picked at the wax, fed it back to the flames. Sometimes there were two flames where, before he'd blinked, there'd been only one.

Sometimes there were a million stars dancing on the brandy glasses. Leslie in red nylons with a slit crotch blurred into a million stars, a million stars danced on the brandy glasses. The girl on the subway with no underwear came and went like the moths and the flame and the stars. He yawned.

"You got a flashlight?" he said.

"You're not going to try to go back through the bush, are you, boy?" said Paddy.

"Oh, come on Paddy," he said . . .

Yes. Let him go.

". . . don't be such an old fart. Live a little. Have adventures. So what'll happen in the bush?"

"You could get lost till morning," said Paddy. "Mosquitoes will love you."

"I'm so sorry," said Mike. "We don't have a flashlight. I've looked all over. I've been meaning to buy one at the hardware store in the village. I keep forgetting to put it on the list. I'll give you a lift back to the cabin."

∽

She heard the car leave the garage. She heard it travel down the driveway, along the road. She heard it stop at the crossroads. She heard it go down the line, pause. She heard it down the drive, the good-byes, the car's departure.

∽

Sheet! "Mike!" Zeeb turned back from the cabin to the open starry darkness beyond the screen door. "Mike!" he hollered after the headlights rocking up the drive.

∽

She heard him calling. In chill darkness she heard him. She knew it was him. But he was calling the other. He wanted the other. She couldn't move any more, her head was wedged as in a vice. When she had first plunged into the pit she could move, but then, every time she had inched up, gripped, with her shoulder, her one good foot, on wet roots, stones, mud, she had lost it, slithered back, finally got wedged. Still, she had believed that, as there is light after night, so mercy would receive her, that way, forward, in the direction away from back there where infinite evil prowled. But now the one was calling the other, shouter wanted whisperer, yes called no, day joined itself to night the way two halves of an apple grow.

Twisted ankle, raw bloody vagina, suffocating on wet wool, mud in her nose, breasts lacerated, legs scraped and torn, whining multitudes of mosquitoes maddening her buttocks, shoulders, arms, neck, earlobes dragging a neon minnow, a little plastic frog — these she had endured. But this she could not endure — the one wanting the other.

Light faded. Sound ceased. She became one with ice mountains.

When the last light is sucked away along the converging lines of trees, Saky, to vanish beyond the horizon, we who resist darkness are driven to strip matter of locale and texture, to reduce reality to planes, to order without time, to monochromes, austerity. We cast a stern eye on nature, lose patience with its outer garments. We abjure our bodies.

ᐧᐧᐧ

The Renault's headlights rocked away back up the drive, turned right through the pines, vanished, and Zeeb slapped his head. Sheet! Sheet! Sheet! How could he possibly have forgotten to take the battery and charger over, how could he? Drunk, too muddled to think, too fucking drunk. He swayed over to the bed and fell into darkness.

⚭

Mike stopped the car at the crossroads across the road from
the A-frame where bush crowded the corner of Paddy's property right to the fence.

*This is no Virgin Spring, Saky. No madonna awaits a
virgin's candles. No mother keeps vigil, no father sweats
his vengeance pure. No rapist will be caught . . .*

He eased the sandal out from under his roped-in waist and
flung it far and wide the way city drivers toss beer cans, styrofoam cups, hamburger papers, doughnut boxes.

*. . . no rapist will be caught selling the girl's clothes. As
yet there is no hero. This, Saky, is the Ontario bush. In a pit
left by a toppled maple Jade/Laverna lies just breathing.*

9

Mike jammed the brown and yellow striped spread in around the mattress of the daybed. He pushed the girl's other sandal into the trunk, slammed the lid, locked it, went upstairs and got the flashlight, and went back out to the compost heap with the dinner debris. He had to bring it out in the sink strainer. There were no spare juice cans because they no longer bought juice in cans. They bought it in bottles because of the poisons of metal seeping into the juice. But you couldn't just suddenly change to a sink strainer and not expect questions to be asked. He must retrieve the can he'd thrown at the chipmunk. He angled the circle of light slowly around. The rise and fall of shadows distorted everything.

∞

Paddy, undressing, gazed out at the night and wondered what in tarnation the kid was doing and why the hell he had said they didn't have a flashlight when it was very evident they did. And then he realized that what was happening was that the kid in saying they didn't have a flashlight was protecting the boy from drunken recklessness and letting him save face at the same time. For sure Zeeb would have got all turned around in the bush and passed a wretched night. He felt the way he used to feel when King and Polly could be seen playing croquet together Sunday afternoons on the back lawn looking out over the hazy city high above the railway tracks, while he and Maggie, and Sal, his sister, and Sal's husband, Paul, drank sherry on the patio, and the roast sizzled. He rubbed his eyes and sniffed.

Sentimental old man, lofty on your patio of memory. You didn't hear/see me, red, shaking, saying to King, You can't just pick up the ball, you have to hit it, you can't just pick it up and move it.

You never saw King smirk, heard him say, You don't make the rules. Girl.

Would have/could have slammed him with my mallet. Did not. Abjured myself instead.

How many rebirths must we make, Saky, before we find the middle road?

The kid must be getting worms for a before-breakfast fishing expedition, yes, that was it. Paddy got into bed and allowed himself to stretch out, to take his ease between the clean sheets. He sucked buttery corn from between his teeth.

❧

Marmalade had slipped out when Mike opened the door to go back in. He framed her in the spot of the flashlight, following her as she searched for a place to squat. She looked back at him, head dipped in embarrassment. When she had finished, she did not, however, waddle to the door and whine to be let in, but, sniffing the ground, the air, headed down around the house. He set the sink strainer and the compost tin by the door and followed her whispering, "Seek, seek."

Around the other side of the house, she focused in on the grass at the place where the concrete walk of the cellar well

that came from his room met the lawn. Her nose made wuffly
sounds among the grass blades. She lifted her head towards the
bush, ducking as she sniffed. She shook herself and wove once
more towards the back of the house.

He pointed the flashlight beam in the direction of the bush.
You could hear the usual wild things, the stirrings and thump-
ings and whistles which disrupted the night. He beamed the
light to the grass at his feet which had drawn Marmalade,
arced it slowly in ever broadening circles forward. It was logical to suppose that the girl had not dematerialized, that she
existed somewhere, that she had left a trail from here to there,
as surely as he was leaving fingerprints on the flashlight, which
technology could discover, that she would have left a trail of
her stenches — pee, blood, even perhaps his semen — that the
bitch sensed.

The lawn seemed to be moving in the beam of light, and he
moved forward towards the movement, and saw worms pulling
back into the earth. Night crawlers. A universal phenomenon.
In the city you looked out the window summer nights and saw
lights like his flashlight beaming on the lawns up and down the
street as gatherers stooped, murmuring to one another, miners'
lamps on their foreheads, and scooped worms into cans to sell
as bait. The worms that ate you up rose, safe, they thought,
from birds, to take the night air, but the gatherers were there to
gather them in. Destruction to the destroyers.

The light led him on. In the stubble where the lawn fun-
nelled into the path through the meadow, the light picked out
a regular shape, a piece, a torn fragment, he saw as he picked
it up, of red lace.

His heart expanded to fill his entire body. His body
thrummed. The external world and the engine inside his skin
had never been more attuned, the one responding instantly to
the other's responses as if omniscient order had fallen into
place after chaos. He moved down the path, beaming his flashlight forward, right, left, forward. He picked up the bent grass
where she must have rolled away when he'd sought her before.

Slowly, surely he advanced down her bent route and encountered, with the light, broken dried brown stalks, flattened raspberry canes, red lace once more and ahead, low in the wall of cedar, unusually bent branches. He crouched, moved past the broken branches. He was absorbing oxygen at such an accelerated rate that he felt his every cell twinkling as brightly as the starry sky that vanished behind him as he entered the bush.

And there, in a declivity ahead of him, he saw black satin gleaming in the flashlight beam, shadowy white flesh, the curve of legs, black in the night, the neon of his minnow. He crouched by the edge of the pit, investigating the details, running over her with the light. She was a mess, muddy, torn, legs splayed, head jammed under where the root wall met the floor of the pit.

The puppy of his childhood had been perfect in death, as if it were only sleeping, not like this.

For a time, after Mother left, he had been convinced he could fly. He had discovered he could get up on the garage roof from the back where they couldn't see him. Father had someone new; bottles, ashes littered the gritty floor inside the house. But he could climb on the fence and then through the lilac bush, using the lilac branches as a ladder, then haul himself up onto the low side of the roof, and from there it wasn't hard to monkey up the asphalt tiles to the peak. He could stand upright on the peak of the garage roof. He could tightrope back and forth on the tiles curved over the roof beam, and survey, through the trees at the fence line, beyond the bushes, into the neighbours' backyards: a circular rose bed, a small glassed-in nursery shed, a brick barbecue, a hammock, and, from the other end of the peak, he could peer down on the concrete of his own drive, and across at the torn curtains drawn over the back bedroom windows.

All he needed to be able to fly, he believed, to glide from foreign hammock to familiar peeling windowsill, from a new life with the neighbours to a clear view of the interior of his own, were membranes connecting wrists to ankles, and these he would construct from his bed sheets with their red, white and blue slogans. MAKE LOVE NOT WAR. SOCK IT TO ME. PEACE.

But first he would test his hypothesis with the puppy.

The puppy was a foundling. It was undecided as yet whether or not he could keep it, whether they could afford the food. He liked the warmth of it in bed at night but not the way it cried and peed. It chewed everything and snitched food out of his hand. Its wet tongue sent shivers through him.

In order to get the puppy up to the roof, he put on his windbreaker and zipped it in, a wiggling scratching burden. But he made it up the fence, through the lilac, to the roof beam overlooking the concrete drive. There he unzipped, raised high the wriggling warm soft body, still squirming around to lick him, and dropped it to the drive, where it didn't move.

When they wondered where the puppy was he said he didn't know. They never went down to the back of the garden. Grass didn't grow under the trees; no need to mow there. No danger of them tracking down the smell of rot, nor risk they'd see the flies. Anyway, he had covered the corpse with rocks and leaves, and peed on it to make it his own.

She lay still under his light, inert, and he laid down the light and pulled out his man, and peed on her.

She groaned. His urine crystallized. She was not dead. A cold film wrapped his body, the active interface between eternal other and himself. He felt as if sparks were flaring off his brain, illuminating every internal resource he possessed.

Quickly he zippered himself whole again. He picked up his light and slid down into the pit, and leaned against the wall of roots which imprisoned her head. He nudged her with the toe of his Birkenstock. She opened and shut her white hands with their black nails.

"Bitch," he whispered.

He set his foot . . .

Paper clip time again.

. . . on the back of her head and pressed. She twisted and thrashed. He pressed with his foot, harder and harder, all his weight on his one foot, holding on to roots to keep himself steady. The flashlight fell and lay illuminating pebbles, sand, roots — a patch of earth. He got his other foot on her face and pressed her down, down into the mud. Her body humped.

"You should have considered that before you decided to leave me," he whispered.

The ambiguity of this messy interval in darkness, a square foot of earth alone gleaming like an otherworldly moon, when she persisted in thrashing and he had to exert all his strength to hold her face in the mud, her nostrils under, it revolted him. He hadn't actually witnessed Father's death. Whatever turmoil there had been was over when he got there. All he had confronted was a corpse. He had lifted his father's hand, the hard hand, the hand that held the belt, the whisky, his mother, the other woman, the hand that threw things, and it fell, curled and white and awkward, not moving. Never again moving. Any idyll must be preceded, he supposed, by a period of messy war in which this, not that, was preferred.

She was limp at last. He stood off her and picked up the light to look. Now she had shat herself. He felt for pebbles and twigs at the edge of the pit and tossed them at her shoulders, her filthy butt. She didn't move. He ran the light over her. Her face was deep in the mud, buried in the mud. Her hair was spread, embedded in mud. He climbed out of the pit and sat cross-legged on the edge and kept watch. Marmalade nudged him from behind. He shoved her away. She nudged again, and he pressed her down flat beside him, never taking his eyes or the light off the girl, the muddy back of her head. At long last he was satisfied that she would not come back and . . .

Resume reading.

. . . he made his way to the house and put the compost can and the sink strainer away and showered again and, in his room, screwed open the windows facing the lawn, and darkened the interior, and got into bed.

He listened to Marmalade's nails above him, clicking into the old bugger's room. He was glad to have gone out into the night and confronted it. He knew the darkness now. It held no more mysteries. He heard the owls hooting and the horse neighing. He could identify them. He stretched his arms out along the rough surface of the brown and yellow Indian bedspread.

Four

Saky?

Saky!

Smooth male idol. Met an old man, did you? A sick man. A hermit. A corpse. The corpse, of course, had to be the woman.

How'd you like a banana in the kisser? Watch me wind up. I can throw.

Attention must be paid.

{Omigod, did I really do it? They're coming. I . . . . . . am chanting holy writ . . .}

A Service in Memory of Jade/Laverna

ORDER OF SERVICE

CALL TO WORSHIP – *King Lear*, 5.3.257

> Howl, howl, howl, howl!

OPENING SONG – Anon

> Oh dig my grave
> Both wide and deep
> A silver stone
> At my head and feet
> And on my breast
> Put a pure white dove
> To show the world
> That I died of love.

READING – *Buddhism,* T. W. Rhys Davids

[Carrying her dead child the woman fled] to Gautama, and doing homage to him, said, "Lord and master, do you know any medicine that will be good for my child?" "Yes, I know of some," said the Teacher. Now it was the custom for patients or their friends to provide the herbs which the doctors required, so she asked what herbs he would want. "I want some mustard seed," he said; and when the poor girl eagerly promised to bring some of so common a drug, he added, "You must get it from some house where no son, or husband, or parent, or slave has died." "Very good," she said, and went to ask for it, still carrying her dead child with her. The people said, "Here is mustard seed, take it"; but when she asked, "In my friend's house has any son died, or a husband, or a parent or slave?" they answered, "Lady! what is this that you say; the living are few, but the dead are many."

SONG – Emily Dickinson

> I heard a Fly buzz — when I died . . .
> With Blue — uncertain stumbling Buzz —
> Between the light — and me —
> And then the Windows Fail — and then
> I could not see to see.

CONFESSION – *Hamlet*, *5.1.297–307*

> 'Swounds, show me what thou'lt do:
> Woo't weep? woo't fight? woo't fast?
> woo't tear thyself?
> Woo't drink up eisel? eat a crocodile
> I'll do't. Dost thou come here to whine?
> To outface me with leaping in her grave?
> Be buried quick with her, and so will I:
> And if thou prate of mountains, let them throw
> Millions of acres on us, till our ground
> Singeing his pate against the burning zone,
> Make Ossa like a wart! Nay, an thou'lt mouth,
> I'll rant as well as thou.

MEDITATION – *A Vindication of the Rights of Women*, Mary Wollstonecraft

I do not wish them [women] to have power over men; but over themselves.

SILENCE

READING – *Encyclopaedia Britannica*, LINGUISTICS 14:70

binary opposition, the contrast of two opposed phonological elements; *e.g.*, voiced/voiceless, continuous/interrupted.

SERMON – Ibid. NUMERALS AND NUMERAL SYSTEMS
16:760

There is one island in present-day life, however, in which the familiar decimal system is no longer supreme: the electronic computer. Here the binary positional system has been found to have great advantages over the decimal. In the binary system, in which the base is 2, there are just two digits, 0 and 1; the number two must be represented here as 10, since it plays the same role as does ten in the decimal system. The first few numbers are

0: 0
1: 1
2: $10 = 1(2) + 0$
3: $11 = 1(2) + 1$
4: $100 = 1(2^2) + 0(2) + 0$
5: $101 = 1(2^2) + 0(2) + 1$

To return to [an] example used before, 256,058 has the binary representation 111 11010 00001 11010. The reason for the greater length of the binary number is that a binary digit distinguishes between only two possibilities, 1 or 0, whereas a decimal digit distinguishes among 10 possibilities; in other words, a binary digit carries less information than a decimal digit. Because of this its name has been shortened to bit; a bit of information is thus transmitted whenever one of two alternatives is realized in the machine. It is of course much easier to construct a machine to distinguish between two possibilities than among 10, and this is another advantage for the base 2; but a more important point is that bits serve simultaneously to carry numerical information and the logic of the problem. That is, the dichotomies of yes and no, and of true and false, are preserved in the machine in the same way as 0 and 1, so in the end everything reduces to a sequence of those two characters.

yes/no
1/0
man/woman
self/other
Jade/Laverna

INFORMATION THEORY 12:247

The parlor game "Twenty Questions" illustrates some of these ideas. In this game, one person thinks of an object and the other players attempt to determine what it is by asking not more than 20 questions that can be answered "yes" or "no." According to information theory each question can, by its answer, yield anywhere from no information to $\log_2 2$ or one bit of information, depending upon whether the probabilities of "yes" and "no" answers are very unequal or approximately equal. To obtain the greatest amount of information, the players should ask questions that subdivide the set of possible objects, as nearly as possible, into two equally likely groups. For example, if they have established by previous questions that the object is a town in the United States, a good question would be, "Is it east of the Mississippi?" This divides the possible towns into two roughly equal sets. The next question then might be, "Is it north of the Mason-Dixon line?" If it were possible to choose questions which always had the effect of subdividing into two equal groups, it would be possible to isolate, in 20 questions, one object from approximately 1,000,000 possibilities. This corresponds to 20 bits.

The formula for the amount of information is identical in form with equations representing entropy in statistical mechanics, and suggests that there may be deep-lying connections between thermodynamics and information theory. . . .

INFORMATION PROCESSING 12:244D

These forms of storage, together with perforated card and tape input, had emphasized the simplification of internal logic made possible by representing data in binary form. This requires two characters only, . . .

Jade/Laverna
Mike/Zeeb

. . . [who] can be identified, with little chance of error, as presence or absence of a hole, of magnetism, or of electric current.

CLOSING WORDS – *Romeo and Juliet*, 5.3.179–181

We see the ground whereon these woes do lie
But the true ground of all these piteous woes
We cannot without circumstance descry.

BENEDICTION – *King Lear*, 5.2.310

Never, never, never, never, never!

Five

Sunday

The rattling of a kingfisher in flight, fishing the pond, woke Zeeb. He sat up, urgent to grasp what he'd been missing. Some light, some message implicit in the sway of grass heads, the cawing of harsh crows, the buzz of flies in the windows, the kingfisher — something was eluding him.

Once he went to the hatchery with King to get fry to restock the pond. A kingfisher corpse had lain squashed and dried in the mud drive alongside the cold coursing tanks teeming with fish. The hatchery guy had pointed to the spines of dead cedars reaching against the sky the other side of the tanks. "They sit there," he said. "Kingfishers. They think it's a free feed here. One of their own lying there like that, dead — that deters them."

It came to him. One of his PowerBook batteries was dead. A couple of hours more work and the other would be too. He slid out of bed.

It had rained during the night. The air over the pond was misty, the sun still behind the pines, the hollow of the pond still in shadow. He wanted to see the kingfisher, to imprint its silver crest on his retina, its long hunting beak, its slash of blue. He crept along the floor, angled his body against the door frame. His stealth was rewarded. Yes, the kingfisher. But also — a great blue heron out there, stalking the tall weeds which bordered the pond on slow long lizard legs, silently, without ripples, easing forward, beak first, pulling one foot forward and gliding, pulling the other forward and gliding again. The ducks squatted on the raft.

His mouth felt like a garbage can. He slid into the shelter of the wall and went on hands and knees to the kitchen. If he stood, the heron, shy and stranger-shunning, would see him silhouetted by front and back windows and sail off. But the heron had vanished anyway when he wormed back with a can of juice. The ducks were drifting towards the silt basin. Only the kingfisher remained, perched on a poplar in the copse where the beaver had been logging before he shot it. The kingfisher dove into the pond and rose with a small trout in its beak. It whacked the trout dead against the branch, swallowed it whole.

Zeeb glugged orange juice.

Then he saw the heron. Not gone. It had circled the pond, passed under the bank below the cabin where he couldn't see it. Now it was stalking towards the silt basin. The sun bugled up over the pines. Light pushed the line of silence back and back. Mist skimmed up silver, curled into illumination, vanished. The heron reached the underwater berm that separated pond from silt basin. It hunkered there, camouflaged by the rock beside the berm, waiting, watching. Soon it would be spotlit and go.

He wondered if it had eaten this morning, stabbed frog or tadpoles or beetles in the weeds. How long without food could a great blue heron live? As he watched, it became a curved dragon, wings arched, swooped underwater, swam submerged, surfaced with a fish crossways in its beak. It thwacked its fish dead on the rock and, lifting its long neck, tilted it down its gullet.

❧

When Mike got up there were deer on the lawn, which darted away at angles, their white flags bobbing, when he appeared at the window, and vanished. Deer, he believed, were vegetarian, and would not beat a path to the relic in the pit. But when he saw Marmalade weaving across the lawn again, nose down, in the direction of the bush — Paddy must have let her out — he began to take stock of his options. Sunday. Even Strickland's machines were silent this morning. The air was so still he could hear church bells.

⌀

"You dirty dog," muttered Paddy. He was brushing Marmalade by the picnic bench. "Where have you been?" He held on to her collar to keep her away from himself. She was filthy — mud and cedar and God knows what all. Fool dog had a terrible habit of rolling in manure, although this neither stank nor looked like normal cow patties, and she didn't usually cover herself with sand and cedar duff, and she certainly didn't often get her muzzle and paws so dirty.

The brush ran through her golden fur like a harrow over soft earth, drawing regular runnels. He could feel the ripples of fat flesh under her fur.

"You're getting old, old girl. Not enough exercise."

Marmalade stood firm, feet planted, in a trance, as the bristles coursed down her body. He wondered why dogs rolled in dirt. What atavism drove Marmalade? Did her ancestors think to disguise the adrenaline of the hunt by making themselves smell of decay?

The kid came out with the compost.

"Well, well," he chortled, remembering the worms. "When are we going fishing?"

Kid halted. "Bear for punishment, aren't you Paddy?"

He chortled again. "Don't try to pull the wool over my eyes, young fellow me lad. I saw you last night. Get any good ones?"

"Good ones?" Kid's head jerked up and back.

"Big fat juicy ones, long thin skinny ones, icky gicky, ooey gooey worms," Paddy sang. He used to have a confident tenor. How his voice now quavered. "Where'd you keep them overnight, eh? Oh, I know what you've been up to. I used to go out to the compost at night myself, just like you. Dig up a few. Keep them overnight in my bait box. Sometimes I'd get grasshoppers."

Kid narrowed his eyes and went off to the compost heap.

Paddy thought of himself creeping up the hillside — this was when they first got the farm and the grass was cropped short on the hills from being over-pastured by sheep — creeping on hands and knees up a hill alive with the whir and leap of grasshoppers, and pouncing on them, and the dry barbed buzz in his hand. Slipping the vibrant thing into the bait box, carefully so as not to let escape those already trapped. The bait box would buzz, belted on his hip. He'd get his bamboo rod. You couldn't cast on the stream. He didn't have the pond then, hadn't built it, hadn't stocked it. He had to fish the stream. The advantage of the long tapered segments of bamboo fly rod for fishing the stream was that you could poke it through the bushes over a likely hole. You'd hook on your grasshopper and drop it, wriggling and leaping, into the cold current where a fish lurked, and like as not you'd haul out a beauty.

But perhaps distance was casting a rosy hue. Sometimes the fish were under the limit, little things, hardly a nibble. He remembered going, with the bait box buzzing against his hip but no rod, to feed a fish he knew hid under that bank, or in that hole. He would watch the grasshopper twitch on the surface of the water, watch it try to leap, watch the dark shadow of the fish swirl under the surface, and grab, and break the surface, and be gone, all still. Fattening fish for future angling.

"There you go, old girl," he whispered. Marmalade licked his hand and went to lie in the shade.

It was too beautiful a morning to go back indoors. Bumblebees sailed past him. Little birds twittered in the sumac up the hill. High above a pair of hawks circled, or were they buzzards? His eyesight was failing, he couldn't tell. But the air was fresh and clean. Marmalade's brush in hand, he wandered down the hill around the house in the sunshine.

Maggie's garden had all gone to pot. The peonies were over and no one had cut off their heads. Still, he was blessed to be here in the centre of this place of perfect beauty. He turned. Behold! The willow tree he had planted when the house was built now towered over the lawn. Behold! The lawn he had carved out of pasture enclosed him like an arena. Behold! The path, which in old times was such a bustling thoroughfare between Big House and cabin, even now, since he kept up the appearance of use by mowing it at least to the edge of the bush, beckoned your eye towards mystery and the unknown, tempted your feet to test the wilderness. Far, far beyond lay the troubled hot spots of the world. Cities encircled by ever encroaching mortar fire, strangling the lifelines of the trapped people within. Food relief cut off, cargoes stolen. Medical supplies, primitive and basic as they had been, long gone. A doctor of Médecins sans Frontières trying to patch a boy's leg broken six months before and festering since then under nothing but a bandage. Women holding the emaciated bodies of children. Men kept at bayonet point in the push-up position for six hours. He brushed at a fly circling his head.

The kid was trotting down from the compost heap. "How do you like them apples?" He held out the compost can. Paddy put his hand into the can, felt in among crumbly compost, and touched the soft bodies of worms. "Where's your bait box, Paddy?"

They were walking around the house to the back again. He was going to quiz the kid about what he'd done with last night's worms. Leave some for the other fellow, he would have admonished. Then the kid put his hand on his arm.

"I don't like to bring it up, Paddy, because I know you're attached to the old bitch, but, well, what's the matter with Marmalade? She's pretty old for a dog, isn't she?"

Paddy squinted ahead to where Marmalade was panting on the back porch. He looked at the filth in the brush in his hand. What would the world be without a worm in the apple?

✧

Mike rinsed the compost can and set it upside down in the dish rack. He brushed the crumbs of dirt around the bait box into his hand, flushed them down the sink, wiped the table, hung up the dish cloth, dried his hands. Carrying the bait box he went down to the mud room and got his rod and his tackle box. He went through to the garage. He could hear Paddy wandering around the living room overhead, talking to himself, looking for his pipe no doubt, stupid old bugger. He opened the back door of the car and laid his rod on the seat, and the tackle box and the bait box on the floor. He got in the front seat. He flicked on the door opener, started the car. Paddy and Marmalade appeared as he'd bid them. Paddy shut the door between the garage and the house, and opened the back car door for Marmalade. She lumbered up, and he helped her. He shut the door after her and then got in and shut his own door. Marmalade panted in the little floor space between the back of the passenger seat and the backseat. She began to scrabble up onto the backseat, clawing at the fishing rod, sniffing the handle. Mike reversed with a jerk. Marmalade crashed to the floor.

"Steady on, young fellow."

"Poor old bitch."

✧

Zeeb lay spread on the deck, cheek on arms, suspended between the imperative to get going and the futility of ambition. A silver dragonfly landed on his shoulder. The old thoughts Polly fed him . . .

temple
when?

. . . angry . . . shamed, great gold god . . . howling around your temple . . . Never. Never. Never. Never.

Never . . . lying like a dog, filthy, pissed myself, stale sweat, snotty nose.

Anger.

Shame.

Women, mauled, molested, children molested, starved, wandering from napalm, collapsed around a begging dish, raped, starved, bombed. Men, fathers of families, beaten, murdered, seeing wives raped, murdered.

While the fat cats sit and watch.

No. Fat cats don't watch, don't bother. They sit in boardrooms, scratch their balls, their cunts. Decide fates.

No. No decisions. They don't even decide. They pick from the ample silver platters before them what choice fruits to pluck, what soft brie to spread on which cracker, whether bourbon or ale will quench their thirsts.

While children starve, men suffer, women suffer, Jade dies, Mike, Zeeb have no fathers.

Fucking fat cats. Don't give a shit.

You. Gold fat cat up there teaching detachment.

Me. Fat cat down here bawling.

Who is this old woman, circling, watching me here in your flickering red/gold silence? Head shaven, beads running through her fingers, mouth moving. Who is she in my night watch, my weeping screaming loss of light?

Go. Go on.

Get away from me.

Leave me alone . . .

. . . the thoughts Polly used to feed him came to him, about trajectories, how he and the dragonfly had intersected at this place and time, how it could not have been otherwise, how they were part of a dense pattern of intersections, so dense that intersections were all there were, nothing more. He was the dragonfly. The dragonfly was him. The entire cosmos branched away from him and the dragonfly at the centre.

Standing on the base ground, he said to himself, my head

bathed by the blithe air, and uplifted into infinite space, all mean egoism vanishes. I become a transparent eyeball. I am nothing. I see all. The currents of the Universal Being circulate through me. I am a part or particle of God — wisdom from the sage of Concord.

The dragonfly had sharp bristly feet that dug into him, light as it was. He himself had an oily warm texture that would suck at the dragonfly's feet. He could smash the dragonfly and the dragonfly would die. He could not smash the dragonfly and the world would be a different place from a world where he had smashed the dragonfly. He saw its silver body, its cellophane hovering wings, his own shoulder darkening in the sun.

A car door slammed. He lifted his head. The dragonfly went flying.

The Renault gleamed behind the cedars. Paddy came around it, pipe in mouth, patting his pants pockets for his tobacco. Mike sauntered after with his fishing rod and Paddy's old bait box.

Fuckers hadn't honked.

He slid into the cabin to put on his jeans. Why not just keep going out the back door with battery and charger?

"Come on out here, son," Paddy called. "See something."

He slouched out onto the deck, squinting against the sun.

Paddy was chortling between the teeth clamped on his pipe. "My batman has caught some worms."

A harsh smell fugged from Mike as he laid his rod and the bait box on the picnic table — stale smoke, sweat, something more primal. Zeeb spat into the grass beside the deck. Why bring your night into the open? Make people twitch? He moved around the other side of the table, levered open the bait box. Inside, darkness was unmoving, and the purplish curves of the worms. A stench rose there too — sex, decay. He pushed the box away. "How about I teach you how to fly cast," he said, "and you help me clear the trail to the Big House."

"No." Mike started to tuck in his shirt to strap on the bait box. Dirty white rope held up his chinos.

"Why not?"

"Do it, son," said Paddy. "That's what I built the pond for." He picked up the bait box. "I'll look after these."

◦◦◦

Mrs. Hagner came out her front door, and locked it behind her. One at a time, because her rheumatics were kicking up, she came down the cedar steps. She swayed slowly down the walk. She let herself out the gate and shut it behind her and stood on the sidewalk, waiting. In the old country her mother would have waited so for friends or neighbours, or hurried on ahead to catch up. She longed here to walk with friends and neighbours, inspecting and discussing the arrangements for living on either side of the street, flower boxes, winding brick walks, Madonna niches, blue painted shutters. But she had no friends here and she didn't know her neighbours, and St. Luke's was half an hour away by car. Joseph pulled up in the polished maroon Chevy Eldorado which he had got from the garage off the lane behind the house and driven around the block. Glancing left and right to see if her departure was noted at all by the flick of a curtain at a window, she fell into the front seat and was driven to church.

◦◦◦

The boy's fingers were trembling as he tied fly to leader, close up so the kid saw how. The kid's straw hat bent over the boy's fingers. The boy's dark curls bent over the kid, his bare brown muscles tense, his fingers trembling.

His fingers were stubby and characterized by strength. Not like his mother's, not like Sibyl's long boneless fingers. Like his father's. Like Long McAdam's square calculating fingers. Their names, the old days, their bodies came tumbling back as Paddy watched the boy tie on the fly. Polly and Sibyl. Long. King and

Gloria. The suntan oil. The raft. The wieners and potato salad. Broiling summer days of young people making earnest use of what nature had to offer around the pond.

"Okay, here's what you do." Zeeb was putting distance between himself and Mike. He was lecturing, loud. He'd scare the fish. Paddy thought about remonstrating, but it was summer, good old summertime. "You want to get the fly out to the middle of the pond," the boy was saying. "You've got to make the fly land first, before the line, so the fish thinks that's what it is, a real fly. It's not heavy like your Walt Disney lures. And the only weight you've got to get it out there is the line. So what you do is you pull some line out so it's lying on the water here."

The line fell and floated. The glistening coils made Paddy think of water spiders walking on water. He scratched his chin. He'd forgotten to shave again this morning.

"Okay. You've got to whip the line up and back in a loop." Zeeb flicked up the rod. The line whistled high above his head through the air. He flicked three times, paying out line, making the line loop back and forth in the air. "Then forward." He flicked the rod forward and the line shot out, and the fly landed in the middle of the pond. Paddy watched the ripples. He couldn't actually see the fly but he knew where it should be, to the left a bit. The wind coming down the valley was why they usually fished at the far end of the pond. There the wind would carry the fly farther and farther from the bank and all hint of human feet.

The boy was pulling in line now, just as he had taught him, looping it again at his feet in the water.

"Your reel," the kid said. "Why don't you use your reel?" He kept his toes in their dirty white socks well back from the bank.

"You're just going to have to haul the line out again," Zeeb said. "No point reeling it in. Now you try."

Paddy moved. Always stand behind the line of fire. The kid, trying to follow the boy's motions, was like a wooden puppet, the line more alive than he, jerking under his hands as if it were avoiding blows. It rose high in the air and clung to the top of a cedar.

Paddy turned and wandered back up towards the cabin. Marmalade lay panting in the shade. He laid his pipe on the deck and went with the bait box around to the forsythia Maggie had planted when they were camping in the cabin before they built the house. Here the sun only got to in the height of the day and the earth stayed dark and cold, and Maggie's lilies of the valley and columbines thrived. They grew, Maggie had died, and yet all of it seemed so deathless — time past when there was no pond, no cabin, only a pasture with black and white cows in it; time now when the two youngsters down there were fishing a pond older than they — all the pictures, then and now, before and to be, all seemed bright and present and accounted for. He emptied the bait box close to the dry arms of forsythia. The worms would have a chance to burrow there before some other creature preyed on them. When he got back to his pipe he was amazed to see that the kid's line was trembling and that there was a fish hanging on it.

"Okay," the boy was shouting. "Now you want to unhook it. It's just a little one. So put it back."

"Back?" Rigid sun hit the kid's jaw.

"Let it grow." Paddy's heart throbbed to hear his own wisdom come back to him. "Fatten it for the kill."

∿

In the toilet bowl the robins floated, water drops rounding on the spread oily surfaces of their feathers. A fly circled over the softening flesh.

∿

The longer they fished the denser the stench from Mike, like the cougar, like a brush fire. It made Zeeb want to run or punch someone. Danger, somewhere, only your five senses to figure out what. Mike had tried again and again to shoot the fly to the centre of the pond. The rod trembled, the line trembled. His casts fell close or caught on cedars. The line tangled on the water. The stench layered out from him.

Zeeb had caught six decent fish. There they were, strung on a piece of cedar. Mike had cut the cedar, had insisted, stropping his knife on his chinos, sawing. Supposed to be a twig. More branch than the twig. Big enough for a whale. So big the tender pink trout gills ripped when Zeeb strung them on. He thought he would barbecue the little beauties, over a fire made from cherry, the way Polly and Sibyl liked best. Show off his cooking skills, feed Paddy dinner. He began to break down King's rod, fit the pieces into the case.

Mike fanned himself with his hat.

Zeeb spat. You could see the dark wet under Mike's arms, on his back. He was whistling, the tune about the teddy bears, If *you* go down in the *woods* to*day* you're in for a *big* sur*prise*. "Better cool off before we go look at the chain saw," Zeeb said.

Mike stopped whistling. "What's the matter with your bike?"

"Bike?"

"Why would anyone want to go to all the trouble of sawing down trees when they had wheels?"

Zeeb clamped the cap on the rod case, shrouded it in its canvas cover, backed upwind.

"I have to charge my batteries every night." He was shouting. "I have to take them over to the Big House every night and recharge them, then I have to go over and pick them up every morning. My PowerBook? You know? I got to get my fucking thesis done. I got to keep up a charge for the batteries of my PowerBook." He headed for the cabin. "The trail through the bush is fastest."

"I'll be your courier." Mike crowded up the stairs after him. "Morning and evening. Forget about the trail."

Now Zeeb was sweating. "Why?"

Mike shrugged. "Little errands like that help to structure Paddy's day."

It was hot and close in the cabin. Zeeb threw Mike a towel, pounded down to the beach, stripped, flung in, stroked out beyond the weeds, face in the cold green water. At the end of the pond he turned over, drifted on his back. Mike splashed past him in an elbowy crawl. Zeeb thought how they were passing and passing over the dead beaver. He stroked hard for the raft, up on it. Mike heaved up too.

All you could smell now was pond algae. Zeeb spread out on the raft. "There's a beaver down there," he said. "I killed it."

"You did?"

"I shot it." He could feel his neck pulsing. "They're pests. They shouldn't come here. They should stay out of the way if they don't want to get hurt."

"Congratulations."

Mike slapped Zeeb on the butt, playfully, but hard enough to sting.

"Hey!"

"Well done. Good show." Mike stood. The raft sloshed, tipped.

Cold water swept under Zeeb. "Jesus fucking Christ," he yelled.

Mike dove. The raft went surfing. Zeeb grabbed the edge. After a while the rocking stilled. Zeeb spread out again, eyes shut. The car doors slammed, one, two. You could hear them going up the drive, up the road to the crossroads, turning.

Little bugger. He'd get him, at dinner tonight. Get the little guy going. Play touch. Finesse him in the bush.

∽

After lunch, Paddy could be counted on to camp out in his armchair with his pipe. Mike said he'd just slip into the village with Marmalade to the vet but he wasn't even sure Paddy heard him.

There were two chain saws in the furnace room sitting on

the shelf under the tool bench, a big yellow one, old dust embedded in its coating of grease, and a small red one, quite shiny. He was pretty sure Paddy had said the yellow one didn't work, he kept it for old time's sake. Certainly it was the red one they'd used when they attacked the black locusts in the spring. A futile task. The thorns made going forward dangerous and irritating. When you looked back from the vantage of the porch to the site of their morning's work, all you'd been able to see was smoke where the couple of trees they'd cropped were dying a fiery death, surrounded by green waving arms of ever more black locusts. He tucked the red chain saw into the backseat. He shoved Marmalade in the passenger seat beside the driver's seat.

The cleft in the rock in Collingwood was exactly what he needed. They had once gone to Collingwood for the day, a family excursion. All they had with them was Mother's shoulder bag, which held what they needed, her lipstick, Father's mickey. They ate in a restaurant. Then they climbed the mountain. There was a cleft in the rock, narrow and deep into unknown darkness, with a wooden footbridge over it. Father said, How'd you like to go down there, eh son? and tipped up his mickey. Mother said, Oh Jim, don't talk like that, he's too little. Father pulled his belt out of his pants and said, Give me your belt, Carol. She said, No, no, Jimmy. He said, I said give me your belt. She gave him her belt. She gave him her belt and the strap from her shoulder bag. Father linked them and looped them round little Mikey's waist, and began to lower him, hand over hand, down the cleft.

Black stone walls scraped hard against his hands and knees, icy, wet. The sky above was a slit, blue, Father's face in it, his fringe of hair in a halo. Father laughed as he paid out the belts and little Mikey hit bottom. Like it down there, son? Snow crunched underfoot, snow in July. His runners skidded. Icy breezes rose up his shorts, and he peed, hot and wet in that cold place, yellow on the snow. Mother cried, Oh, my baby, my baby, let him up Jim, let him up, he's just a kid. Father said, He's tough, my son. Mother said, Oh Jesus, bring back my baby.

Father's face was a white cloud behind Mother. Sideways the slit narrowed, but little Mikey could see water, the blue lake, the blue sky. In his cleft in the rock he was warm and held. He would never come up. He began to loosen the looped belt, to wriggle out of the loop. Mother said, Oh Jesus, he's trying to get loose, stop Mikey, come up now, come up. Father yanked. The belt tightened around his waist. Father hauled. Willy nilly, he rose. He banged the sides of the cleft with knees and elbows, though he tried to fend them off. Mother grabbed at him, Oh Mikey, my baby, my baby. He pulled away from her. He stood by Father, held on to the rough wool of Father's jacket while Father looped his belt back on. Mother knelt and said, Oh, my baby, you're bleeding, you're wet. Father looked and laughed and said, Little pisser.

That cleft would be perfect for the chain saw. He could drop the chain saw down there, under the overhang. No one would find it ever. But Collingwood was too much of a drive. He thought of secret places in the neighbourhood. The loft in the cabin where there was a gun. The pit in the bush where the girl lay. The pond where a beaver lay.

He thought of the culvert where the road ran over the stream. He eased the car out and away along the sideroad, down the line, Marmalade flopping and panting beside him. She wanted to get out when he stopped. He had to cuff her back in. Holding the chain saw, he slid down the steep grassy slope to the edge of the stream. The culvert was almost high enough to stand up in, the stream gargled through, and hamburger boxes and styrofoam coffee cups had caught on the rocks along with slimy branches and weeds.

He hung on to the edge of the culvert and heaved. The chain saw landed echoing. He hauled himself back up the bank on long tufts of grass and drove to the village.

But it was Sunday, of course. The vet was closed.

He grasped Marmalade's muzzle, blocking her wet nostrils with his palm, clamping her jaw shut with his other hand. She wiggled and squeaked, and people were going in and out of Becker's across the way. He wiped her slobber off his hands on her fur, started the car.

cℳɔ

"Jesus fucking Christ." Zeeb said it over and over. The spare battery was still by his work when he got up to the cabin. Fucking H Christ. He jammed battery and charger in his pack, pushed the bike round the cabin, got on, coasted across the dam to the hill, got off, pushed the bike up, remounted, began to pedal. He reached the end of the drive without cramp, turned right. His legs were warming. The right one wasn't kneeing in. He gained momentum, geared down as the hill to the crossroads approached, pumped clear to the top.

Those girls' car was still parked beside Sam the Man's truck. That short one knew Chaucer. Good tits. He cut down the drive. The door of the A-frame was open. No one was around so he went through and out to the deck, looked down towards Taylor's pond.

In the shade by the big boulder Taylor's kids called the Council Rock when he used to play here, Sam and the girl lay on a sleeping bag, his bare back to the sun, the crook of his arm over her bare belly.

Leslie.

He heeled hard away.

So what if he had hit her. Got her once — maybe twice. So what. It was her fault. She shouldn't have said what she said. He wasn't a rapist. A rapist was a fucking coward. Anybody in their right mind would have seen red. How was he to know there'd be blood? Why hold it against him? Not a big issue. Tit for tat. Eye for an eye. She should know that.

He swung his leg over his bike, wiped his nose on his shirt shoulder. He'd said he was sorry.

Cunts, faithless cunts. Fuck them all.

He started to pedal. The Renault was stopped at the cross-roads, about to head up towards the Big House. He sped out yelling, "Stop!" He had to see the old man, speak to him. The car slowed, came towards him. He skidded up to it, braked.

Marmalade, fuggy with dog breath, was crawling all over Mike towards the driver's window. Zeeb bent to look. No Paddy. Mike smelled like anyone now. Just sweat and sex, like himself. He snapped his fingers at Marmalade and pointed. "Down," he said in a low rough voice. "Down." She cowered. He and Mike both laughed. "Fucking bitches," Zeeb said. He handed over the battery and charger. "Go plug it in and come back for dinner."

ᢙᢍᢛ

Mike woke in the night to high haggish laughter. He jerked upright. The red light on the egghead's charger glowed in the dark. Outside a thousand hags cackled and screeched down from the hills, closer, across the road, into the bush. His heart thundered. Upstairs Marmalade stood up and barked.

ᢙᢍᢛ

Paddy hushed Marmalade, and she lay down, but he could hear her tags clicking. He lay with his hands interlocked behind his head. He tried to count chores that needed doing, like counting sheep. Clear the black locusts. Behead the peonies. Mow the grass. Locusts. Peonies. Grass. But it was no use. He was as awake as ever. He curled in a ball and let the mocking primal laughter engulf him.

ᢙᢍᢛ

Zeeb heard them drift yipping, yapping, over by Taylor's, into the bush, around the far side of the pond, away downstream, off into the distance. He tossed, thinking of that girl with Sam. He got up, got some water.

He'd never seen a coyote. They saw a fox once, him and Polly and Ma, on one of their walks around the concession, sniffing the bank across the road. They were still, downwind probably, and the fox never noticed, turned and sniffed its way back up the bank and away under the trees.

Coyotes pursued chipmunks, and the fawns of deer at speeds of up to sixty kilometres an hour, through bush, over hills, but they were nocturnal and preferred cover. All the notice you ever got of them was this ghastly laughter.

✺

Mike slid back down under the covers. They were gone, whoever they were. It was apparent they weren't after carrion.

Monday

Zeeb dreamed it was dinner still. He and Mike had filleted Paddy, sliced bloody strips from the old man's back. They were roasting them over coals with the sticks they used for toasting the marshmallows. The strips spat and hissed, writhed like live things. He tried to conceal his weeping but he couldn't help muttering under his breath, Jesus, Jesus, and weeping. Then Mike was walking into the cabin, a wicker basket over his arm, Paddy following, yawning. Grey dawn lay out the windows.

Zeeb flailed his legs against the twisted sheets. "For fuck's sake, what time is it?"

"Early bird gets the worm." Mike pulled the PowerBook battery out of the basket, put it on the table beside the PowerBook, went into the kitchen. Paddy trotted after. Shortly, he came out over to the window with coffee, stood bent sniffing steam.

Zeeb got loose finally, dressed, went into the kitchen. Mike's unwashed stench jangled through him. Mike had bacon, eggs, bread, jam, butter spread on the counter, had got down the frying pan, laid in strips of bacon. Spitting, hissing.

"Jeez." Zeeb poured coffee, breathed bitter dark shapes.

∽

Mike scrubbed away at greasy plates, the fishy ones from last night, the eggy ones, hardening already, from this morning. He watched the egghead and the old bugger heading down the path into the bush, the egghead lifting up branches that would whip into the old bugger's eyes, the suck. When the two were out of sight he wiped his hands down his chinos, dragged the stepladder out from beside the fridge, and set it up under the trapdoor. Heat buzzed in the attic. The papery grey of a hornets' nest hung from the ridge pole. He held still while his eyes adjusted to the half-light. There was the canvas-covered rod case. And there, in a green plastic bag, was the long narrow shape that would be the gun.

He slid it down, closed the trapdoor, put away the stepladder. He pushed a space clear on the kitchen table, set down the gun, unwrapped layers of plastic and cloth. He raised it, heavier than you'd think, pointed it through the window, laying his cheek against the wooden handle and squinting the way they did on TV. The trigger moved with a soft spring. All he needed was their two heads on the far side. He would have to get some instruction on how to shoot it though. He added bullets to his mental list of things to get in the hardware store. He rewrapped the gun, took it to stow in the trunk of the car. As he passed Marmalade, who was flopped on the deck, he bent and let her sniff the plastic-covered bundle. "I say unto the wicked, thou shalt surely die," he whispered.

❧

Paddy lowered himself to one of the pieces of corduroy that had never got made into proper trail. He pushed a grass stalk between the spaces of his teeth and sucked. Bacon up his gums. And still peaches-and-cream corn from last night's dinner. "Got this far." He looked around but the boy had forged on to the other end of the tumble. And then Maggie died.

Zeeb turned. Undone things lowered on him like swamp fumes. He couldn't go back to the cabin. Not with Mike look-

ing over his shoulder, stinking excitement. But he couldn't go
forward either. Chained to the old man sitting there picking his
teeth on a log. He tried to see ahead to where he'd come to a
halt yesterday — fresh cuts, tangled green branches.

"Get up Paddy." He wanted to lash the old man. "We'll get
the chain saw, come back cutting."

Paddy considered his fallen logs. They were a memorial of
sorts. You should pay them honour, become one with their
implications. When he'd digested death, when he'd digested the
fact of Maggie's death, of his own death, which hovered in the
air, you could smell it this sticky early morning, then he could
move on beyond this arrangement, straighten the crooked,
observe the straight and narrow once more. Make trail. But did
you ever overcome death? You look back. How many years
was it now since Maggie died, since he'd worked the trail, half-
worked it? Whenever you wanted a clear vista you came up
hard against a memorial of tumbled corduroy, bark peeled off
by wet weather, green moss growing down the slimy sides. You
look forward for the hand that will lead you on and you see
that twitching boy where what you would really want to see,
deserve to see, was your own son and heir, his strong shoulders
ready for the falling of the mantle. King, King, King, he
mourned. What would become of the farm? Would King cut it
up into a subdivision? He envisaged bulldozers and plumb
lines and orange boundary markers dividing and gouging the
land, the way they'd cut through Maggie's body, as if they
could stop that rot. "She didn't ever really like the bush. She
liked the garden."

Zeeb sloshed back, stood over the old man. "Let's go." He
didn't recognize his voice, husky, cruel.

"We brought those peonies from the city." Paddy looked
up. "Do you remember them? You used to catch the ants on
them. You used to fry them on the back walk with your magnifying glass."

Not me, old fool. I'm no fucking murderer. Others, maybe.
Sibyl once flicked a cigarette into the reeds. A frog flipped it in

as if it were a dragonfly, out. Polly set a fire once. A snake was sleeping in the pit. How it had writhed. Of course it died.

But the beaver. Remember the beaver.

"Let's go Paddy." He shook the old man's shoulder. "Let's go. Let's go find a magnifying glass that will burn the trail clear."

Paddy squinted up at him, then stretched out his leg, reached down his pant pocket, and pulled out his pipe and his tobacco. He filled his pipe, tamped down the brown shreds with his thumb, put back his tobacco, and reached down his back pocket for a wooden match. He tried to strike the match with his thumbnail, but the nail was pared too short. He struck it on his zipper, lit his pipe. He gazed around. He needed to think about Maggie, about death, about the green vistas extending around him and how they were broken by black trees. The meaning of the moment, here, now, was the reason for being on the farm. You planted trees, raised the water table, harvested trout. You could do this because you reflected, and made connections between now and what would come and what had gone before. He puffed. "What's your hurry?"

"I told you, goddamn it. I've got to fucking defend. I'm thirty years old. I've never had a real job. I've got to make my fucking life happen." Paddy was taking his pipe out of his mouth. "Let's go. Get the chain saw. It won't take a morning with three of us. I can zip back and forth whenever I need."

"What?" Paddy was gawking up with watery blue eyes. "Thirty?" He laughed a hard astounded laugh and clamped his teeth on his pipe again. "My God, man. When I was thirty, I'd got my man and I'd begot my man. What in hell have you been doing?"

"It isn't so easy." Zeeb coughed, spat. Who could pinpoint why? They all suffered though. Barnie, old baseball pal of Huron Street days — cooking in a seniors' home. Arun whom he first roomed with at Guelph — a wife, her two kids, a job in construction — nights only for his guitar. For himself everything had come together once, when he and Leslie rode in tandem — to school, to the market Saturdays, to the river to swim. But what was left? Where was he now? Locked in a green shade with a relic of the past whose tentacles barely made an impression on the present. He took a log, whacked a cedar, whacked, whacked. Bark flew. The bush thundered. Bird whistles ceased. The brook babbled between blows.

Paddy stood up. "Stop that." His watery blue eyes were blinking. It was amazing how short he'd grown, shrunk by age, outstripped by Zeeb's own maturing. "I don't like that," he said.

Zeeb threw down the log. "What would you know about it?"

They faced each other. Zeeb saw where the tops of Paddy's ears were peeling. Paddy saw the black of the boy's eyes, a dark spirit of another order.

Then Mike was beside them. "Your chariot awaits," he said to Paddy.

Paddy took the lead back to the cabin. He moved slowly and stopped to look at the old well, saying, "The old well," and looking back at Mike and pointing at the well and then carrying on. Mike turned and gave Zeeb a wink from a green auburn-rimmed eye.

There was movement on the pond as they came out of the bush. Paddy said, "Oh, oh." Mike and Zeeb halted behind him.

The mother duck had brought out her ducklings to teach them how to feed. The flotilla of duck and small brown ducklings was circling the verge of the pond, in and out of the reeds, up in among the irises where you couldn't see them, back in the water, fourteen of them, Paddy counted aloud. They were connected like the intervals of a whipped rope. They looked like fleas scrabbling around the hair roots of a dog. So many of them, blown like milkweed down.

"Swim, said the momma duck, swim if you can," sang Mike in a phlegmy tenor.

Zeeb was back in grade six, the Huron Street choir. "So they swam and they swam," he sang in unison, "all over the dam."

∽

Finally Zeeb could open the PowerBook, flick it on. It boinged. His fingers flicked over the keys. His mind flicked after them, jogged thoughts on the screen. He flipped pages — the tall stack yet to deal with, the short stack of corrected sheets. Back, forth, his fingers flicked, his mind flicked, pages to keys, keys to pages. He called up the calculator, ran his formula through new numbers, refigured a graph.

There were other women in the world. There was that girl — Futzy? Melissa? — who used to bring him espresso when he wrote essays. Back in the dorm, first year, the cold concrete dorm. Warm Futzy/Melissa. There were many girls like Futzy/Melissa in the world who would spread their legs, stick their asses in the air for you, who didn't exhibit the gaping wound Leslie always brought to his attention. Girls who wore lipstick, whose lips didn't go tight like Leslie's, reading the paper, going out to meetings, who didn't chew their lips over statistics. Fourteen women engineering students in Montreal. Two out of three married women. One child in ten.

He flipped pages. Paddy — another gaping wound. Bogged down in unfinished corduroy. Following Mike's lead, over here for breakfast at ungodly hours, back to the Big House on demand. Unsparked by thoughts of the chain saw. Letting someone else structure his day.

He could hardly wait to get away. He vowed never to get that old. He'd shoot himself first.

∽

temple dormitory
day

Wake! — the hour? — morning, must be tomorrow . . . stopped watching, Saky . . . must have lost a day. She brought me to this dormitory, that old woman . . . slept.

Apologies, great gold god. You don't sleep. You keep your golden silent watch — while Zeeb squirms for a way out.

The old chant for comfort — om mani padme hum, om mani padme hum, om mani padme hum — the jewel in the heart of the lotus, you, the Buddha, all is sorrowful — birth, growth, decay, illness, death, separation from loved ones, hating the inevitable, craving the impossible. All sorrow. No way out.

Oh, these stinging tears — I repudiate them. They startle me. The old woman watches from the doorway.

⌘

After lunch, once the old bugger was napping in his armchair, Mike went down to check on the charging of the other battery. It didn't suit him that it should take six hours. The egghead would be sitting idle. There must be some way you could speed up the process, the way you would put a penny under a low amp fuse so you could use the power mower on the circuit. But the system was unresponsive, a black box in a black box with just a little red light glowing, warm to the touch. You had no idea what stage it had reached, just the knowledge it had been there from ten to two. He put it back down.

His fingers — how had his nails got so black, and torn? He stuck them in his mouth, curled his tongue and lips around them, sucked at the dirt. How warm his tongue was. How it undulated. But his fingers tasted sour, his nails were rough. He began to bite them to even them out.

He needed to check on the girl. What besides worms ate corpses? There was a kind of beetle, wasn't there? On a school trip to the Museum they'd seen a room where the curators put the corpses of animals whose skeletons they wanted to study, and the beetles ate the bones clean. Then they could transport them as they wished, white and clean-smelling, take them home with them even, to mull over at the dining room table. He could cart the girl's bones around in the trunk of the car, once they were clean, deposit them across the countryside, like throwing away empties the way Mother used to distribute Father's in the neighbours' garbage cans before dawn on garbage day.

But what was the beetle?

He glanced out the window and almost bit his finger in two. There was the old bugger, up, not napping in his chair at all, dressed in his rubber boots and his red plaid shirt, heading off across the lawn. He'd even combed his hair. His pink and white baldness was rounded and smoothed down. He was carrying the little saw with the bowed yellow handle and the hatchet. Marmalade was cavorting beside him. He and the bitch were heading for the bush.

He ran outside. "Hey!" He began to run down the lawn. "Hey!"

The breeze was blowing the wrong way and the old bugger seemed to have added deafness to the ailments of aging. He felt as if he was running in molasses, voice bunched up in throat, fortune about to slide over the waterfall and him powerless, yelling and pounding along the bank. One of his Birks came off as he ran and he wasted precious seconds dithering whether to stop for it or get it on the way back. But the accident was in the long run a true blessing for it shocked him from his frenzy.

What had the therapist said? That he could control any situation if he could control himself. He halted and took a deep breath and let it all the way out. He slid his fingertips down the front pockets of his chinos and began to saunter towards Paddy and Marmalade who were turning down the path, vanishing into the tall grass. He clicked his tongue. Marmalade at least heard him. She stopped, and raised her nose, sniffed. Turned and saw him. Turned again and slunk, tail and nose down, beside Paddy. Paddy's old feet made clunking noises as he clumped forward in his boots with little steps. But his steps were regular. He was covering the ground. The distance between him and the bush was diminishing.

He pulled a stalk of timothy in passing and thwacked his leg with it as he proceeded, his temporary swagger stick. He wished he could break off a branch of the black locusts as a goad, but he had no gloves on and the locusts were violently thorny. He made himself taller. He opened his stride.

What would he do if Paddy came upon the girl? He'd been found out once before, hadn't he? The worst could happen.

It was after high school, when he had run away. The playground shelter had held change rooms. He preferred the smell of the little girls'. There was a false ceiling. He had removed a panel. You could lie up there and watch the little girls, their tiny smooth pubis mounds, their long skinny torsos, their long solemn faces as they talked to one another. Smell their sweet farts. Almost taste the crust of Coke on their soft unlined mouths. You could make your meals from their peanut butter and jelly sandwiches, and cheese cubes, and celery sticks, forsaken in the playground garbage pails for the glockenspiel siren of the ice cream truck.

Crumbles of insulation fell as he masturbated up there, glazed and rhythmic, groaning, watching the sweet flesh below. One little cherub looked up. Then another. Then they began to scream, shrill nymphet screams goading him, and he came as he never had before. Even his anus had pulsed in terrible splendour. He tightened his buttocks, remembering.

And then the cops.

And then the long long dance with the therapists, the social workers, all the different psychiatric wards, treatment rooms.

He ground his teeth. If the old bugger saw the girl, caught a glimpse of that black satin, caught even a distinguishable whiff of rotten flesh amidst the compost and the smell of Strickland's septic tank/topsoil enterprise and went to investigate, he would beat him, haul down his trousers, his boxer shorts, pull his belt out of his belt loops, lash his saggy buttocks. Watch him writhe, cringe. Promise silence. There were areas of privacy where you could not permit trespass.

Interception was, however, a more elegant solution than suppression to the problem of intrusion. He came to a standstill. He whistled like the egghead when he came limping out from under the pines Friday.

Paddy halted and turned with a glad smile.

He lit a cigarette, tingling at the old bugger's look of confusion. He blew smoke into the air and muttered, "Come to Daddy, you stupid cretin, come to Daddy and let me reason with you."

Paddy frowned and cupped his hand around his ear.

"Come on you stupid old fart. Polly is on the phone. King is coming for lunch. Maggie will be joining us from the dead."

Paddy began the slow ascent back up the path, the yellow saw dragging like a teddy bear, Marmalade's tail drooping. He stopped once, looked back to the bush, and wiped his forehead on his red plaid cuff.

He went to meet them. He gripped Paddy's forearm. "I can't find the chain saw," he said. "We need to get it sharpened. Where did you put it?"

∿

This time they honked, Zeeb noted, but why come now? — two hours before the spare would be charged. He had his bike on the deck. The chain had jammed. He was black with oil. The stack of corrected pages was at last higher than the uncorrected; the battery had given out. He poked grass heads, grunge clogging the chain.

Mike hunkered beside him. Zeeb turned away to breathe.

"Paddy's having one of his spells," Mike said in his ear. "Could you keep an eye on him? I have to do some errands."

Zeeb leapt up coughing. "Spells?" But the Renault was spinning up under the pines, gone. That black streak on his arm — bike oil? Dirt from Mike? Fuck the little prick. Goofing off. And where was the old man anyway? Nowhere. Out of sight. Spells. Fucking excuse, lazy little bugger.

He hoisted the bike down to the drive, mounted, coasted to the dam, pedalled. Good enough. The ride back to the city was downhill. He should be gone by Wednesday. He caught his breath. Defending. He began sweating, scary, you had to do it, face the jury. Jump. Hurry. Be a man. Do it, do it. But after. Well, after he'd start his life over again, without Leslie, fuck her. He hoisted the bike back up.

A hawk was flying straight across the pond. Why? Hawks don't fly straight. Hawks circle high. What was amiss? Then he saw the shape hanging from its claws — a rabbit, the quarry of the circling, still running, still squealing. The hawk would have a nest, young in the nest. Soon it would be feeding its young.

Crackings came from the bush, breaking branches. Over there, beyond the well head, beyond the rock where Polly put flesh leavings.

You didn't want fish heads, steak fat, bones, gristle, greened cold cuts, chicken skin in the compost heap with the vegetable matter. Dead flesh attracted the kind of live flesh which killed to live, thrived on carrion, fought, not browsing nor grazing, whose snarling squealing struggles pierced the night. You left animal offerings on Polly's carrion rock . . .

back in the temple

. . . the old woman fed me. I mailed my card to Paddy. I'm with you again, Saky, watching in your red/gold space. Still raining out there. Joss throwers still racket here, fruit still moulders. Across the continent, the young king . . .

. . . at the edge of the bush. It was as if spirits cleaned up in the night down to bare rock by morning. Nothing they wouldn't take, the predators that came from the bush.

"Paddy?" His voice echoed. "Paddy!"

Like a shot from the .22, the cracking of a dry branch rang from the bush behind the carrion rock. What now?

You couldn't enter the bush here. The trail where scavengers came and went was too low for a man. He went round where thistles grew, high as his head. They grabbed his bare feet, arms. He lifted up, swam through. The ground sloped, he lost his footing, fell, slid, halted under the wall of cedars.

Before him twisted the split rail fence which once marked a pasture — fallen, mossy. Beyond, trees in a tangle.

Again he heard a crack as of a rifle. To the left a big white birch waved diseased arms. Widow maker. What they called those trees. Even windless, the hour when it let go, thundered to the ground, was there in its configured leafless branches. You could be under.

He crawled over fallen split rails. He could cross the tangle on that fallen cedar. Then he saw Paddy's red shirt far to the left.

"Paddy!"

What was the old fool doing? — pulling dead branches till they snapped, almost falling, righting himself, gripping another branch. Pulling. He batted twigs from his eyes, sought footing in leaf-covered muck, roots, hollows, pressed on, almost within touch.

"Paddy, what the fuck are you doing?"

"Looking for the chain saw." Paddy broke another branch. "Kid says I lost it."

"Here?"

"Kid says I lost it." He pounded his foot down on a dry branch, almost fell. The branch snapped.

You couldn't see beyond the wall of cedars. You could see the animal trail though. It would lead out.

"How'd you like a raft ride?"

Paddy stopped.

"We'll go on an inspection tour of the pond."

"You think the chain saw's there?"

"You think it's here?"

Paddy wiped his sleeve across his forehead, looked around. "I never cleared here. Thought about it. Planned to, don't you know. But I never got around to it."

Zeeb made him crouch down the animal trail. They emerged at the carrion rock. He got towels, Paddy's trunks, put on his one pair of bikini briefs. Paddy's white shoulders hunched under the towel while Zeeb swam out, untied the raft, flutter-kicked it in. Paddy got on. Zeeb pushed it out, waded after it, dunked, got it churning.

Wouldn't think about — fuck the beaver anyway.

~~~

Light bulb for the drier, Mike, driving, listed in his head. Composting compound. Bullets. Anything else? His hand on the wheel, yellowed between index and middle fingers, reminded him he was low on cigarettes. He'd get a carton at Becker's. He'd get briquettes too. And a new lure, a couple. The empty compartments in his tackle box made him sick.

He parked in front of the hardware store, got out, came around the car, smoothing his hat over his hair. The wares that usually lined the sidewalk — trampoline, composters, scatter rugs, wheelbarrows — where had they gone? He pushed the door.

Locked? Why was it locked?

He shielded his eyes against the glass. A couple of lights at the back pulsed. Otherwise the store was dead.

He leaned his forehead against the glass, pressed his hands against the cold glass till they were white. He could get in the car and just go. He had a wad of housekeeping money. Head east, back to Newfoundland. A trawler, work there. They'd never find him.

Then the sick feeling passed. He saw a sign on the door announcing a fireworks display on the soccer field near the town hall this evening at sunset.

Canada Day. It was Canada Day. That was why everything was shut up tighter than a drum.

He shook out a cigarette, lit it. Inhaled smoke till his hands stopped shaking.

~~~

Paddy wanted to see the fireworks. He and Mike got Zeeb, drove to the soccer field, lined up with the crowd. A sphere of red and white lights swelled in the night sky, rockets thundered. "Munich," Paddy muttered. He had his pipe clamped in his mouth, fists in his pockets. "Dunkirk," he said through his teeth.

"Jeez," Zeeb breathed on Mike's other side. "Jeez. Have you ever seen them done over water? You get the rockets going up into the night sky and the reflection going down in the water at the same time. Leslie." His voice was shaking. A light flared. You could see his cheeks were wet. "Leslie. At her island. We sat on the rocks. The night was massive. The rim of the mainland — diamonds. And oh, the rockets, the rockets." His hands wiped down his cheeks.

Mike had his hat well over his face. He didn't raise his head. The pulsation of the fireworks, like strobe lights, could be your downfall. You could fall on the ground and wail and twitch. The brim of the hat protected him. But he changed his cigarette to his left hand and let his right hand just brush the egghead's hand.

Zeeb caught his breath. The air was like guns. He put his arm on Mike's shoulder. "Oh my god," he said. "Look at that. Look at that."

∾

Zeeb sat kicking the deck after they made the battery exchange, headed off. Tomorrow he'd be done. Water, sky — all was stars here, reflected stars. These stars, other stars — part of night everywhere, land or sea.

An explosion from the far end of the pond sliced through his thoughts, the ducks quacking like machine guns, wings hammering water. Silence. Snuffings, footscrapings of whatever the predator. He felt his blood pounding, like when you watch dogs fucking or hockey fights.

Everything's got to eat, he told himself. Cougars. Coyotes. Isn't that why God grows ducklings?

∽

The old woman has told me to sit on this bench, Saky, padded, running around the walls. She has chided me in words I don't understand but whose tone I do, that I must not put my pack on the bench. Must put it on the floor. Must not put my pamphlets nor the Buddha instruction book on the bench, nor the photo of your fellow statue, golden Kuan Yin standing over there — she of the thousand golden hands and thousand golden eyes, which the fees taker gave me and to which I still cling. Must put everything in my pack. That I must wait.

Wait. For life to unfold. For paths to converge.

Wait. That pushing down movement of the old woman's palm, her flattened hand, that gesture is the same the world over. Wait. Be silent. Obey.

Tuesday

Zeeb hurled a stone at drifting duck feathers. Where the fuck was Mike now? This was like a prison. Or being on a long leash. In sight of light. If he were to go get the battery through the bush, Mike would be sure to come down the drive the instant he was far enough away not to be able to hear him. If he were to go by road, he'd get to the Big House to find Mike gone to the village and coming to the cabin from there.

The stone arced, plunked. The feathers bobbed. Circles spread the way circles spread when fish rise, only fish weren't rising. Not because he was hurling stones at duck feathers but because the air was thickening, the blue of the sky turning opaque, still, pressing on the pond and his chest like a shroud.

He prowled the flat space between beach, wellhead, carrion rock, looking for stones to throw.

There weren't stones on the beach. Wherever the sand came from it had been refined. For gardens, cement. Horsetails grew out of it — remnants of prehistoric forests, the way newts were remnants of dinosaurs. Pointed deer tracks picked through it to the pond. Tracks of blue heron etched the shallows.

He loaded up, hurled. Tried to outdo each heave with the next, to excel.

The air was suffocating, closed in over the passing of his arm. Even the ripples were subdued, oily circular groovings of green water. Impatience diseased his blood, rotted his concentration. The dawn hours had been so fine, so forward-moving. Now, with no Mike, no power, no pages turning — now was a backed-up sewer, a retreat from Moscow, a subsidence under the foundations.

The sun darkened. Now there was another kind of circle on the pond, sharp, shivery, the sky emptying. Warm thick rain hit his arms, face. He ran to the screened porch.

The world became water falling — pines, sky, pond, grasses all one rushing grey. Driving rain on the roof became a cascade jetting from the drain spout into the green garbage can/rain barrel, overflowing, running into the grass. Light split the dark sky. Thunder rolled. The pond water rose so the dimple where the downpipe usually broke the surface was lost in swirling grey.

He hunkered in Sibyl's chaise longue. Why shouldn't he take up smoking? Mike did. Ma did. What made him different? Bunch of losers.

ᴄᐱᴏ

Lisa ran out of the A-frame, a newspaper over her head, splashed through lakes around the Dumpster. Mud flung up her legs. She'd left the car window open and the rain was pouring in. She was wet through by the time she got the window rolled up.

At noon she was supposed to be lecturing to the summer engineering students, Ethics 100. And she hadn't been able, just couldn't get it going to get herself out of the warmth of Sam's bed.

Till the table saw whined.

He'd turned it off to say good-bye, just.

The ignition went thump. Imagine having to go back in. Don't flood, she prayed, turned the key again. The engine caught. Muddy water sprayed as she backed and spun out. She scraped her hand over the condensation that fogged her in, headed south.

But you couldn't hurry. A dome of rain came with you, as if you were a snail and it was a snail shell. Beyond the dim line of trees was nothing, grey darkness only. Fast as the windshield wipers swished, the glass remained molten silver. Frogs splashed through the tunnels of her headlights and fell behind with the other roadkill.

Would oncoming cars have their lights on, the macho drivers? Hemales. Pemales. Scromen. Inverted toadstools.

Then the vent began to blow the glass clean. The world grew lighter. And then she was out of the rain, travelling fast and silent as if all that back there were another land. And on the horizon ghosted the minuscule CN Tower.

cⱱɔ

A faint busy phraseology like the singing of asteroids electrified a thin line between Mike's ears. He could feel his eyes staring through the condensation on the windshield at the white stucco wall of the hardware where they provided parking. Trucks thundered by. Who else would dare to be driving? His eyes stared so unblinking he was beginning not to be able to see. He simply sat, hands knobbed on the wheel, the downpour cascading.

There was a spider who maintained her web in the back porch of the Big House between pillar and doghouse. She would catch bees and moths, large insects. With crabbed fingers she would spin white winding cloths around the items in her insect deep-freeze. Circles of white spider waste had thickened on the concrete floor under her web. Husked discarded corpses drifted away when you passed. She would repair her spirals, wait at their hub.

Marmalade turned and turned on herself on the backseat. Doggy breath vapoured into the fug. On the seat beside Mike lay the egghead's battery and the plastic bags containing his own purchases. Bullets. They came out of a locked drawer in the hardware, which was all very well and good, but there were no instructions for them. And the only lures the tight ass in the hardware would sell him, when he said he was fishing for trout, were a dull little Meps and something he called Al's Goldfish, a vaguely fish-shaped curved piece of gold-coloured metal. Nothing pretty at all. No bright jiggling minnows, no soft rainbow frogs. Remembering the puppy, the stench of rotting flesh that had made it difficult to approach anything close to the furry little corpse, he had also got a packet of plasterer's masks.

He'd been able to leave Paddy snoring in his chair, though it was only morning. He'd dosed him with some old medication, a tranquillizer tablet crushed into his porridge, had watched him in his armchair loll and fade and drool. Chemical straitjacket, like himself in the ward when words had failed him, when words became tips of icebergs below which had moved welded ice mountains which crushed flesh to crystal. With each word had moved a mass of ice, below the surface of speech, a ponderous memory bank of which the edges might for a moment from time to time come clear through blue ice seas. Upper. Crust. Mom. Apple. Snake. Case. Worker. Black. Widow. Spied her. Red. Satin. Doll. Eyes. When he had tried to link words in a sentence, the jagged masses below the blue surface collided and ground with the roar of titans. Speech sent words roiling apart, monumentally, inexorably. Words slid their exploding ways. Each found and sank its Titanic. A salad was made of words. They played with one another like political kittens. He had had to learn to speak again. To bite down on each moment. To beat time. He had learned to sever connections so each word moved on and made way for the next. He had excavated meaning. He had repossessed what Gaiter had called his gift, had begun to speak again with the tongues of men and of angels.

His head cracked against the windshield and his breath snapped in. He sat up. Still raining. Forever raining. Lost forever in a world of rain. He opened the window and the rain chilled his cheek, arm, shoulder, sated his ear. He lit a cigarette against the stench of dog.

ᴄᴧᴐ

The terrible stench that hit Lisa when she opened the door was, she discovered on investigation, something in the toilet. Something feathered. Bloated. Beaked.

Baby bird corpses. Rotting.

She dropped the seat cover, flushed, hung over the wash basin heaving.

She stumbled out of the bathroom to open windows, hers, the front room, up into Jade's loft. Even under the sun-blasted eaves and the reaching dormers, the odour was overpowering. Her stomach heaved and she lurched to open the window.

Swirling flies in all the rooms were what got her most, their stupid slow buzzing, bungling into her arms and face. "Go away!" She swatted air. They would have been feeding on the dead things. Her sweating hands shook as she tried to gather her books and papers from her desk for her lecture. In the kitchen she buried her nose in the dry coffee mug she'd left Saturday, but it didn't help. She heaved again anyway.

Right after class you will go to Health Services and get a morning-after pill, she told herself. Holding her breath, she flushed the toilet again on her way out.

ᴄᴧᴐ

"Cats and dogs," Mike was saying. "Cats and dogs." He was swabbing at his hair and arms, breathless still from running into the cabin through the rain. He was using the tea towel.

Zeeb moved to the screen door. "Where's my battery?" he said.

"In the car." Mike lit a cigarette. He blew a cone of smoke towards the screen door. "Tell me about shooting the beaver."

Rain drove across the pond. Marmalade had her muzzle pressed against the car window. "She came at me." Zeeb spoke to memory. "I hit her. She wouldn't give up and I hit her again."

"Yes, yes," said Mike. "You told me all that. But go back to the beginning. Tell me step by step."

"Jeez." Zeeb turned. Mike was tapping his cheek. Tiny smoke rings came out in a stream. "I got down behind the grass there, the other side of the car. I loaded. I shot. The fucking asshole kept coming." He turned back to the door.

"No, no," Mike was saying. "Make it concrete. Tell me how you loaded the gun."

"What's it to you? First I cleaned it."

"Cleaned it?"

"The pull-through. Paddy made a pull-through. We keep it with the rifle."

"Pull-through?"

"Oh, fuck, I'll show you." He headed in to the kitchen to get the stepladder.

"Never mind." Mike was spreading the tea towel on the table. You'd want to boil it before you touched it to a dish again. "But it is curious, isn't it, that an English major like you can't give me simple instructions without resorting to show and tell."

Zeeb flung out. The screen door slammed.

The rain had almost stopped. Cracks of blue sky scudded between the growling clouds. Where sun spilled out and lay on the deck, steam rose. Robins were cheering in the cedars. Mike came out behind him, stood on the edge of the deck beside him looking out. Some women found short rutty guys like Mike a big turn-on. "So, what's your girlfriend like," Zeeb said.

Mike flicked his butt into the grass. "She wears satins and laces and smells of cologne."

Zeeb jammed his fingers down his pockets. The mallards were making a ruckus on the stilled pond, the duck quacking furiously, circling the drake. Post partum hysteria, no doubt. Did she remember the death of the ducklings? But it was strange out there, the drake riding high on something, as if the rain had bred a rock from the pond. He rolled up his jeans, went down, Mike at his heels, picking his way through the wet, brushing grasses aside.

What was it under the drake? Something with strands of weeds draped over it, the drake paddling for a foothold on it.

"The beaver!" The bloated corpse of the beaver floated out there, the drake on it like a raft. "That stupid drake is riding on the beaver. It's come up from the bottom of the pond."

Mike snorted, let out a whinny. "On the third day she rose again from the dead," he said.

Zeeb started to laugh too. He laughed till he wept. He dropped his head, to Mike's shoulder. He looked sideways again at the outraged duck quacking round, the proud drake rocking on the unsteady corpse. He crowed with ever more laughter. He felt weak. He wanted to lie down. Mike put his arm around his shoulder, laughing too. They laughed so hard their faces pressed together, wet, slippery. They whooped. They stomped their feet. They wiped their noses with the backs of their hands.

The ducks flew away.

Heat plummeted down on them. Mike hustled out of the sun into the car. Zeeb leaned in through the window. He asked Mike for a cigarette.

"I'll have to beach her," he said. "Get her out of the pond. She'll stink."

Mike flicked his Bic for him and then went honking up the drive.

Zeeb let the cigarette droop from his mouth. With slow fingers he untied the raft. Smoke got in his eyes. He snorted phlegm, pushed off. The life of dead things possessed him as he approached the corpse, how it tilted in the water, the strong green weeds that floated from it, silver dragonflies mating on it, taking off. It had swollen round, the snout absorbed by the roundness. The tail floated. The body was tinged green.

He jammed the forward ends of the raft logs against the corpse, paddled. He headed away from the beach, away from the cabin to the far end of the pond. The raft moved its figure-head across the water. We are a stately barge, he murmured, a strange invisible perfume hits our senses.

With a final knee bent punt of the paddling pole in the muddy bottom he heaved forward. The advancing beaver parted the reeds, bobbed against the shore. He moved the raft sideways so he could jump off. The cigarette was burning his lips, semi-blinding him by the time he poled the corpse onto dry land.

But the goddamn raft had taken off on its own. He'd have to swim out for it later. He dropped the hot butt on the beaver, walked back to the cabin, parked the pole against the deck, headed in to the PowerBook.

But Mike still had the fucking battery.

∽

"And that's situational ethics," Lisa was explaining to the engineers. It was really weird that Jade hadn't once in God knows how long flushed the toilet.

∽

Marmalade wouldn't stop barking, hadn't paused since the car crested the hill driving away from the pond. She stood on the backseat barking hard sharp alarms. Mike jerked the wheel to make her tip, but she righted herself and stood up on the seat barking again.

He turned west. He wanted this next episode to function with the dignity of a firing squad but the stupid bitch wasn't playing her role right. He pinched his thigh. If he'd been on his toes he'd have scoffed a rope from the cabin to keep her in check.

A passing car had a barking dog too. The people slowed and giggled through their window into his face. He braked hard and Marmalade tumbled to the floor as they passed. He turned left and left again and parked on a road so remote it was sand, not even gravel. He slipped the bullets into his pocket. Marmalade tried to get out with him. He shoved her back. She continued to bark at him, at the road, at the fields against the windows.

The fence here was wire and there were pliers with a wire clipper in the tool box of the car. He got them, climbed the grassy bank, snipped off two lengths of fence wire. Back in the car again he twisted the short length tight around Marmalade's muzzle, sitting on her to make her still, digging a furrow of wire into her fur and her shallow muzzle flesh. The long length he looped around her collar. She had almost the strength of the girl bucking and whimpering. He tugged her, feet digging in, up the bank to the field side of the fence and, with the pliers, secured the loop to the fence. He lingered, watching her bark and whine. Then he went and got the gun.

The loading of it would have to be logical. If you pulled that knob back, you could put in a bullet, and if you twisted that spring it would be set, and then you would pull the trigger.

The first bullet plowed into the sandy soil at his feet. But he had it. He'd reasoned it through. The stupid bitch was in a frenzy at the sound of the shot. He reloaded the gun, stood at a distance from her — he'd seen blood spatter executioners and he didn't want to get messed — and fired.

He hadn't exactly got the aiming down cold. Marmalade was pulling so hard against the wire that . . .

temple

Oh, stop! dull sight — the wheels of the gods move so slow. Again a night in the dormitory, back now to the bench — what ties me to this bead-telling old woman?

You are silent, Saky. So silent up there. Great gold god.

Silence is golden.

Silence is yellow too, as in not brave.

But the fees taker — this heavy, smiling, halting-speeched man in his sports shirt and his grey pants — he is approaching. He says someone is coming. Someone who can talk to me.

Someone here who can talk to me? What can be said here, in this red and gold place? What lust makes us want to come together in your golden silence for the purposes of communication? What hope? Is there any hope?

. . . her collar was up around her ears. He reloaded, tried to hold the gun steady against his shoulder, and squinted that bead here into that notch there, in line with the bitch's torso. Disable her, then let her bleed — or do her in, he'd make a decision about that when he got her. He shot again and that was the moment Marmalade sucked her head out of her collar and took off.

He couldn't tell, as he shot one last time at her retreating form, whether or not he'd actually hit her. But it didn't really matter. With her jaw wired shut she couldn't eat or make more alarm, and she was far from home, without identity.

∿

Hadn't even used the toilet, Lisa thought as she waited at Health Services.

∿

In Zeeb's dream, Nemesis, daughter of Night, swam by, nose cutting water, weaving left, right in pursuit of him, whichever way he rowed. She wanted to board his boat. He wasn't ready, not old enough to copulate with swans, fish, goddesses. She reached hooked fingers over the gunwales — even in his dream he laughed to think he'd absorbed enough *Boys' Own* to know he had gunwales. He dropped the oars, pried off her claws. She hooked them on. He thwacked them with his oar. She let go, bloody, mewing, thwacking the water with her broad tail.

But he was moving, rowing, his boat was becoming, became, a huge multicoloured balloon, he in a basket suspended below. Hot air whooshed into the balloon from a blowtorch. He was moving, light, silent, over sand, scrub, animals stretching in all directions, herds of zebra, elephants, a pride of lions, a cheetah running down a little deer-like animal, giraffes splayfooted at a watering hole, hyenas, flocks of long-legged birds in flapping flight. Old cities, new villages passed beneath him. Mike, who'd been trying to take a bead on a lion, now turned his rifle on a village. Six of one, half dozen of the other whether they would shoot their bullets down into a dry well or up into the hot balloon. A chorus of male voices sang Shoot my beaver to cheer them on. He laughed at the puns dreams made, rolled over, woke on the hard deck.

Shadows lengthened eastwards, his skin smelled of sun. Birds, contrails cut through the sky. He had wasted his entire life. He stood, strode into the bush to get his battery.

cᴎ৲

Hadn't been bugged at all by this lingering puke-making smell, thought Lisa.

cᴎ৲

Mike ran water over the dinner dishes in the sink. He'd only half-emptied the dishwasher of clean dishes and he didn't want to take time to finish the job while there was still enough light for him to do the other things he had to do. The dishes could profitably soak till he got back. Reconstituted mashed potatoes tended to glue if you didn't soak them.

Paddy was making little whimpering noises in his sleep in his chair in the living room. Another crushed tranquillizer in his mashed potatoes and a before-dinner dose of Mortlach had seen to that. Into the hardware store bag with the composting compound and the masks, he put a pair of painters' plastic gloves. There wasn't any special meat composting compound, the salesman in the hardware store had said. Probably they didn't carry it.

But what about ashes? The chemicals in ashes certainly promoted decay in the outhouse at Children's Summer Bible Camp. Why wouldn't they work on the girl? He took down an old plastic honey container from the cupboard. Maggie had bought her honey in two-pound lots. He wondered that Paddy's bridge was as small as it was. He'd better cart the old bag of bones off to the dentist pretty soon. His understanding was that King expected him to maintain health, even at the risk of a certain amount of pain.

It was a lovely summer evening out the back door. But he didn't have time for that now. With the honey container he scooped ashes out of the barbecue. His hands became dusted with grey, masking the grime that even the making of hamburgers and the rinsing of dishes hadn't disturbed.

Uncleanliness wasn't necessarily ungodliness. Consider hermits. Consider saints in caves.

The kitchen door slammed as he went back in. He hearkened. But still the same pathetic little sounds came from the living room. He put the container of ashes into the bag. He took a look at the old bugger as he passed by. Long ropes of slobber hung from his slack mouth and trembled as he let out his little whimpery breaths, snored on.

∽

Zeeb was almost at the Big House side of the bush. He scratched, slapped yet another fucking bug, wiped sweat from his eyes. His jeans were soaked from rain shaken off branches. A strange odour came from near the fallen maple. Something rotting. What wanted to die in peace should be left in peace, but he was a reader of texts and the bush was forever rearranging its data, rendering new meaning. He buried his nose in the sweat of his palm, tiptoed closer. Whatever it was was in the pit left by the fallen maple. Maggots bubbled in it like macaroni.

No fur. Not an animal.

His scalp began to crawl.

Skin. Green skin. Bloated green skin. Hands. Bloated green hands curled over each other, ragged nails. Red.

Legs. Red pantyhose. Bursting out.

Roiling cunt.

A jade bangle.

His heart thundered. He couldn't hear his breath.

⌁

Mike stopped. Already at the edge of the bush you could smell the girl. He got a mask out of the packet and strapped it on. In here, he believed. And to the left. Not that the smell left any doubt about which direction to take.

⌁

Zeeb saw Mike coming. He had on a white mask, was pushing through as if he was going to wake the girl for breakfast. Fear bellowed through him. Get back. Hide. Get into the shadows.

⌁

The mask didn't filter smells. Mike ripped it off. The side of his face trembled.

Bountiful Mother Nature had got to her ahead of him in the great levelling power of maggots. How could he have forgotten about maggots after the years in his father's house where garbage so irregularly met its pick-up day? There was nothing for him to do now. Ultimately, once she'd devolved to bones, he would retrieve them, dispose of them, and what would link them, his belt. The stockings, the sock, he could see, would simply rot along with the rest of her flesh. Certainly there would be no point in removing them, for already the sock was sodden and frayed and the stockings were bursting and, around her orifices, overrun with the seething of maggots.

This was instructive, that the maggots were not on her green unbroken arms, her back, but only where orifices had made entry easy for the laying of eggs by the parent flies. It followed then that if there were more orifices where there weren't yet maggots, soon would there be more maggots, and her flesh would vanish sooner. Ergo, since what he'd brought to rot her was useless, in fact worse than useless, for the ashes would probably dehydrate the maggots, he must employ himself in the making of more orifices.

He dropped the plastic bag, reached the knife out of his back pocket, scrabbled into the pit, crouched by her. He opened the knife, jabbed at a leg. The knife was pretty dull. It bounced off her. He had to raise his hand and slash.

∾

Zeeb saw Mike's arm rise, come down slashing. Rise. Slash. Silver blood began to lace the girl's bloated skin. He retched. His stomach heaved. Mike was grunting, slashing, grunting, slashing, grunt, slash. Blood everywhere — Leslie, Leslie — he choked, gagged, coughed till his eyes, nose streamed, fell on hands, knees, heaved in a hoarse guttural rush.

∾

Mike arrested his arm. The bitch, was it? Marmalade? Could it be? That she'd made it home?

He scrambled from the pit.

The old bugger?

He moved towards the sound, pushing aside undergrowth, stepping high over roots.

The egghead. It was the egghead, on his knees, puking.

He rushed at him, knife fisted high.

∽

Zeeb jerked back on his heels, stood. Leslie. Fucking bitch had a knife, raised silver. She'd kill him. He backed. Blood whistled in his ears. She kept coming. He grabbed her, twisted her wrist back. He locked the crook of his arm round her neck, yanked her warm body against him. Her hard little ass jerked against his thigh, soft hair engulfed his nose. He smelled rut. Their breath drew hot together.

She stiffened, arched, shook like a live wire, then, as if a current had shorted, she went limp. Her dead weight unbalanced him, pulled him over. They fell, he heavy, winded, on top of her. He scrabbled up, looked down.

Her eyes gleamed half open. He toed her ribs. She didn't move.

The racing of his heart had become a high sizzle that deafened him. What had he done? You always kill the one you love. But how could he have killed her? He couldn't have killed her. But there was blood. He had drawn blood. He had killed her.

The bush reeked of an animal sickness he could not nurse. He backed, stumbled, turned, moved, crashed away. The reeking stench came with him. He yanked out of his T-shirt, crashed on, unzipping his jeans. Halted. Hauled off boots, peeled off jeans. Ran. Paused, yanked off briefs. Ran panting.

Ahead, over and under and through, water was running, the stream.

Six

on the bench in the temple

Saky. You've been holding out on me. This isn't your tem-
ple. It's hers. She owns it. Up there, that other statue.
Kuan Yin, she of the thousand golden hands and thou-
sand golden eyes. Lady of compassion. Your monks have
blinded me to the shaved-headed women who dapple this
red and gold gaudiness, like brown leaves in the evening
stream.

It's the nuns who have been watching me, Kuan Yin's
nuns, watching out for me, maybe, watching over me. She
whom they said I was to wait for, this child, this little
novice, who has come to spend her holiday with the chief
nun, the old lady, her teacher — she speaks English.

Is it a relief or a discipline to have been brought to this
bench to wait to have the existence of this temple, this phi-
losophy explained? — how the chief nun watched soldiers
throw the idol of Kuan Yin from her home temple in
China into the river, how she watched as they destroyed
the temple, how she vowed to rebuild, and did, here, in a
Canadian suburb.

She says to me, this child, "How are you feeling?" I'm
thinking, what courage to flee your land, however bru-
talized and no longer your land, to come to a new land
and create such a tactile tribute to your high ideals with
only the animal language of faith. What peace to have
such a faith.

And Zeeb runs.

Turn back, beloved. There is no exit, no answer. You can't escape yourself. Witness me here, myself with me always, forever seeing, foresightful, unending images of you before my eyes, running.

Night

Running, Zeeb was running, breathing hot, jabbed by branches. The stream, ahead was the stream, the babble of the stream, here was the stream, his feet were on rough moss. He must crouch, slide to stand in the brown rush of leafy water, feet yellow in the water, slipping. Must grip with toes on stones, gravel, sand. Must crouch, kneel, hands down. Hold on to slimy rocks, fingers yellow, wavering in icy water. Lie down in rushing ice, all down, lie flat, face under, breath jamming. Down, all down. Heart shrinking, stuttering. But stinking death back there with hell hole eyes, hell holes, her hell holes — must not be part of her, no part of her, not know her who touched him, died under him, be ice, in ice, odourless, motion-less, timeless — event only, only this event. Forget. Forget.

Breathless.

Raise nose, nose only, breathe. Get back down, stay down. Ice. Now he was ice.

He was no more.

Lift slow reptile limbs then, slither onto the bank.

Body, white in the dusk.

Must not be a body.

Go backwards, back through the grass, away from the rushing water, back, under branches. Slide back under scratch-ing branches, over duff, to reeds, marsh, mud. Daub mud on hair, visage, limbs.

Become shadow.

☙

Mike opened his eyes on ferns, grasses, black earth. Cool, he felt cool, and melded into what he lay on. He let himself fall back flat. Above leaves laced around intervals of dusky light. He need never move. And then the smell of the girl wafted to him and his heart began to tick. Tingling set into his toes, hands, legs, arms, into his torso. He pulled himself up, saw his knife, fallen silver in nearby ferns, retrieved it. Stood up.

He was shaking. Slime. There was slime in his shorts. He had wet himself. His knees buckled. But no. He had come, he had come! Unknowingly! A languid mellowness smiled over him.

Yet don't gloat yet. He must gather himself to himself, for he had an enemy, the egghead, on his way to the Big House, to report to Paddy, to phone the police. He must pursue and silence him. Yet the unfolding of events ahead of him, the scene that would take place at the Big House — it made him weary. There they would be two, linked, like father and son, against him. Yet he did have an advantage, for he still had the gun. In the trunk of the car there was still the gun. He would get the gun from the car before he got to them.

He imagined rounding the corner into the living room. The old man would be in his chair, the egghead standing above him telling his tale of woe. He imagined the horror growing in their eyes when they saw the gun, saw him with the gun, aiming the gun ready to fire. The egghead would pull the old man to his feet. They'd back away, they'd run for their lives. He imagined picking them off as they ran, the egghead first, then the old man.

Then he remembered he hadn't been too quick picking Marmalade off as she ran.

He would not be able to let them run. He would have to corner them, shoot them in the corner, one two, leave them bleeding and dead.

He was skirting the pit where the girl lay, heading away up onto the next stage, when back there to his left something alerted him, something white, something which was not part of the bush, which hadn't been there before. He altered direction to get towards it. Twigs cracked under his feet. Shadows and shapes were beginning to mingle. He tried to steal ahead but his limbs were lazy and branches slashed at him. He fended them off with his knife. At last he reached it.

A T-shirt. The egghead's T-shirt.

He picked it up, smelled it — rot, and sweat, and vomit. Then where was the egghead? He looked around. Ahead the branches were broken as if something had crashed through. Farther on there was something else, deep blue. He pushed forward.

Jeans, the egghead's jeans.

Excitement gripped him. He needn't go to the Big House. The shoot-out need not yet take place. They'd broken rank.

∽

It wasn't exactly snooping to be looking over Jade's things, Lisa told herself. She just wanted to be sure Jade had gone home to her mom and dad, and how could she find her home phone number to check except by going through her things? But no phone number was turning up, no address, nothing. There was nothing in the desk. Not even in the address book, the new one that had come from the Bell with the phone. Nothing under Hagner. Nothing there at all except a doctor under D and, in the front, their own number here. Nor on any of the bills and receipts — made out to L. Hagner, the father probably — stuffed in the desk drawer among ballpoint pens and paper clips and scotch tape and scissors and magic markers. It wasn't even on the sheet of paper where Jade had written her name, Jade, in a multitude of different scripts. Nor had she written her number with her name in any of her art catalogues. Nor in her textbooks. Not even in her old high school biology text — the father's old book, must be, belonging to L. Hagner. There wasn't even an in-case-of-emergency-call-so-and so card. Anything like that would be with her in her wallet.

She fingered the reproduction of a Lauren Harris glacier,

thumb-tacked on the wall of the dormer window, as if the stripped white planes could give her a clue. She turned over the framed snapshot on the dresser of Jade, smiling, with her arm around a smiling little girl — a sister? a niece? someone she had babysat? — to see if there was anything on the back, but no. Jade's hair was longer in the picture and she had on a long pleated grey skirt. Weird how you could live with someone and know so little about them. There was no other picture on the dresser, none of the ones you'd expect. No mom. No dad.

She slid the cupboard door open, pushed through ironed red blouses, clean cotton pants, khaki and white. Hangers squeaked along the rod. Everything was neat and new. No old running shoes. There were no laddered pantyhose in the dresser drawers. Even the manicure equipment was new, a packet of emery boards broken open, one used. A bottle of cuticle remover. An open packet of Q-tips. A barely consumed bottle of polish remover. The only object in the entire room that spoke of a past life for Jade was that doll lying naked on the bed. She sat it up, propped it against the pillows.

There was an Uncle Freddy. He had a farm. But there was nothing here that spoke of an Uncle Freddy even. Anyway, the Uncle Freddy was dead.

✿

The trail of the egghead's clothes ended in his briefs lying luminous in the darkening bush near the stream. Mike hooked them up on the point of his knife. Brown ass smear. So. The egghead was scared shitless. So much the better. It might be possible then to silence him without actually terminating him. It might even be possible to implicate him. Guilt by association. After all, the girl had met her end halfway between pond cabin and Big House. An explanation of that would be an interesting addendum to any accusation anyone might contemplate making against anyone else.

The stream rushed glinting over its dark bottom. There were crackling noises, the swoosh of wings, distant yipping. The egghead would have washed himself, headed to the cabin for clean clothes. The cabin was where an intelligent stalker would locate him.

He turned downstream. He needed the bridge in order to cross the stream dry. Branches grabbed at him. He held his arms over his face. Darkness was encroaching apace, and it was becoming difficult to distinguish solid footing.

Yet here, as it should be, was the bridge, slippery, but he made it across, and here was the path leading up to the cabin. You could see the clearing through the dark bars of the trees and in the clearing the hulk of the cabin against the dusky sky. Black windows reflected the wall of trees, the upper branches interlaced with sky.

But why was there no light inside? He had thought he would be able to see through the window undetected, the egghead spotlit as in a play, and he would plot his strategy based on what he saw. Instead, he on the outside in what was left of daylight could be observed by him on the inside in the dark.

He eased through grass, his legs swishing like rain falling. He leaned to one side, squinted into the screened porch. But there was nothing. No one there, only the chaise. He swished through the grass around to the side window. He could pick out the sheets on the unmade bed, the papers on the table under the window, dishes in the dish rack. But there was no movement, no sound. The back door whined when he pushed it open. He waited. Nothing.

When his eyes could distinguish shapes inside he crept forward, crouched, looked under the bed, the table, stepped out onto the screened porch, opened the door of the toilet cubicle, stood back against it, knife at the ready. But there was only the toilet, the shower stall, towels. There was no person in the cabin at all.

But the egghead was out there somewhere without any clothes on. To trap him you need only attend him here where his clothes were.

He sat down on the egghead's bed to wait. His eyes were like sand. After a while he slipped under the covers, stroked the underside of his arm against the flannelette sheet.

∽

The sky had become the kind of luminous navy Lisa had always wanted in a bathing suit when she finally found from information that there was an L. Hagner in Oshawa. She dialled the number. The phone rang. A woman with a German accent answered saying, here was the Hagner house.

Lisa's heart did a little flip. "Mrs. Hagner?"

"Yes, I am Mrs. Hagner."

"Oh, I'm so glad. Is Jade there?"

"Who is this calling? Who is Jade?"

"This is Lisa, Jade's roommate."

"Who is this Jade?"

"Your daughter."

"I have no daughter Jade."

∽

Now Zeeb was only shadow. Only movement marked the whereabouts of his mud-dulled hands, knees, feet. The hoot owl was a sound he was inside, the mouse rustlings, the rabbit squeal. In this darkness a shadow could wander free, forward, backward in time, to his den, identity. He could remember who he was.

He hesitated forward on hands and knees. He sighted with the planes of his face and shoulders the warm dry aura of twigs, branches, trees. He sniffed ferns underneath, marsh to that side, stream to the other. He heard — what? A bell? A cat? He froze, returned to invisible darkness. But it moved away, whatever it was, and his knees and hands resumed forward probing.

A gap presented itself to his right shoulder, right ear. He turned his eyes, saw a cabin in the open space beyond the darkness. He stood, slid along the edge of the bush.

The light grew easier, he almost remembered this place, his name. He opened the door.

∽

Mike dreamed he heard a voice cry out. He smacked his lips, shifted, tried to force his eyes open, to look into night shadows he didn't know where. What? Anything?

∽

But, see? Zeeb froze. Beyond the whining of the opening cabin door? In the bed? Look. There. Already someone was sleeping in that bed. It wasn't for him. These walls, this cabin, were already occupied by another, some rightful sleeper after his hard labours.

Then who was he — this nakedness under mud-daubed skin? This animal shadow he inhabited, who was he?

What afflicts my child, Saky, is a fugue state — temporary amnesia induced by stress. Women fail to recognize their husbands, men forget they have wives, soldiers walk away from a war. Same route as fugitive, flight.

He slipped back out into darkness, into the bush, down towards the stream. Not downstream, for that was the way of men. He picked his way upstream, guided by the babble of the water, the cold and heat of the air, the quality of the ground cover. He needed to find shelter somewhere where something would cover his back.

⌒⋎⌒

You dialled 911 only in emergencies. An emergency was when you heard a prowler downstairs or a car had hit a pedestrian. This was not an emergency, not that kind of emergency. Jade just seemed to be missing. But, To Serve and Protect. That was the police motto. So look up Police in the phone book. The phone book said to dial 911. So, okay, dial 911.

⌒⋎⌒

Another form of fugue state afflicts my little lady of compassion, Saky, my Kuan Yin manifestation.

She is seventeen. She comes from San Francisco. She flew up this evening.

She used to translate for her father who held Buddhist study sessions. One day, when she was sixteen, she was reading a newspaper, and she saw that suffering was everywhere, and she knew she had to be a nun.

She lives in a religious community. She goes to ordinary school because she knows her work will be to translate her community to the world around her. She will never marry. She will never dance again. She used to love dancing but not any longer. Oh no, she doesn't miss her hair.

Dawn

Paddy woke with a jerk, tightening his seat muscles. But it was too late, no use. A creeping mess of his own warm feces was spreading beneath him. "Oh," he groaned.

But his voice echoed. Where the hell was he? He rotated his head. The cloth his head moved against was familiar, but it was rough and he was sitting upright. He blinked, to make his eyes adjust to the darkness. The shapes around him began to gather meaning: the chesterfield, the other chair on the other side of the fireplace, the round table beside the glass doors that slid open to the veranda. He was in his own chair, for God's sake, in his own living room. His after dinner coffee cup was gleaming at his elbow. His mouth was dry and his lips tasted of Mortlach, his legs had been crossed too long and were all pins and needles when he unfolded them, and he was chilly, and filthy.

He must clean himself up before the kid came in and made remarks. But how to move?

The house creaked. The refrigerator was purring. Distant barking came in through the window. Once the postie in the city had asked Maggie if he could use their bathroom. The ignorant cuss left turds up the stairs. Didn't even offer to clean up after himself. Left it all to Maggie. Ignorant cuss. But maybe he was too embarrassed. What, after all, could you do if you were a postie and nature called and you were stuck in your rounds where there were no shops, no restaurants within a mile, where the houses all had polished brass doorknobs and knockers, edged flower beds, raked lawns?

He clicked on the lamp, undid his belt, his zipper. He pushed off his slippers, shoved them to one side, grunting, peeled off his socks. Inch by slippery stinking inch he slid out of his trousers, shorts, slipped them to the floor, stood, stepped free.

Or children. So often when King was stalking around Slater's Acres and making remarks about how the entire pasture would soon become lawn if Paddy continued to mow round the house in ever advancing circles, or when King would just look past the neighbour farmer woman, who dropped by in her jeans and her tattered hair to see if they'd seen a couple of her steers, as if she was too low to focus on, Paddy would want to stare King right in the eye and say, I know you, sunny Jim, I've changed your diapers.

Kid would soon be suggesting he needed diapers.

He jammed together his messed pants and scuttled with them down the hall to the bathroom, drew the curtains, shut the door, turned on the light. A button popped when he ripped off his shirt. He turned on the shower and when it was warm enough he got in and let the water pound on him.

The soap was the last of Maggie's Allenbury. He would tell the kid to get some more.

Or Maggie herself in the hospital. Dirtying herself. Perhaps he too didn't have so many years left, dirtying himself like Maggie. What else could have made him lose control of his bowels if not age? It didn't bear thinking on.

And Marmalade once, locked in the house. They'd got held up by a snowstorm, held up overnight in the city at King's, the radio said there was a blizzard, the roads drifted over, not even centre bare, and when they got home here finally, and got Strickland's blower to blow the drive out, there were turds inside the front door, and a pool of urine by the back, and the

poor old bitch was under Maggie's bed. They only lured her
out by opening the back door and propping it open and sitting
in their coats in the living room shivering, Maggie's cigarette
drifting against the smell, till they heard her nails clack down
the hall and out through the kitchen. And then when she came
in she wouldn't meet their eyes. Poor old Marmalade.

Poor old man.

He snivelled a bit under cover of the warm water. And then
he thought he better get out of the shower quick and finish
cleaning up before the kid woke and came up and provided
himself with material for more tales to tell King.

He dried himself, and drove his thoughts to pretty things,
Maggie's peonies in full pinkness, Polly swimming, his
mother's fur collar, while he washed out the soiled clothes in
the toilet, flushing, and flushing again, every time the tank
filled up. He rolled the shorts inside the trousers and left them
on the counter, and washed his hands again and dried them,
and went into his bedroom for his pyjamas. He turned on the
light and stared at Maggie in her little Italian frame.

"Oh, damn, damn, damn."

But be quiet.

He found his pyjamas, almost tripped and fell trying to get
into the bottoms.

One thing at a time. Easy does it.

When he was tied up and buttoned into them, and ready
for inspection, he went and looked at the little travelling clock
beside his bed.

Four o'clock? Was it possible?

"I couldn't have slept in my chair all night," he muttered to
Marmalade on her blanket under the window, and went to pet
her, to knuckle her warm familiar head under his fingers.

But Marmalade wasn't there.

And then he remembered the kid had said he was taking
her to the vet. Lord, he hoped there was nothing too much the
matter with her, he was too old to train a puppy. He found
himself tiptoeing as he went back into the living room to sur-

vey the site of his accident. Good thing he had gone to look. Things had come through onto the chair and the floor. He would have to scrub them. He trotted into the kitchen, clicked out the cleaning pail. The dinner dishes were still in the sink. Disgusting. He pushed them aside and put some warm water in the pail and some dish soap, got down some dusters, a linted pair of red shorts, a stained khaki shirt.

He couldn't understand why the kid hadn't been up yet to check on the racket. But don't look a gift horse in the mouth. Be grateful for small mercies. Sufficient unto the day. He got down on his knees by his chair and scrubbed at the soiled spot, rinsing the dusters in the soapy water, scrubbing again. Something about the dusters as he wrung them out niggled at him. He had peered long and hard at this very shirt, and not too long ago. Now, wasn't this that girl's? Yes. Look at the stains. He remembered these stains. Mustard. He thought again with loathing of the coarse white bra, the saggy underpants. She was an uncouth young lady altogether. And weren't these her red shorts? Yes. Yes indeed. There he was kneeling in his own living room, rotating these soggy rags of clothes in his hands, and what he was thinking was that if these were her clothes here in his hands, then what in tarnation did the young gypsy go back to the city in?

But probably the kid had lent her something. One of his, Paddy's, own old shirts, probably. After all, wasn't that what the boy went home in? Or maybe, goddamn it, the kid had let her use something of Maggie's.

He felt a furious impatience in his legs and arms thinking about people disposing of his and Maggie's possessions without asking if they could. He pushed himself up and sloshed the pail of dirty water into the kitchen and dumped it in the sink, watched how it backed up against the red shorts, the khaki shirt, the dirty dishes, how it drained slowly.

Giving away Maggie's clothes to strangers. Wasn't this grounds for reporting the kid to King, turn and turn about? Furthermore, how had the kid come to shut the house down,

turn out all the lights, and go to bed, and leave him, his pur-
ported charge, sleeping all night in his chair? He banged the
pail into the cupboard. If the kid woke up, so much the better.
In fact, he would go down and wake him up on purpose,
demand to know what the hell that girl had gone home in.

He stomped down the stairs, turning lights on as he went,
stomped down the hall. The door of his study was ajar. He felt
his way in his bare feet across the tiles and the rag rug, over to
the desk, and flicked on the desk lamp.

The brown and yellow cover on the studio couch was
smooth, undisturbed, the curtains not drawn. The blue trunk
sat under the window, a bit of green gauze or some such thing
sticking out of it. There was no evidence here of any person at
all. His nose, his eyes were streaming. He yanked out one of
the kid's faux tulip tissues.

He heard the cardinal, always the first of the dawn chorus
to wake and announce the light, the bird that needed to be
most wary because of its bright colour. Day already. Him and
the cardinal alone. No one else in the entire universe.

Except, of course, the boy over at the pond cabin. What he
would do was he would hike over there. But no, no. What
he would do was he would drive over to the pond cabin, drive
over, and rouse the boy. He would drive over and consult with
the boy about the kid's absence, about his own night in the
chair. No need to mention his accident. They would have coffee and toast, he and the boy. He would ask him what he
thought about the girl's red shorts and khaki shirt being in his
duster cupboard.

ᴄᴠɔ

Zeeb heard the cardinal. He jolted awake as if its brightness had
flashed across his eyes. He hadn't really been asleep. All night
water gurgled and echoed on the edge of his consciousness, he
had to be careful not to fall in. Now he saw light at the ends of

the tunnel. The pun amused him. This really was a fucking tunnel. He turned to share it with her. "There's light," he began.

His voice echoed, hollow, watery.

He was alone.

Put out the light, and then put out the light, I kissed thee ere I killed thee. He shuddered. Mists crowded over his mind.

He was hunkered, knees under chin, arms around shins, on a rock in a tunnel. Water was running through it. The tunnel arched above him and was hard against his back. He wasn't sure he'd ever be able to straighten out his legs again. Cold was something he was so far beyond he barely felt numb. But it was beginning to be light. And he had heard a cardinal.

Cautiously he picked up one leg under the thigh, began to extend it, to lower the foot, all pins and needles, into, because there was nowhere else to put it, the water. His heel hit the shallow bottom. He picked up his other leg, stretched it out too, into the water.

Culvert. That's it. He was in a culvert. He had spent the night in a fucking culvert. Unreal.

His foot, when he picked it out of the shallow water to shake some feeling into it, looked much whiter than his leg, as if it had been washed. He held out his hands to the light, rotated them. They were filthy, grey, fingernails black. He examined himself — legs, arms, body. He was filthy everywhere.

The guys. Must of been the guys. Who else would have done such a thing? Horsing around. They would have brought him here as a gag, drunk, dumped him, gone off. Left him to find his own way home, fuck them. These weekend bashes could get really out of hand. You got together with a bunch of goddamn Aggies and goddamn Vets and a stack of goddamn two-fours, and who knew what the fuck was going to happen?

He didn't have a head though. Wasn't sick.

Couldn't recall any party.

Couldn't quite say his name.

He concentrated on flexing and straightening his legs, pounding his thighs and calves to make them feel something.

A din of bird calls now occupied the space where the dawn-announcing cardinal had earlier reigned alone. He could distinguish robins, song sparrows, jays, crows, possibly a brown thrasher, maybe chickadees, although chickadees were predominantly winter birds. An old tire, lodged upstream, grew visible, the stream gliding around it. Probably the strands floating from it — like girl's hair, girl's hair, stinking girl's hair — he passed his hands over his face. Probably just algae.

There was something else up there, near the tire, taking on colour now, red, showing a dark blade. A chain saw.

The chain saw! He should take it back.

Yes! Back. Turn. Become the agent of your own salvation.

Back?
Back where?

Back to face the music. Back to Paddy alone in the Big House, Mike on the loose. Back home.

No way. He wasn't going back. He dug his fingers into his scalp. Black back there — no going back, only forward. Onwards, upwards. Push against the rock. Lever up.

He stood. He could sense the water now, icy. His feet slid on slimy pebbles. He staggered, slipped, righted himself, through the shallow water, out of the culvert. The sun was lighting the tops of the trees. Above the culvert, up that steep grassy bank, would be a road, egress.

He hauled up the bank onto the road. He heard a car stop at the crossroads, start towards him, flung back down the bank. He couldn't be walking on the road. He didn't have any clothes on. The car whooshed past overhead.

But he did recognize the layout up there. Where the car came from, this road went north, became part of the Bruce Trail, ran along the back of the conservation area. He bet anything he'd find the guys at the conservation area with a couple of two-fours and their fishing rods and a tent or two. That's what guys from Guelph did weekends, lacking girls, went into the bush. And if he didn't find the guys, fuck them, well, at least he'd find someone, some clothes, some wheels. He could get back to school.

He didn't want to walk through the woods though.

Bears.

Bares.

He shuddered. If it was so punny why wasn't he laughing? But he couldn't walk bare down the road.

❧

When Lisa opened her eyes the clock was ticking faint and fast, like her pulse, but it was only 5:45. She closed her eyes again. When it was 6:00 she would get up and phone Sam. Traffic growled through the shutters. Cars, trucks, buses. People running to catch buses. Kwami pounding his basketball on the sidewalk in early morning practice. The streetcars had started down Bathurst at 4:00 and she'd been awake, sort of, since then. It wasn't just the cramps and the blood, though she was going to have to wash the sheets and eventually go out to the corner store for pads, tampons wouldn't do it. It was the knowledge that she'd done something wrong that kept her awake. She'd talked with the police last night. But she hadn't talked with Sam. She'd talked to the police before she talked to Sam. In the course of their investigations, a police cruiser would soon be pulling into the muddy yard of the A-frame.

She imagined the colour draining from Sam's face when he opened the door. In fatigue or anger Sam turned grey, greyer. In sun he tanned, burned. You could see the line of exposure on his arms and neck, light and dark brown. After they'd been in the sun, he had got quite red. When she pressed her fingers into the skin of his back they left prints, which slowly filled again with blood.

5:50. She hugged her knees. Warmth gushed from her, down her. In the toilet in the night there were clots.

But she was damned if she did and damned if she didn't. She couldn't phone Sam last night, couldn't bring herself to. What would she say? How would the conversation have gone? The fact was that she was morally bound to hand Jade's absence over to the authorities, but the issue, the life and death of it was that the air between her and Sam had got so murky by the time she left the A-frame that there was no breathing space left in which to say, casually, one to one, What do you think?

She'd handed Sam over to the authorities. In effect that's what she'd done. The police shot black people, no questions asked. Whatever way it turned out she would always know she'd spoken to Pontius Pilate before she spoke to God.

⌃⌄

An unholy screech brought Mike upright, his back to the wall, arm raised against the shining light, the blows Father flung from nowhere, from rage, from bile, alcohol. But the light was the sun streaming in. The screech probably some bird. Birds glided blue past the window.

The egghead. Where?

He jerked up his chin, stretched his mouth into a smile.

Nothing moved in the cabin. He turned his head slowly, left, right.

No egghead. Not sitting, watching, ankle on knee, for him to wake. Not bent over his computer. Not at the sink. Not eating.

He uncurled his legs, lowered his feet. Something clattered.

He froze.

His knife. On the floor.

He bent for it.

It slipped from his fingers.

He dragged his clammy fingers across his thighs. Now there were dark streaks on his chinos. He grabbed for the knife again.

The bending made him nauseous and he swayed, grabbed the iron fireplace. Cold hardness resisted his fingers. The cabin spun. He held on for dear life. Blood drained from his forehead, his scalp. His eyes fuzzed.

Breathe.

Breathe.

The cabin slowed, stopped. Intervals of silence broke up the screeching buzz of bird call, tintinnabulation. His knees shook, but he could walk. He could think.

The back door, look out there first, look for the egghead's bike. See if he'd taken his bike. He emerged. Something flapped against his face. He cringed, squealed. But it was only the girl's drawers on the line. He imagined reassembling her. He imagined retrieving the parts of her from space and time. Replaying the tape. No, rewinding the tape. Erasing it. Forever thereafter, he and the old man would go together, with the dog, to the mailbox. The bike was in its place against the outside wall.

He eased around the corner of the cabin. Wings lifted off the pond. He ducked. A huge shadow dinosaured over him. He peered after it. Only some bird. But the silence was dreadful. A truck thundered down the road. You could be the only living breathing person in a world of robots. Not even Strickland was moving yet this morning. The soft frayed red of Paddy's plaid shirt, the stubble on Paddy's chin, the sloping chest, the shiny bald pate materialized in his mind. "Now I lay me," he whispered. It steadied him. He eased towards the bush, got down to the stream, stumbled over the broken bridge, began the long slippery trek up through fallen logs, clutching branches. Breathing.

◌◌◌

Just about the time the gravel trucks began heading south down the second line, Johnnie Strickland headed out of his house, up past the end of the vegetable garden and across the yard to the shed. The shed was the old barn. He remodelled it in '81 to house the machinery. It wasn't big enough now. Six of the machines had to sit in the yard. The well borer was off on a site near Paisley. The crane at Macville. One front loader permanently in the pit back of the house where he ran his topsoil operation.

Nobody'd been by to purchase topsoil yesterday because of the rain. Soil too heavy to move. There were still puddles by the fence. The soil was clayey here in the yard and some clown with a flatbed from Wildfield had backed into the weeds behind the barn last week and got stuck in clay up to his axle by the fence. They had to get the winch back from Ebenezer to get him out. He hadn't got around to grading it yet. The standing water reminded him now.

Today was bright day. Full summer. The housing development north of Lockton needed sixty yards and since they didn't come for it last week, and couldn't come over the long weekend or yesterday, he had told them they better come early this morning because he had to go on to the job up near Mono.

He detoured to unlock the gate, so he wouldn't have to do it when they got here, and what should he find lying at the gate, muzzle pressed under it, but Slater's bitch. Something wrong with her. Backed away. Wouldn't come close. Shaking her head like she had a fly in her ear.

He walked off and sure enough she followed him and he whipped around and grabbed her. Almost didn't get her. No collar. Grabbed her tail.

Then he saw her muzzle was wired shut. What clown would do a thing like that? Barbed wire around the poor bitch's muzzle.

Well, he hollered for Cathie, and she came out of the house with the baby, and he told her to get the pliers, and he cut the wire, and, bloody as she was, Slater's bitch headed straight for that puddle and drank like she'd wandered forty days and forty nights in the wilderness. He went in and called Slater, but there was no answer. The old man must be up and about real early this morning. But the bitch there drinking at the puddle just showed you there was sometimes a good reason why you didn't get to chores just when you thought you should of.

Now which key was the one for the ignition? Paddy hadn't driven the car for so long he wasn't sure. That was the front door key. This one might be the one for the back door, though it seemed to him they didn't keep the back door key on the same ring as the car keys. These two were the same size. This one didn't seem to fit the ignition though. It must be for the trunk. Then this one must be for the ignition.

At the maple pit, in sight of the big pasture, Mike paused, sweaty, scraped, and looked down once more at the girl. She should have cooperated. For women are infatuated with death. If she had danced howsoever willingly he would have given her whatsoever she wilt.

The busy inhabitation of her flesh had grown to municipal proportions. Only an ordinance of God would halt its multitudinous purposes. He hastened towards the light.

Seven

by the temple shop stall

They want me not to want, Saky, just like you. Nonetheless, there in the shop stall you can see my little lady of compassion bent over — I think for my benefit — looking at the wares.

The custodian has pulled out trays and trays of bracelets — gold chains set with stones, priced according to the number of gold carats and the value of the stones, quartz or amethyst — like that. He has laid out the trays on the glass top of the showcase, and it's over them that the shaved head of my little lady of compassion bends.

She tries the bracelets on — this one, that one — she turns them over in their trays, teenage longing unmistakable in the angles of her bent grey-collared neck, her crooked brown-swathed elbows, her grey-tunicked knees pressed against the glass case.

My bullshit metre is screaming. Dissonance! Dissemblance!

Forgive my bitterness, Saky. Betrayal flourishes everywhere — Zeeb's flight, your materialism.

My heroine, my go-between, my interpreter, my little lady of compassion with the thousand outstretched hands — she doesn't want bracelets — and if she does, she is not allowed to — where could she ever wear them? She has renounced the world — as you, they, wish me to renounce delight in objects, lust for life, Zeeb.

I see what's happened here. My little lady of compassion

has been instructed to seduce the sentimental questing round-eye into buying her bracelets, which they, her mentors, will later return to the stall. The temple will reap a profit on the sale of one hundred percent.

Break, heart.

What is her life, little shaved head? — it isn't a life, it's living death. This young fresh person in her uniform and restrictions is as buried here as surely as Jade is buried in her pit.

Oh Saky, what what what have you done? If I were to stretch out my finger now and touch her — my little lady of compassion — I wouldn't even make a dint, not a wrinkle in her brown sleeve, no impression in her soft cheek — she wouldn't even turn her head. She's utterly safe here — walled off, walled in — our voices cross, they don't twine. We are as distant, close here, as if she were in China, as distant as Zeeb.

Oh, lord, I'm huge, I stink, still wearing this grungy skirt and shirt. No toothbrush. Let me out, let me go.

But I've taken up so much of their time — your time — your, their space and time — and commerce rules us, I can't leave without paying my rent.

My wallet — where did I put it? — fingers slip slide.

When did I last really eat? Do I actually have any money?

What is the weather doing now, out there, out the door?

I'll just dash back, drop a bill — a two? — was that a fifty? — it's gone, anyway, into the contributions box — scoot back to the doorway.

Wednesday

Zeeb decided to keep to the road — the roadside mounted a steep grassy bank to a wooden snake fence, beyond that — dank bush. He would flee there only if he had to hide.

Traffic was getting heavier. He heard a car, scrabbled up, tugging on grass, slipped, scrabbled, slid, slipped, scrambled at last over the fence, rolled on hard dry cedar duff, lay panting, staring up through branches.

He imagined the people in the car.

Did you see that?

What?

A naked guy. Going into the bush. Didn't you see him?

In case you hadn't noticed, I'm driving. What are you on anyway?

Don't be rude. Let's go back.

And be late for work again? Asshole.

He had to stay in the bush. He got up, went on, low like an animal, close as he could to the fence, batting branches, skirting raspberry canes, slapping bugs. He wished he hadn't washed. The mud would have kept off the fucking bugs.

The going got easier. Grass grew close to the fence. Styrofoam cups had got into the grass, flying McDonald's hamburger papers, some girl's sandal. The flimsy intricate lacing of the leather thongs of the sandal filled him with fury. He heaved it away. He was sweating, skunky. He spat.

At some point he was going to have to expose himself if he wanted to keep going north. The crossroads was coming up soon. He was going to have to get across.

The bush got dense again. Cedars grew to the fence. He had to crouch, creep under. Dry branches scarified his back, arms. But he could see through to the red and white stop sign at the crossroads.

To his left, across the road, he made out a white A-frame. Suddenly he remembered. There was a girl.

cᴧɔ

Well, that works, thought Paddy. The car was purring nicely. Now, what the hell did you do to open the garage door? Wasn't

there some gizmo? He turned to peer in the backseat. Was that
the boy's battery? Well! He was going to get a fine welcome
indeed. The boy would be very glad to see him. Maybe he'd
make scrambled eggs.

ᴄᴧᴐ

In the A-frame, Sam lay flat on his back on the floor. He had
put his back out jumping up from a sound sleep to answer the
phone. Or was it while Lisa was telling him she'd called the
police? He pulled his stomach in, down to his spine, slowly
tilted up his pelvis. He stretched out full, fingertips reaching,
toes pointing, relaxed. He rotated . . .

in the temple doorway

> *Squinting, no sunglasses, it's bright out there. But no sun
> blinds my mind's eye. I too have been a three-legged dog,
> like Sam. The pack turns on the one who is different. Egg
> on the windows. Unbenefited.*
>
> *The world loathed the entity Polly/Sibyl. Long
> McAdam gathered the glory, the power, made us beg. We
> circled the edge of society, perpetual refugees, making do
> with less, with laughter.*
>
> *If I were in Sam's shoes, I'd leave now. Get a head start
> on them. Before they swagger in.*

. . . he rotated his hands before his face, surveying the dark
rivers of life that ebbed against the pink palms, the pearly nails,
work-torn, dirt-embedded. Then he curled . . .

> *I'd get in my truck, head straight home. I got on a plane,
> didn't I? Headed here? Ah, but you're old, Polly. The
> spark that drove you — she is dead, ashes in the wind.
> Your life is no longer on the line. The future is behind*

you. You can afford to run now. All the credibility you'll ever have is what you bring with you — we were exiled, yes, but we kept faith with Zeeb. I keep faith with Zeeb.

. . . Sam curled slowly up, stretched tall, breathed, looked . . .

But how nice it would have been to drop sunglasses over my mind's eye sometimes, to see no more evil, hear no more evil, to run, to use paper clips when the news made my stomach heave.

. . . Sam looked out the window. Sunlight sparkled on the granite boulder by the pond. He plugged in his little yellow portable automatic percolator . . .

So Sam won't run. He fears no evil. We must sometimes, we three-legged dogs — be foolhardy, show courage in the face of disaster — to save our souls, whether or not the Lord is with us.

Yet — does Sam fear no evil? I see no fault, no way in to what he is thinking, no getting inside his skin. Only, above blowing sand, I make out sometimes a peak like a pyramid.

. . . tidied socks, the bed, went upstairs to the shower.

✑

Sadie's other tenant — the short one — she was in early. She was hovering over the sanitary napkins and tampons, so Mel looked away. Anyway Mo was jumping up and down the other side of the counter and there seemed to be more on his mind than just yesterday's numbers.

"You heard the latest about that sex case?" he said.

Mel only grunted. He was leaning on his elbows on the

morning paper spread out over the glass case that held the lottery tickets. He'd had it up to here with these people who acted like they knew something they weren't supposed to know about that sex case. They'd walk around looking like they had a pickle up their ass till you just had to ask them what was bugging them. Then they would explode. Nyah, nyah, nyah. I know more than you do.

Meshugas. Craziness.

"There's a guy at the shop," Mo was saying. "He knows someone who knows a guy who met the wife's lawyer's sister at a wedding." He was wiggling his black eyebrows like bat wings, jumpy as he used to be in spelling dictation.

You couldn't tell whether this one had good legs or not, like the blonde tenant. The blonde had worn shorts. This one had on jeans. Good tits though. Tank top. No bra.

He turned and walked through the back of the store into the storeroom. There had to be some way to get a little privacy.

But Mo was following. "Terrible. You wonder why they don't stop publishing these things. Then people wouldn't get these ideas." He jiggled his change like dice rattling. Pocket pool, they used to call it. "You know what I mean? A five-letter word that begins with s?"

You wouldn't think you'd have to leave your private space so you could get some privacy. That's old friends for you. Anyway Sadie's tenant was waiting to pay. And the dairy delivery had come, and he had to check to make sure about the special on yogurt. And Jason, the motherless kid from down the street whose father worked all day — he wanted bubble gum.

"Sure, Morris," he said as he rang up Sadie's tenant's purchases. She was buying pads and tampons both. Don't ask. "Everyone knows a five-letter word starting with s. Talk to you later, eh?"

Mo got the message and sauntered out. And Sadie's tenant hurried out too. Jason stayed chewing bubble gum and reading *Archie*.

There was too much vanilla yogurt. What sold was fruit flavours. But there was pure sour cream at last. Mrs. Steele had been asking for it. He had to shelve everything before he could get back to his paper, and even then he still felt sick about Mo's inside dope. He had to admit that this was a wrinkle he hadn't thought of.

Snuff.

Zeeb stared at the A-frame. Something he didn't want to think about a girl. A cop car was nosing up the road. He ducked. It turned down the A-frame drive. He fell back breathing hard. No fucking cops for him. He heard a garage door screeching open over the hill.

It's Paddy, beloved. Listen.

He had to get across the fucking crossroads. Now. Dash. He swarmed up the fence the other side, stood astride barbed wire, lifted a leg, fell into grass. He heard the far-off scream of a car engine.

Listen. Paddy's in danger. Attend.

His heart pounded. He crawled on his belly away under branches till he was sure he couldn't be seen, got up, thrashed on.

Mike

Somewhere Mike had lost his hat. The sun was higher now, glowering between the raised scraggly arms of the black locusts. The back of his neck prickled with heat and his hair lay on his forehead like an electric blanket. His ears were ringing. His breath came in gasps.

He halted because there was no sense mounting a pulpit unrehearsed. When you crested the rise you confronted the house head on. What was he going to say? What could he justifiably have been doing all night?

He sidled in amongst the black locusts, and attempted to proceed in their shadow. He wanted to reach a vantage where he could see without being seen. Yet thorns grabbed at him, ripped the sleeves of his shirt, dug into his chinos. They clawed at his face and arms worse than anything had in the bush. Red streaks bubbled on his arms. He held his arms over his face, moved his hips sideways.

Then he caught a light glinting.

He stopped, uncovered his eyes. He saw through spiked shadows the white Renault backing out of the garage. It stuttered in a wide arc onto the lawn, jerked around, and began to dust away down the drive.

He had to have the gun in the trunk. He thrashed through the last of the evil branches, out just into the open. He needed the gun as backup. He kept his back against the trees. Thistles grew to his knees. The Renault scrunched to a standstill at the mailbox. He started to run after it, knees up and shoulders hunching against the thistles. But the Renault erupted once more, skidded into a left turn, no signals, headed west, disappeared behind the trees that lined the road.

He froze.

Who might now be observing him from the dark eyes of the house? He pressed back into the thorns. Who went in the car? Who was left behind? The world was beginning to spin again. For whom should he prepare lines? He heard an old voice saying, You are cursed above all cattle, and above every beast of the field. Upon your belly shall you go and dust shall you eat all the days of your life.

"Help!" he cried.

Father, too, had cried out, "Help!" near the end. His own strength then had been to resist getting the hospital chaplain. He had stared into the staring eyes. In thought he said, I'll care for you, I won't let you succumb to this weakness. Only weakness ever let you let your only son be taken by Children's Summer Bible Camp. You couldn't provide. You were down to your uppers. You were homeless and fearful of starvation. The best of you never bowed your head to any God.

He opened his eyes, looked up into the sky, gave God the finger. Ah, he would dazzle any watchers with his fancy footwork. Giant steps and baby steps would mark his passage. He would consider the eyes of the house, see all was still, and then he would stride. If there were a lash flicker of watchfulness he would take only baby steps. He would circle. He would come at her from the rear.

By slow degrees, freezing at each jay call, chipmunk squeal, grass flutter, he worked his way in the hot sun around the periphery of the mowed meadow, taking giant steps or baby steps according to the instructions of his heart, but when he was within range of the compost heap, he halted. Here were his windows and here was where he laid him down to sleep. The house was smiling at him and he leaned into her magnetic embrace, walked to the back porch, entered the spidery shade, opened the door and was in the kitchen.

Silence.

Who had driven off? Where was the egghead? What had befallen the old man? The house creaked as he tiptoed into the hall to see into the living room. The old man's chair was empty. He sneezed, stifled. He tiptoed to Paddy's room. The bed was made up but his pyjamas lay on the floor. The bedside clock ticked. Breezes rustled the screen. Somewhere a tap was dripping.

Dread began to prick him all over. The house was abandoned. Any second now there would be people come to the rescue once again. King would tear down the drive. The egghead would spring out of a cupboard. The Renault would return, bulging with neighbours.

He must flee.

He darted into Paddy's room. He gathered to himself from the jewel box Paddy's old one-dollar bills and the pill bottle of pennies, for they would have collector value. Tilting his head this way and that to listen, he jabbed through all Paddy's pockets for change and found about seven dollars in coins. In the dining room he clicked together, in their blue cloth bag, Maggie's sterling silver teaspoons. He scuttled down the stairs to his own room. He would have to wear his jean jacket, for the pockets. He would also have to wear his one pair of jeans for they were tight enough he didn't need a belt.

In the little dark windowless bathroom, he wiped his hands and face. He would not shower. Under cover of the pounding water they could lay siege. He wondered how fast they'd be back. Would he be slipping out one door as they entered the other? He glimpsed his white skin, his coarse reddened neck, slammed shut the three-way eyes of the mirror against the seductions of reflection.

He thrust his possessions into his blue trunk, dirty clothes, clean clothes, TV, tackle box, broken down rod. Birkenstocks. He would wear his runners. Even his wallet with all his ID he pushed down into the trunk. Even his bank book. A string of withdrawals across the continent would mark as clear a trail as bread crumbs. Into the pockets of the jean jacket he put his wealth — coins, bills, change, spoons, the wad of housekeeping money.

His heart hurt him. He wanted to take at least the red nailpolish. He slapped his face briefly. He would send for the blue trunk at some future date. He locked it, pocketed the key.

He got Paddy's yellow hard hat from the mud room, tucked it on. He skittered out through the garage. He hesitated between a concealed route through the bush and a clear dash down the drive, and chose the drive — the bush begrimed you. He must look civilized or no civilized person would pick him up.

At the mailbox he turned east, turned his back on the familiar route west, away from the crossroads, away from the A-frame, away from the village, the pond. This new road took him up an unfamiliar rise, and then another, and then another. He was looking at cows in a field he'd never seen before. He came to a new crossroads. The shade of maples cooled the hard hat. He began to whistle a campfire song from Children's Summer Bible Camp:

> The cabin boy, the cabin boy,
> The dirty little nipper.
> He filled his ass with broken glass
> And circumcized the skipper.
> Away, away, with fife and drum.
> Here we come, full of rum,
> Looking for women who peddle their bum
> On the north Atlantic squadron.

Paddy

Cars might be honking and screaming past him, but Paddy kept crawling at a snail's pace down the road, and with very good reason. When he'd crested the rise, there, at the crossroads, had been a red and white stop sign. He had done his damnedest to stop, but somehow the car had gone jerking right through. He almost hadn't made the turn, and then he'd been honked at and overtaken by some damned fool who'd been stopped all the time he was negotiating the turn, and now the damned fool was racing away ahead of him at breakneck speed along with all the other damned fools.

They must have put the sign in overnight. It had never been there before. Why, when he and Maggie first came up here there were no signs of any kind on the roads anywhere, no labels. Everybody knew where they were. Airport Road. Second line. Fifth sideroad. Tenth sideroad. These roads were all gravel back then, and maples arched over them. Mr. and Mrs. Eddy Edwards had summered in a tin garage near the crossroads, just beyond the little red brick school house on the corner. They were going to build the house one day, but they never did. Eddy Edwards had a stroke, and Mrs. Eddy moved into town.

The school was in use then too, kids running around in the grassy yard. He had given them all his old *National Geographic*s when he moved up. But then they built those big schools and began to pick the kids up in buses from all over the countryside, and drive them miles every day to the one big school, and the little old one-room school had been bought by a couple of bachelor girls, and converted, and landscaped, so's now you wouldn't know it had ever had a functional purpose. God alone knew what happened to the *National Geographics*.

The car was behaving very badly, dragging and pulling, and then jerking ahead like a rabbit that's decided the grazing here is terrible and it better just lollop along. Furthermore, his mind was interpreting something else he'd seen at the crossroads. Parked in the yard of Thompson's A-frame, beside his yellow truck, was a white car, a police car, and he was remembering he no longer had a driver's licence. His knuckles were white on the steering wheel and he was hunched forward to peer through the windscreen.

But he was making some progress. He'd crossed over the stream where it ran way down there through a culvert and he, on the road, went high and straight over it.

That was a sad thing. Years ago, when he'd bought the farm, before the roads were labelled and paved and the maples on the roadside hadn't yet been poisoned by salt running off in winter and gone dry and stiff and leafless and been cut down — long years ago, longer than he could actually calculate just at the moment, concentrating on his driving as he was, the road had run down there too, just a few feet above the little stream which had run through a much smaller culvert. The road had curved down there to get around the hill.

He thought of the men laying out those first roads, wanting the sun on their backs for such hot work, not wanting the sun in their eyes, and so, as the day progressed and the sun moved across the sky, they made the road curve around the hills.

No one would dream of speeding round that twisting little sandy road back then. In fact, it was a joy just to walk along. Cedars, not maples, lined its damp curves, so there you were with the spice of cedars in your nostrils and the tinkle of the little brook in your ears and the shush of sand under your

boots. If it was a hot day still it was always shady and cool
down there by the stream under the cedars. A cardinal nested
yearly on one side of the road and hunted on the other so
whenever you walked down there in the summer, red would
flash back and forth in front of you. And in winter, even after
the plough had been through, you could ski on the edge of the
road and hearken to the winter life, jays, chickadees, squirrels,
and mark the tracks of deer and rabbits and mice.

Then of course he had cut the trails through their own bush
for getting around. And King had made his circular cross-
country ski trail. And the township had straightened and raised
the road, paying him a tidy sum for the curve which had orig-
inally been surveyed as part of his property and which they had
cut off in the process of straightening the road. He'd put a
fence in with the money. You couldn't say progress was entirely
a bad thing.

Another car went screaming past him and he came out of his
reverie. What in hell was he doing? It was breakfast time, a
crazy hour to be driving over to see the boy. Why wasn't the kid
driving him? And why were his hands all sticky and cracked?

Then the red shirt appeared in his mind's eye, those khaki
shorts. No. Those red shorts, that khaki shirt, that girl's belong-
ings — that's what he saw, them blocking the drainage of the
soapy water in the kitchen sink. He tightened his knuckles again
and sat straighter.

The kid had abandoned him. The boy would make him
breakfast.

There was another turn coming up any minute now when
he had to get off the road and onto the driveway and into the
shelter of his pines. His bowels were rumbling again and he
tightened his anus. You wouldn't find him caught short a second time. But he had to get on. He pressed on the gas and went
forward in jerks. Yet he mustn't go too fast and miss the drive.
How would he ever get turned around and back again?

He was passing over the marsh now and the pond gate was
right after. He slowed. Now he wasn't going even at a snail's

pace. Now he was more like a sick cat crawling. Another car, and another, and another whirred past him. The car window was shut and he couldn't get his arm out to signal his turn. He had to come to a full stop at the side of the road, open the window and start up again. Even just to start up again, he flapped his arm out the window, holding on to the steering wheel for dear life with only one hand.

He caught sight of what was going on in his rearview mirror. A whole line of cars crept along behind him, three or four, and another one, and another one, far in the distance. If he didn't watch it the ones at the rear, who couldn't see the reason for the slowdown, they'd overtake him, zoom, and zoom, and he'd never be able to make his turn.

But there now was the gate. And there was the cool pine tunnel. No one was coming up towards him, unless they were hidden ahead, beyond the rise by Strickland's and he didn't want to think about that possibility, so he shot out his left arm and spun the wheel with his right hand, the car jerked forward, and he was home free at last, off the road and on the pond driveway.

He thought he'd just stop a while and catch his breath. When he came to tug out the hand brake he found it wasn't there under the dashboard where his hand was reaching out for it. He peered around the interior, and there the goddamn hand brake was on the floor and it was already on.

Well. No wonder he'd had such trouble, jerking all over the map like that. What an idiotic place to have a hand brake.

He left the car idling and got out and went in under the pines and undid his trews, and let them down, squatted and relieved himself. He was twenty yards from the road into the bush here and the only sign of civilization was the scream of the cars. Safe home. He got back in the car and cruised on under the cool tall pines.

He had reached the hill and was heading down when he felt the car beginning to slide and he remembered the thick bed of pine needles. He braked, but it was like on ice, he skidded, braked again, pulsing. But he couldn't get to a full stop. Would he be able to make the turn at the bottom? Would he just keep straight on going into the pond? But at the bottom of the hill he wrenched around onto the flat, and then he wrenched round again onto the dam.

But again he was crawling, now for fear of driving over the side of the dam. He wrenched again and heard willow branches scraping the car roof and so he scooted up to the parking place by the cedars and killed the engine and braked and waited for the boy to come out and greet him.

The sun beat in through the window. The roar of cars sizzled from the line. The smell of the cedars came in through the window. But the boy didn't appear.

He'd forgotten to honk at the top of the hill. He honked now and waited another minute to give the boy time to come out on the porch.

But he didn't come.

He got out, got the battery from the backseat. He was feeling a little shaky now, doubtless from hunger. He dug his feet up the bank to the cabin, climbed up onto the porch, knocked on the screen door.

But there was no response.

He called out, "Anybody home?" Not a peep. The boy must be really lost in dreamland. There wasn't even the sound of snoring. He screeched open the door and walked in.

The cabin was empty. The bed was kind of tousled, but the boy wasn't sleeping in it. He put the battery on the table by the boy's work and went through to the back. Maybe the boy was out there fussing over the trail. He opened the back door and saw that girl's sad underthings hanging from the clothesline.

His gut contracted again but it wasn't his bowel problem this time. If the girl's clothes were all still here — khaki shirt, red shorts, saggy under things — how had she got home?

Or had she gone home?

If not, where the hell was she?

Where were all the young people? Where was anybody?

He puckered his lips together and tried to whistle Polly's

whistle but his lips were quivering. He called out, "Zebu?" But his voice fell short. He couldn't muster a shout. He felt in his pockets for a handkerchief but there was none. Not even a Kleenex. He wiped his nose on his cuff.

He went back into the cabin and there on the floor by the bed he saw the knife the kid used to cut off fish's heads, gut fishes, pare toenails, — the one he'd removed from his work-bench. He stared at it lying there, in the wrong place, grimy, dull.

He went back out onto the porch and stood looking at the pond. A fish nosed the water. But the day was too hot for fishing. The air was putrid and heavy. There were crows down at the end of the pond cawing softly over some carrion. Strickland's machines were starting up. The world was beginning its workday.

He thought of King and his hands began to shake. King didn't seem able to provide, even where he'd excluded anybody else's provision, even for his own kith and kin. What he wanted to do now was just whistle up Marmalade and walk home through the bush. Just forget the boy had ever shown up. Forget the kid had ever been his caretaker. He wiped his nose, his eyes on his cuff. His stomach growled.

He slammed himself into the car again and got the damn thing going. He began backing down. His neck didn't want to turn. His hands were so tense on the wheel, for fear he'd just back through the reeds and right into the pond, they were numb. He had to keep looking into the side mirrors, the rear mirror, the side mirrors again. He had to go forward and back up again twice. He clipped the mud bank on the rise to the cabin, and the willow branches screamed so loud on the roof he thought he'd driven right into the willow.

He turned the car and inched forward back over the dam. He wrenched the steering wheel around the first curve. He wrenched again and headed up the hill. But the wheels were spinning. The car was skidding again. He was slipping backwards down the hill towards the pond. Turn, he told himself. Turn the wheel. Pull on the hand brake. He'd forgotten again about the ruts full of pine needles. You had to drive beside them. Give her one more try, he told himself. He let out the brake and got onto the top of the ruts and crested the hill.

There he came to a standstill. He put on the brake again and got out of the car and went back to where he could look out over across the pond to where the cabin nestled in the cedars. He wished he had his pipe. One time, when he had gone to visit Maggie in hospital, he had taken the route along the thirtieth sideroad, taking his time, admiring the new stone fence someone was erecting under the cedars by the roadside, dawdling past the marsh with the marsh marigolds, knowing any he picked would be limp as noodles by the time he got them to Maggie, but wishing she were there with him to marvel over the bright yellow, the paddy green of spring. Some guy was tailing him. The road was too curvy there for passing. The guy was so close he could be crawling up his back. When he came to a stop at the Airport Road the guy behind him began honking. So he put on the hand brake, got out his pipe and began to fill it. The guy nearly had a conniption fit. He backed, and skidded around him, yelling and honking, and spun out onto the Airport Road, and almost ended driving himself into the ditch.

Maggie had laughed till the tears rolled down her face when he told her. Saint Patrick, she'd said. Then she had put her hand with the intravenous taped into the back of it over his hand. But who will look after you? she had said. Who? Who? Her hand had been cold, and light.

His hands had stopped shaking. He went and got back in the car and started off again. There wasn't so much traffic going down the line now. It was easy to get off the driveway. He turned south, down towards the village, towards the stores, the firemen, the police.

Zeeb

Zeeb stumbled to a stop on the bush side of a wide green close-cropped lawn with a spread-out brown house beyond. He was shivering, sun dappling him through leafy maples, hiding his nakedness. There was a little kid out there on the lawn in a pink and black T-shirt, orange shorts, pink runners. Pushing a goddamn yellow and green plastic doll carriage over the lawn. Talking to herself. Lips moving. Maybe she was singing, singing a lullaby, singing her fucking doll to sleep. Coming, coming closer, Jeez — but she stopped short, crouched on the lawn, grabbed something, went running, her fist clenched, towards the screen door. Her voice came to him thin and clear, "Mummy! Mummy! See what I got!" A skinny woman in white shorts let her in.

He let out his breath. Okay. Now. Go. Flash across to the garage, get behind it, plan your next move.

But what if he didn't go fast enough?

He held out his hands trying to press forward. He was losing it, his hands were shaking, he was beginning not to be able to keep his plan in focus. What the fuck was he doing here naked anyway?

To his left, after a metre of leafy bush, there was a split rail fence, then the road that went south to the city and the CN Tower. But he was taking it north to the conservation area. Right? To the guys.

Why? He pressed his head with his hands. What made one way better than another? To his right there was more bush. He could see distant undulating pasture, a thin line of smoky-blue hills merging with sky. Up, there were wispy little clouds.

Pray for rain. If it rained all these interceding people would get inside their houses, attend only to the insides of their precious cars. He could think, in solitude he could think. He shut his eyes, blotted out the landscape, willed wind, rain. His love in his arms again.

He shuddered.

The screen door slammed. The little girl was back on the lawn. She was squealing, "Ladybird, Ladybird."

"Leslie, Leslie," his voice echoed.

Jesus. He had spoken out loud. His voice had come out in a high cry like a rabbit in a hawk's claws. He jerked back. The little girl was peering up, starting to walk towards where he stood naked, shivering. He slid behind the maple. A satiny maple leaf ran its surface through his fingers. On the underside, warts marked bug egg cases. He squeezed the leaf, ground it. A wintry cold was spreading across his chest. The leaf squeaked in his grip. His fist was so tight it was shaking. His face was wet. The kid was coming, she would see him.

But no one could see him. He was a jungle animal, a ghost, the murderer of a ghost, and you always kill the one you love. Leslie, Leslie, Leslie. He couldn't stop shaking, saying her name and shaking in ice. He pressed his green-bloodied hands against his head. Fragments of leaf fell down his bare shoulders. He staggered through the maple branches to the fence, crawled over, cold, numb, crossed the ditch, hit the gravel which would take him north. He turned for one last look back down the road. A white Renault was heading south.

Little fucker. Played chicken with him all the way up the line. Wha?

Pins and needles were stinging his brain, like a foot waking. Fiery blushing overcame him. He hit his head, hit it, hit it again, hard.

"Fuck you, fuck you, Mike." He was snarling.

From the beginning, the very beginning, Mike was there, the villain, the bully. The murderer. He should have known. Why hadn't he noticed? Why didn't he put it together? He was aflame remembering it all. The girl. In the car. In the pond.

In the bush.

Maggots, roiling, white, in her body, inside her. Mike lifting his knife, slashing.

Her bangle.

He choked, wept.

Jade.

Dead, she was dead, mangled, murdered in the bush below the Big House.

"Oh, no." He clutched his gut, twisted down. This knowing was unbearable, torture, he'd rather be a rock, a robot, not know, never, nothing, forget everything.

And Paddy?

The world stopped turning.

What had happened to Paddy? Forgetting everything forgot Paddy.

Sun gnawed at his back, arms. Daisies glared at him. Trees shook their fists. In the high white wispy clouds he saw the beloved old man who called him son, spoke his name. Zebu. He felt in his arms again the cool softness of the old man's embrace, felt him thumping him gleefully on his back when he arrived a week ago. Heat spread from his heart to the tips of his toes, his fingers. He let a breath out from the bottom of his gut. His face drew down, down.

Paddy? His eyes fuzzed blind. Knifed too? Bleeding?

Dead?

"No!" He beat his thighs. "No!"

He could hear his voice echo against hills and trees back down the road. It reached before him. He began to run towards it, back towards the Big House. Faster, faster. Running, running. Leaping over stones, roadkill, hair streaming, legs flying, fingers reaching forward to pull himself to Paddy, feet fleet on gravel

like wings. He turned at the crossroads, ran, leapt the fence, cut
down across the field to the back door, flung in.

"Paddy!"

Silence.

He imagined the old man, bound in a huddle somewhere,
hidden, squirming, dirty, a gag through his teeth, eyes bulging.
He picked up a knife in case of Mike, ran through the house,
everywhere, opened every closet, turned round in each of the
bathrooms, both the bedrooms, the living room, dining room,
thundered down the stairs, into the study, into the basement
bathroom, calling, calling, Paddy.

Nothing.

Nowhere.

Nobody.

He went through the house once again slowly, banged open
all the doors, trying to puzzle it out. There were things that
didn't add up. In the kitchen sink the girl's red shorts and her
shirt lay in a sodden mass with a heap of dirty dishes. The living room had a smell of cleanser. Cleanser, for fuck's sake.
Cleanser? He prowled, hearing his breath like a pump in the
silent emptiness. Paddy's bed hadn't been slept in. Paddy's old
study was clear of all Mike's stuff, the fucking TV, the bag with
the hearts, the Birks in their pairs. Morning light came through
the south window. You could see dust on the desk where
objects had not stood. The blue trunk was sealed and locked.
A wisp of blue gauze hung out of it. He got out of the study
quick. The garage door was open and a chipmunk skittered out
when he went in, scolding through the empty space.

He went back upstairs, stood by the table in the hall looking out the window over the bush towards the pond. He wanted
to go back, to Friday. He wanted to take the other road, be part
of another set of intersections, change the direction of the story.
There was a postcard on the hall table, a picture of a pagoda
with dragons on the roof. He fingered it, picked it up, read.

From Polly. Thinking of you all.

He wanted to sit down on the floor and cry. Everyone had

slipped away from him. Leslie. Polly. Paddy.

But Paddy hadn't left him, no, Paddy had welcomed him with open arms. What Paddy had was life, location, presence of heart and mind. Paddy kept faith with man and beast. Paddy was always there, like the proverbial old wise man, the swamp man, the bush man, the sod man, the old man of the mountain, the wizened wizard. Old — he'd dealt with things, figured things out, knew all the stories. Zeeb was crying now, dissolving. He wanted Paddy more than tongue could speak without drink. If he ever got Paddy in his arms again he wouldn't ever let him go, no, not ever, not till they were singing together like birds in a cage. He'd follow Paddy around, trail blazing, he'd ponder the old man's old tales of Maggie, women, his woman, shake their meaning out. He'd make Paddy puzzle out loud the mystery of tumbled corduroy, he'd compel him to show him his reasons. They would go fishing, just the two of them, silent, purposeful, become one with the watch and the water and each other in falling dusk. Never ever again would he let hurt master him, blind him, make him stiffen, turn away. The one true line was Zeeb/Paddy. All between was filler. The gap in him craved definition by Paddy, Paddy alone, only Paddy. What did anything mean if you couldn't finally lean back, your feet up, in conversation with a knowing old man?

But Paddy wasn't. Nowhere. Not even his hard hat, it was gone.

He laughed a sudden hard unreal laugh. The chain saw though, now — that he could locate. In the culvert. Jesus. He'd spent the night in the fucking culvert. The fucking culvert.

He looked up, away, out towards the distant hidden pond. The girl lay in the bush between here and there. He should go down to the bush. That was the next task. Face that hell. Look for Paddy in the bush.

Rotting.

"No."

He could not. Not alone. Unlocated. Disconnected.

What he should do was he should phone Leslie. Leslie would

be sure to come if he told her all the details, Leslie wouldn't let him down under the circumstances. Leslie would come.

He imagined the call.

There's a madman on the loose up here, honey.

Silence.

There's been a murder. Paddy, my old man — he's vanished.

Silence.

Oh, God, I'm in deep shit, Leslie. Please help me, please come.

Yes, then she would come. Leslie would come.

And he'd be beholden always, apart, together, whatever transpired between them forever, child to her woman for the rest of their lives, the rest of his life. That was not what he could live with, no. Living death. Gagged and bound. He might as well die. No, the only way he was ever going to see Leslie again would be level, looking her in the eye.

Then who?

Not Polly. No, not that either. That nurture was exhausted, ripped to fur on the ground, the nest crawling with starved lice, full of dry bones. She-hawk had flown to a place of pagodas. He had to make it solo now.

Beloved child.

He was crying again. He thought of all the things he'd never done. He'd never been to Spain, Florida, Tierra del Fuego. He'd never eaten satay in Thailand or clams in Boston. He still hadn't finished his fucking thesis.

He wiped at tears, snot, with the back of his hand. You couldn't see the pond from here. The bush intervened. But you could see where the treetops dipped down to the hollow which held the pond. The jewel in the heart of the lotus, that's what Polly would say.

Beloved.

The centre of the universe. The womb of the world. It would be quiet over there now, it was almost noon, the fish would be hiding from the heat in the depths. The ducks would have flown away, their brood dead, eaten. Only the dragonflies would be hovering. He pictured their red and blue bodies, darting, mating, laying eggs, hatching, the circle of life, sex, love. It made him smile. In spite of everything, tears, snot, he was smiling, thinking of darting dragonflies over the pond. Though he wasn't there now, the pond was still going on. If he could only ever go back to it like this in memory, he would never forget it. Besides, he sniffed, giggling, his beloved yellow T-shirt was there, the one with the frogs leaping. He couldn't leave that, he had to get his T-shirt. He went into the kitchen, got out the phone book, looked up Roy Taylor's number.

"Sam?"

"Who's this?"

Sam sounded in rough shape. Then Zeeb remembered the white cop car nosing down the drive of the A-frame. His heart beat fast and hard. Hang up before they track him down too.

And then? After?

"It's me, Zeeb. From Polly's place?"

His throat caught. He grabbed a breath. He'd said his name. Now, now it all had to come out. But where, where in all this chaos could he possibly begin? Paddy, gone beyond heart's reach? The girl, rotting, the maggots? Mike, the fucking little bastard with who knew how much blood on his hands? What made sense, any sense at all?

At least he'd stopped shaking knowing Sam was there waiting on the other end of the line with his cool stare. He wasn't crying any more. He gripped the phone tight.

"Listen, Sam. You've got to listen." He began.

Polly

*My face wet with grateful tears, loose with laughter —
he's made it, he's come back, the young king, my Zeeb.
He's come home.*

Older? By a week.

Wiser? Not very, at least not yet.

*And more princely than kingly, like the jeans we
bought him each June — room to grow.*

*But not a villain either, praise be, nor a victim. A sur-
vivor. Today's hero, the survivor, the one who lives to
worry the tale until meaning falls out, like ripe apples.
It'll take him a lifetime to locate himself, always measuring, separating, examining. A slow man, a watcher, a
thinker — the tragedy over, the rest of his life to live.*

*But he has made his choice — Paddy, the careful fish-
erman. He has come home. He will hold the old man again.*

*The little white Renault negotiates the turn into the
village at the* Globe & Mail *box.*

*Jade rises from herself into the treetops. They will come,
they will come. They will find her, they will find her.
Her mother will truly weep.*

*Mike walks east, still whistling, in Paddy's yellow
hard hat. How far will he get? Belleville? St. John's?
Maybe only as far as Palgrave, the next highway over.*

And then the years of waiting, assembling evidence, settling lawyers, and then the courtroom.

Oh, how horrible, what filth, what pain. Turn, turn. And now?

I hear flapping, like film at the end of the reel. The sound track has gone silent. The lights are coming up, and now I have to strain to see them, these afterimages which have occupied me for so long. Paddy turning into the police station. Mike taking off the hard hat and scratching his hot head. Zeeb thumping the phone book, listening, speaking.

Oh, put on some clothes, dear heart. People will be coming. At least wrap a towel around your waist.

But — you can't live other people's lives for them, the lights are coming up, and I am here, stopped in the Buddha's doorway.

Back at the beginning of the eighties interest rates sky-rocketed. I had money in two banks and by means of that I was working a little scam. If I wrote a cheque on one bank and deposited it in the other late Friday I got interest on it twice over the weekend, until the first bank got the cheque back Monday or, if it was a long weekend — lucky break — Tuesday.

Gold! Silver! Dollars! I was as inflamed by the game as a gambler. I darted from bank to bank like a lover. My bank books were my missals, I studied them like chicken entrails.

Until suddenly one day I could no longer see it. What had entranced me? Dollars? Dollars?

And now I can suddenly no longer see them, even those I have loved so long, Paddy, Zebu, they are gone from my mind's eye like dreams in the morning. Next time we meet and they tell me about this they've been enduring — what has it been, what have they really been through? Can we tell each other our stories?

I am standing in this doorway. Darkness, religious

commotion are behind me. The sky over the courtyard is huge, blue, bouncing with fluffy clouds.

Oh, hurry, hurry, down the steps, across the stones, past the shrine, along the high wall to the gateway. Look! Look! It's the highway, the Steveston highway. Cars going back and forth. Buses. A bus stop.

Across the highway a suburb. Streets lined with houses carefully asymmetrical. Grey stucco, white stucco. Yards, driveways, bushes, flowering bushes. Flung down bikes.

And now out of the suburb comes a young woman pushing a baby carriage. She's trim in beige slacks, tight over her hips. She looks cool in a white blouse. She stops to wait for a toddler trailing behind her and calls and the child dawdles closer.

Now she looks over and sees me staring.

Well, I must look a sight. Days and nights in the wilderness. I shrug. I sort of smile. What can you do?

She raises her hand, smiles.

One look back, Saky, at your temple, Kuan Yin's golden temple. You did say if we met you on the road we should kill you. If you meet the Buddha on the road, kill him. That's what's happened here between you and me, I guess. I can no longer see you.

But there, beyond the gateway — her smiling, I can see her shiny teeth. The toddler catches up, she takes the child's hand, they turn down the highway, and I . . .